THE
KIRKFALLEN
STOPWATCH

Jan-Andrew Henderson

Black Hart Entertainment

Edinburgh. Brisbane.

First published 2009 by Oxford University Press (as *Colony*)
Reprinted 2019 by Black Hart Publishers.

Black Hart Entertainment.
5 Leven Terrace Edinburgh EH3 9LT.
Blackhartentertainment.com

Cover by Panagiotis Lampridis (BookDesignStars).

Book Layout © 2017 BookDesignTemplates.com

The Kirkfallen Stopwatch. 2nd ed.
ISBN 978-1-64570-609-0 (print)
ISBN 978-1-64570-610-6 (eBook)

The Doomsday Clock is a fictional timepiece which has been maintained since 1947 by the Board of Directors of the Bulletin of Atomic Scientists at the University of Chicago. The clock measures how close the human race is to catastrophic destruction – midnight being the point where the human race will wipe itself out.

It currently stands at two minutes to midnight.

It is estimated that there are approximately 8,000,000,000 humans on earth

And 100,000,000,000,000,000 ants

For Harper and Scarlet

1

1 9 8 0

The teenager woke up in the back of a bouncing jeep. A full moon swung sickeningly in the inky sky as the vehicle pitched and juddered across uneven ground. His jaw was clenched and his muscles ached with cold. All he was wearing was a thin paper gown.

He rolled over and found himself face-to-face with a dead soldier. The man's pupils had rolled upwards and his lower lip quivered in time with the vehicle's vibration, making it look like he was praying. Jerking back, the boy collided with a limp pair of legs. Another soldier was sprawled over a pile of Jerry cans - blood saturating the back of his jacket. The teenager let out a rasp of terror.

The jeep slewed to a halt. The boy scuttled back to the tailgate, holding out thin white arms to ward off the driver.

"It's all right, son. I ain't gonna harm you." It was too dark to see the stranger's face but the voice was female, gruff yet deliberately reassuring. "Dan, isn't it?"

"Dan Salty." The boy replied shakily. "I got dead guys on either side of me."

"Yeah. Sorry about that." The figure turned off the ignition and climbed awkwardly into the back of the vehicle. "But we're gonna need these fellas."

Now that she was closer, Dan could see the woman had a broad, pretty face with thick black eyebrows, bright blue eyes and a gap between her front teeth. Her chin and hair were hidden by a fur-rimmed parka hood.

"Got you some clothes here." She pulled a bundle from under one of the seats, elbowing a corpse aside to get it clear. "Better put them on fore you get hypothermia."

"What happened?" The teenager croaked. "I remember everyone was dying!"

"We've got to reach the foothills before the sun comes up." The woman thrust the pack onto his knees. "Get dressed. I'll explain when we're moving again."

Dan Salty looked down at the flimsy gown, barely covering his body.

"Could you turn away? Please?"

"Sure, honey." The woman swivelled round and returned to the driver's seat. "Just don't hit me with a lug wrench when my back's turned. I'm on your side."

She crunched gears and the jeep jolted into action again.

"Why haven't you got the headlights on?" Dan struggled into oversized combat fatigues and a roll-neck jersey, then pulled on a pair of boots. None of it was easy to do in the darkness of a bouncing jeep with two dead bodies knocking him from side to side.

"Out here, a spotter plane can see headlights miles away." The woman hunched over the wheel, peering into the darkness. "Don't even dare light a damned cigarette. You get up here with me when you're dressed and shout if you see any obstacles. Like this boulder."

She wrenched at the steering wheel and the jeep leapt into the air, landing with a tooth jarring crunch. One of the soldier's arms jolted up in what looked like a casual salute.

Dan gave a moan and clambered quickly into the passenger seat. The woman winked at him.

"Name's Louise Martin." She swerved to avoid a shallow ravine that had materialised out of the gloom. "When we reach the foothills, we're gonna hide this jeep in a gulley. Then we're gonna walk till we drop. Try and cover as much ground as we can before the sun gets too high. It can get pretty toasty out here in the daytime."

She gave a low chuckle.

"Don't wanna spend too long in the heat. Not with my condition."

"Your condition?"

"I'm pregnant, son. An I already got a ten-year-old daughter. I need to whisk that young lady off somewheres, before the army realises I'm still alive."

They didn't speak for a while. The boy heard the howl of an animal somewhere in the darkness.

"Coyote." The woman cocked her head. "Means the foothills are close."

"I recognise you," Dan said. "You helped them do tests on the prisoners. And on me."

"That I did."

"Do you still work for *them*?"

Louise glanced back at the lifeless men behind her, then sideways at her apprehensive companion.

"I reckon I quit."

2

2000

Mr Gacy sipped a lukewarm mug of tea. A blue clipboard lay across his knees and an old-fashioned doctor's bag squatted on the floor between his legs. The Flintheart family - mother, father and daughter - were perched on their couch opposite, looking sheepish. Mr Gacy placed his mug on the coffee table and took a pen from his coat pocket.

"So," he began pleasantly. "What makes you think your house is haunted?"

"It was my wife's idea to let you come here." Mr Flintheart looked distinctly put out by the stranger sitting in his living room. "I dinnae understand how you even knew about the stuff going on in our house."

"I'm psychic." Mr Gacy gave a cheesy grin. "I know that must sound daft..."

"Aye. And I'm the tooth fairy."

9

"If you're not comfortable with my being here, I can leave." Mr Gacy pushed the mug aside. "I realise it must be a bit freaky, having me call you out of the blue."

"No." Mrs Flintheart held up a trembling hand. "I want you to stay. We need to talk to someone."

Her husband lapsed into surly silence.

"All right." Mr Gacy clicked the top of his pen. "Just what seems to be troubling you?"

Mrs Flintheart cleared her throat.

"Well, it sounds stupid. But, a while back, we all began to act a bit... strangely."

"When exactly did this condition start?"

"About six months ago."

"Haunted is the wrong word," the daughter broke in.

"Could you give me a better word... eh?" Mr Gacy consulted his clipboard.

"Elspeth."

"What word would you use, Elspeth?"

"It was like we had a Guardian Angel. To begin with anyways," she added ominously.

"And would you agree with that?" Mr Gacy turned to Mr Flintheart, who was still glowering at him. "A Guardian Angel?"

Mr Flintheart sighed deeply.

"I used tae have a drink problem," he said finally. Behind the man, photographs of the family cluttered the mantelpiece. "A bad one. Six months ago, I gave up. Just like that."

"Lots of people quit drinking."

"I never could."

"I stopped smoking around the same time," Mrs Flintheart added. "Plus… you know… we always used to fight over what was on TV."

"Not fighting, really. More an animated discussion."

"Andrew likes sport. I like my soaps. Elspeth always preferred music shows."

"And?" Mr Gacy was finding it hard to hide his impatience.

"Then, suddenly, we always wanted to watch the same channel."

Mr Gacy's smile became pained.

"We'd turn up to breakfast," Mrs Flintheart continued falteringly. "And find we were wearing the same thing as each other."

"Must have been embarrassing for at least one of you." Mr Gacy gave Mr Flintheart a sympathetic wink.

"She means the same colours," Elspeth chided. "Even yellow. And I *hate* yellow."

"But not anymore?" As far as Mr Gacy could see, they were all dressed differently.

"Not anymore."

Gacy made a quick notation on his clipboard, more for show than anything. He had no intention of keeping any record of the conversation.

"I don't suppose there are any physical signs of this, eh... manifestation."

The whole family nodded.

"Elspeth and I use our mobiles." Mrs Flintheart got up and went to the dresser at the back of the room. "But Andrew is old-fashioned. He still has a Polaroid Instamatic."

She opened a drawer and pulled out a bulky camera. "The kind that makes instant pictures?"

She handed the camera to Mr Gacy.

"Hence the name Instamatic," he said, trying to work out where the on switch was.

"Take our photograph."

"Now?"

The family nodded again.

"Ok." Gacy pointed the unwieldy machine at the couch. "Say booger-man."

Nobody smiled. Mr Gacy looked through the viewfinder, clicked, and a small square of plastic slid out of the bottom. He pulled it free and waved the photo in the air.

"Nothing shows up on digital images," Mrs Flintheart said. "But look at what you've just taken."

Mr Gacy watched the film develop as air reacted with the chemicals on the photographic paper. Slowly, an image began to form. He could see the Flinthearts sharpening into focus on their couch.

"I don't take a very good picture," Elspeth warned.

"No. It's a nice shot." Mr Gacy kept watching. Then his eyes widened.

"What the hell is that?"

"That's our Guardian Angel."

In the picture, a blurred figure stood in the background. The Flinthearts were now perfectly clear but the person behind them was like a creature made from fog. The features were indistinguishable but its shape was definitely female. Her pose was hunched and threatening, as if she were about to strike the family in front of her.

Mr Gacy looked up. There was nobody standing behind the couch. There had been nobody behind the couch when he took the picture.

"Can I keep this?" he asked quietly.

"Certainly. We've got dozens." Mrs Flintheart looked nervously around. "At first... this girl... she just seemed to be watching. We even thought she was smiling. Now it looks like she means us some kind of harm."

"Anything else?" Mr Gacy attached the photograph to his clipboard.

"Insects."

"Insects?"

"We keep finding ants in the house."

Mr Gacy gave a visible shudder.

"I don't like bugs," he said by way of explanation.

"Ach, I dinnae think that has anything to do with it," Mr Flintheart interjected, his gruffness returning. "Perhaps if we washed the dishes more often."

"I wash the dishes plenty," Mrs Flintheart shot back, anger roughening her voice.

"If we can get back to your Guardian Angel?" Mr Gacy said.

"See? We've started fighting again. But now it's over the smallest things, not just the TV." Elspeth looked uneasily at her father. "Like whose turn it is to wash and whose to dry."

"I can see that would be a dilemma."

"I hit my wife last week." Mr Flintheart made no attempt to hide his shame at this revelation. "I have flaws, like anyone, I suppose. But I never lifted a finger tae anyone in my life before. Especially not the woman I love."

"We're scared." Mrs Flintheart reached out and took her husband's hand. "At first, the things happening to us were just weird. Now they're frightening."

"What about your neighbours?" Mr Gacy made a few more imaginary notes. "They experience anything?"

"The people on the left, the Warbecks, only moved in a few months ago," Elspeth said. "They seemed dead happy to start with - but now I think they're having the same problems. I've heard them fighting through the wall."

"Have you talked to them about your... spirit?"

"Of course not. We don't want them to think we're crazy."

"All rightee." Mr Gacy stood and picked up his bag. "Well, I have quite a workload but your case is certainly an... eh... interesting one."

He strode over and shook Mr Flintheart's hand.

"I don't think you're in any danger and I usually find that manifestations like this vanish of their own accord. I'll give it another month or so, then check back."

"Is that it?" Mrs Flintheart looked somewhat put out.

"Actually, no." Mr Gacy clicked the pen and put it back in his jacket. "I would not mention this to the media under any circumstances. The papers tend to make a laughing stock of anyone who believes their house has an entity."

He spread his arms disarmingly.

"I believe you, of course, but most families bitterly regret media exposure." He looked at Mr Flintheart. "The father often loses his job because employers don't want a nutcase working for them."

"I telt you this was a bad idea." Mr Flintheart glared at his wife.

"Oh, shut up, Andrew," the woman snapped back. Mr Flintheart clenched his jaw.

"If I may continue." Mr Gacy held up a hand. "Elspeth will get a lot of stick at school and people may accuse you, Mrs Flintheart, of attention-seeking. I'd get rid of those photographs too."

The women nodded.

"Like I say. Give it a few weeks and, if the condition persists, call me again." Mr Gacy put away his pen with a flourish.

"Don't get up. I'll show myself out."

As the front door slammed, Elspeth turned to her parents.

"Mum?" She looked warily at the empty space behind the couch.

"If that man's really psychic, how come he didn't know the girl was there?"

Mr Gacy crossed the neatly kept lawn and climbed into an unmarked white van. On the side was a logo.

G.B. Paranormal: Psychic Investigators

He threw his bag into the back and fished the ignition key from his pocket - but his hands were trembling too much to start the vehicle. He leaned back in his seat and took deep, quivering breaths, fingers curled around the steering so tightly that the nails cut into his palms.

"Oh Christ." He stared through the windscreen into the starless suburban night.

"This was *not* supposed to happen."

The Sheridan Disaster

*The world is a dangerous place to live, not be-
cause of the people who are evil, but because of
the people who don't do anything about it.*

Albert Einstein

3

Sheridan Research Facility: Mohave
Desert

1980

Three Chinook helicopters buzzed out of the haze and settled like pendulums on the open compound, whipping up swirling curtains of sand. A dozen figures in protective suits emerged, some carrying automatic weapons. As soon as the passengers had alighted, the choppers rose into the air and headed further into the desert. The pilots had orders to land twenty miles away and not return to the base until an all-clear had been given.

The leader of the party strode out of the billowing sand and headed for a low cluster of square buildings. A pall of hazy smoke hung over the compound, drifting out from shattered, wire-latticed windows.

Another figure, smaller in stature, caught up and pointed to the ground. It was mottled and black, moving slowly as if a layer of soot was drifting across the desert floor. Both knelt and dug gloved hands into the sand, using their fingers like sieves, until only the squirming mass remained, sticking to their palms.

The smaller figure spoke into her headset mic.

"Ants," she said. "There must be thousands of them."

"Hundreds of thousands."

Her companion moved his head from side to side, trying to see the extent of the black carpet, but his visor had fogged up. With a grunt of exasperation, the figure struggled to his feet and pulled off the hood.

"Doctor Kelty!" His assistant glanced up in panic. "With all due respect. Are you insane?"

Kelty grimaced and wiped perspiration from his forehead. A few stray ants stuck to the sweat, a rash of oily droplets below his hairline.

"Everyone here is dead, Naish," he replied matter-of-factly. "If what killed them is still hanging around, protective suits won't do the slightest bit of good."

He took a deep breath and exhaled slowly. Nothing happened. He nodded confidently to himself.

"Take the suit off, Naish. We've got work to do."

"I don't mind keeping mine on. Really."

"It makes your ass look big."

"I'll take it off."

Kelty took another deep breath and unzipped his suit. "Seems like we're safe and I can't collect samples wearing a pair of damned oven gloves."

Under the hazard gear, both doctor and assistant were wearing olive overalls with military insignia. Kelty's denoted the rank of Colonel. Now that their helmets were gone, they could hear the wail of Klaxon horns echoing round the deserted complex. Kelty signalled to the other members of the party to follow his actions. Reluctantly, they removed their biohazard gear.

Without the protective suits, the doctor could see who was who. Those with guns were wearing U.S. army uniforms. The members of his research team were unarmed and had olive coveralls similar to his own.

A tall Lieutenant with cropped blond hair marched over and saluted briefly.

"Orders, doctor? I mean, Colonel."

Kelty nodded towards the boxy buildings in front of them.

"The fire must be localised or the whole place would have burned down overnight. Lower levels, most likely. Send some men down with respirator gear and make sure it's out."

Sheridan Research Base was still brightly lit. The complex had its own power supply and strip lights shone in sickly lines through smoke that still drifted across the ceilings.

Doctor Kelty was correct. The occupants of the base were all dead.

Researchers in white lab coats lay at strange angles in the antiseptic corridors. Uniformed soldiers were draped over consoles. Legs stuck out from under tables in thickening pools of blood. And each body was covered with swarming black dots.

"Jesus, doctor, what caused this?" The Lieutenant sidled up, looking distinctly queasy. "Was it the fire? Was it the *ants*?"

Kelty turned over the body of a researcher with his foot. A kitchen knife protruded from the man's chest.

"Don't think so, Lieutenant." He turned dispassionately to Naish. "I want blood samples from a couple of these bodies."

But Naish was staring at the dead researcher.

"Dr Kelty. Look at his face."

Kelty felt the hairs rise on the back of his neck. The man's eyes were wide open and so was his mouth, white spittle crusted around the lips.

It was a look of absolute terror.

"He's got a knife stuck in his chest." Kelty strove for composure. "You expect him to look pleased?"

"It's not just one man." The Lieutenant was inspecting another body. "This guy's got the same expression." He moved quickly to the next corpse and turned it over. "This one too."

He stood up, wiping grimy hands on his jacket.

"Doctor. If I didn't know better, I'd say some of these men died of fright."

"You leave the diagnoses to me," Kelty snapped. "What are you waiting for, Naish? The poor boob to show you his organ donor card?"

Naish knelt resentfully beside the nearest corpse and opened a medical kit. Long dark hair swung round her face, hiding a grimace, as she injected a syringe into the body's stiffening thigh.

"Notice something odd about these ants, Naish?" Kelty bent down and peered at the scurrying insects.

"They've all got dead bodies under them?"

"There are half a dozen different species. Species that don't normally mix."

"Ow!" Naish jerked her hand back, releasing an arc of crimson from the syringe. "You little...."

"Yeah. Some of them are bull ants. You wanna watch those suckers."

The Lieutenant's walkie talkie crackled. He held it to his ear and listened for a few seconds.

"The fire was in the research labs below, Dr Kelty. You were right. It was extensive but it's pretty much burned itself out."

"See if your unit can salvage anything. The computers up here are just for administration and the ones below are probably reduced to ash. So tell them to look for classified file cabinets or any hard data that might have survived – not that it's likely."

He took Naish by the arm and pulled her into one of the offices lining the corridor.

"Get one of these PCs up and running. I want a list of all personnel on this complex, and that includes the prisoners in the lower levels."

He stuck his head back into the corridor.

"Lieutenant, I need a body count. And it has to be accurate."

"The soldiers have dog tags, but my men say the other staff on the bottom levels are too charred to be identified."

"We'll cross that hurdle later. For now, I just need to know if anyone got off this base."

"Will do, Doc." The Lieutenant turned sharply and strode away. Naish sat down in front of a computer and dropped the syringes into her medical kit.

"Well, it looks like the Stopwatch Project is an unmitigated failure," she grunted, turning on the machine.

"Oh, I don't know about that." Doctor Kelty stroked his chin thoughtfully.

"I'd say we got precisely what we were looking for."

Kirkfallen Island

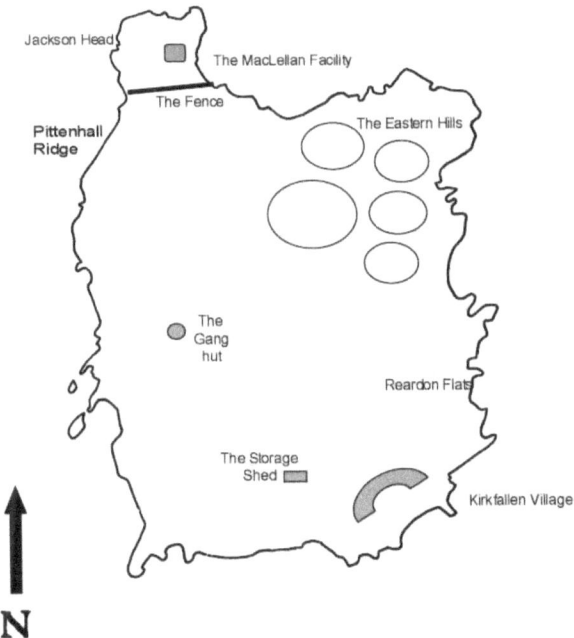

Jackson Head

The MacLellan Facility

The Fence

Pittenhall Ridge

The Eastern Hills

The Gang hut

Reardon Flats

The Storage Shed

Kirkfallen Village

N

4

Gene Stapleton sat at the edge of his world, legs dangling over the cliff top, watching the sunrise. In front of him, the Atlantic Ocean rose and sank in muscular green swells, buffeting the rocks below his perch and showering him with misty droplets of freezing water. Guillemots screamed overhead, angered by the boy's closeness to their nesting area, circling above his head in flailing clouds of frustration.

Kirkfallen Island, or 'Fallen' as the inhabitants referred to it, was the only home Gene had ever known and its isolation was near-absolute. Four miles long and two miles wide, it was hours by boat from the Outer Hebrides, a cluster of larger islands off the west coast of Scotland. And the Hebrides hardly constituted a bustling metropolis – the only inhabitants lived in a few villages or made up the personnel of Radcliff U.S. Naval base.

Gene had never really minded the remoteness of his home. Sure, it could get boring. The land was an unbroken expanse of brownish-green, as if the island wore camouflage, and a peculiarity of its location meant Kirkfallen was almost permanently shrouded by low-lying clouds. TV signals didn't reach that far into the Atlantic and the island's electrical generators were for essentials - Gene didn't even have a computer, never mind internet access.

But Kirkfallen housed a small self-sufficient community and he had lifelong friends he had grown up with. Gene could catch a fish with his hands, gut and cook it. And, though he was only fifteen, he could shoot like a marksman and do a hundred-yard wheelie in the communal land buggies – though he wasn't supposed to touch them at all.

If he had to describe Kirkfallen, Gene Stapleton would have said *harsh* but *idyllic* - words he had looked up in the big dictionary in the information hut.

Until three days ago.

Three days ago, a young married couple called the Orbisons, the newest addition to the island community, had committed suicide. They were found on the rocks below Pittenhall Ridge where, it appeared, they had jumped to their deaths.

The Orbisons had arrived the month before, on a trial period, to see if they could handle the rigours of island existence. At first, they had kept themselves to themselves. But recently, they had taken to life at Kirkfallen, praising the inhabitant's uncomplicated ways and joining in with communal activities. In fact, they seemed delighted to be there.

It looked like their happiness had been an act.

But there was little time for mourning on Kirkfallen. Life here was a continual struggle to wrestle a living from the land and it had to go on, no matter what disasters befell the inhabitants. Some even muttered that the Orbisons had brought disaster on themselves by being at Pittenhall Ridge in the first place. It wasn't exactly off-limits, but few adults ever ventured there and the children were forbidden to go near it.

Because Pittenhall Ridge ended at the fence.

The fence had been there when the first islanders arrived. According to dilapidated warning notices, it was once electrified and still posed a formidable barrier - ten feet high and topped with broken loops of rusted barbed wire. The fence separated the bulk of the island from a small but towering promontory known as Jackson Head and the only gate was padlocked. Bolted on the front was a weather faded sign.

Property of the
United States Navy
Trespassers will Incur

the Severest Penalty

A few hundred yards further on were the remains of a low concrete building, now crumbling and overrun with weeds. It was a place that inspired rumours. Some kids theorised that scientists conducted secret experiments there until a massive explosion destroyed the place. Others swore the promontory was haunted.

Whatever the truth, Jackson Head was an absolute no-go area for a very practical reason. The cliffs just behind the abandoned complex were sheer drops and the land at the top was dangerously unstable, often jutting out over the ferocious Atlantic waves. The whole promontory had been deemed unsafe, riddled with caves and holes, some of which plunged in deadly funnels down to the jagged rocks at sea level.

The day after the Orbisons died, a helicopter from Radcliffe naval base airlifted the bodies out. Then life on the island had continued. Nobody wanted to dwell on the tragedy.

But Gene Stapleton couldn't stop thinking about it.

Because he didn't believe the Orbisons had committed suicide.

He was sure they had been murdered.

5

The sun was beginning to crumple the air into a shimmering haze as the jeep reached the foothills that marked the northern fringe of the Mohave. Louise lurched down a ravine and brought the vehicle to a halt by crunching the front into a rock face with a jutting overhang.

"Brake's the middle pedal, Louise," Dan offered dryly.

"Last few minutes in the shade." The woman unzipped her parka and pushed back the hood, revealing curly black hair. "Make the most of it. Time to lose the sweater and pants. There's a shirt and shorts under the passenger seat."

Dan Salty jumped out and went behind a rock to change. When he emerged, Louise was also wearing shorts with a light purple top. He watched with macabre fascination as she pulled the stiffening bodies of the soldiers into the driver and passenger seat.

"Should take the army a while to find these fellas. If we're really lucky, they'll think they killed each other." She manoeuvred the men so they were face-to-face. "Though I gotta tell you, good luck has never really run in my family."

"Is everyone back at that place dead?"

"Far as I can tell."

"What caused it?"

"They did, honey." The woman hauled a small rucksack onto her knee. "C'mere."

The teenager sidled over and Louise pulled a tube of suntan lotion from her pack.

"Better get this on." She squeezed ointment from the tube and began to smear it on his arms, legs and face. Dan remembered his mother used to do the same. He looked into the bag. It was filled with bottles of water.

"You've thought of everything,"

"I was always an outdoor type, son." The woman applied lotion to her own face and arms. "It's just a basic survival kit. Easy to put together."

Dan stuck hands in his pocket and squinted at the sun.

"Louise. How come you and I are still alive?"

"That's something I ain't figured out yet." Louise tucked the empty tube into her pocket. She wiped the interior of the jeep with a rag to remove any fingerprints, stuffed the extra clothing into her rucksack and shouldered it.

"This way. Stay off the sand and on the rocks until we're a goodly distance from here, so's not to leave footprints. We don't want to broadcast the fact that we even exist, never mind the direction we're heading."

They walked at a steady pace, never getting too far from some sort of shelter. Twice, they heard the noise of a helicopter and scuttled under the nearest rock formation until the sound was gone. After a while, Dan tried to start a conversation but Louise dismissed this with a wave of her hand.

"Save your breath, son. We ain't done tramping."

Before long, the boy was glad to heed her advice. Sweat slicked every inch of his body and his breath came in short searing bursts. But he kept pace with his long-legged companion, who seemed unfazed by the heat or her pregnancy, which hadn't even begun to show. Partly Dan kept up from pride. Partly, it was because he suspected Louise would leave him behind if he started to flag.

Slowly the foothills levelled out and rock was replaced by scrub grass. Sequoia trees began to dot the landscape. Forty minutes later, they came to a road. Louise sank to her knees and Dan collapsed beside her, panting with exhaustion.

"Highway 58. We can hitch from here. Driver asks? You're my son and we were on a camping trip. Couldn't get our car to start. In fact, don't say anything at all. I'll do the talking."

"Can't speak anyhow," Dan rasped. "Feel like someone's stuffed a pair of Jockey shorts down my throat."

Louise gave a chuckle. In the distance, they saw a plume of dust moving slowly across the deserted landscape.

"That's a car." She struggled to her feet. "Could be you've changed my luck, honey."

The Lieutenant marched into one of Sheridan's sparse living quarters and saluted. Naish was asleep on a bunk but Kelty was alert as ever, sitting at a table, studying files.

"We've gone over the base with a fine-tooth comb, Sir."

"And?"

"As far as we can tell, four people are missing."

Kelty slammed his palm flat on the table. Naish's eyes shot open and she sat up quickly, wiping saliva from the corner of her mouth.

"Do we know who they are?"

"No, Sir." The Lieutenant smelt of smoke and his cheeks were streaked with soot. "There are about twenty bodies in the lower level, too badly burned to identify. Some of the corpses are prisoners - they couldn't get out of their cells - but there were only twelve of them, so the rest must be personnel."

"Are you searching the surrounding area?"

"The choppers are doing aerial sweeps in a fifty-mile radius of the base but there's no sign of life anywhere."

"Which means they left in a vehicle. Aren't there tyre tracks out there in the sand?"

"Hundreds," the Lieutenant replied. "Base security patrols this area three times a day in jeeps to make certain it's secure."

The doctor shut his eyes.

"Then tell the choppers to look for the only tracks going in a *straight* line," he sighed.

"Yessir." The Lieutenant saluted and turned on his heel. Then he stopped. "Excuse me, Sir. What do we do if we spot the fugitives?"

"You do not land or approach them under any circumstances. Shoot them down where they stand."

"Sir?"

"You heard me."

The Lieutenant swallowed hard. Then he saluted once more and barrelled out of the room. Dr Kelty lowered his head into his hands.

"Shall I get us some coffee, Sir?" Naish leaned over his shoulder, yawning. Her eyes were bleary and gummed with sleep. "The vending machines on this level still work."

"Get back to the computer," Kelty barked, holding up a clipboard. "Match every identifiable body on the base to this list of personnel and prisoners."

"And then?"

"Find out the name of everyone you haven't ticked off the list. Check if they were billeted here or not – I know some staff were bussed in from the towns on the fringe of the desert. If any outsiders are unaccounted for, send what limited forces we have left after this debacle to find out if they've shown up at home. If they haven't, check the houses of relatives, friends, lovers, workmates... their favourite store where they like to go get an ice cream soda."

Kelty thrust the clipboard into Naish's arms.

"I want the survivors who got off this base *found*."

"That could take weeks!"

"Good job you got some precious shut-eye then." Kelty's voice dripped with sarcasm. "Cause you'll be awake till this is sorted."

"Can't remember the last time *I* had an ice cream soda," Naish said wistfully, then scurried out of the room before Kelty found something to throw at her.

6

Gene Stapleton ate lunch with his parents in their stone croft, like always. As usual, it was simple fare – potato salad and smoked fish. As usual, Gene's curious nature got the better of him and he asked his daily awkward question.

"Shouldn't we be saying Grace before meals?"

"Say *what*?"

"Thanking the Lord for the potato salad and that kind of thing."

"Well, it *is* good." His father ladled a large helping of white mush onto his plate and offered some to his wife. "You want to say Grace, Annie?"

"Not really," Gene's mother gave a serene smile. "I've never been much of a public speaker."

"Me neither. You're outvoted, son." His father gave a sympathetic shrug. "God bless democracy."

Gene's mother sniggered, then quickly straightened her face.

37

"Don't make fun, Eddie," she scolded. "The boy's entitled to his views."

"You're right, of course." Edward Stapleton took a swig of water and stretched. "Say Grace if you want Gene. Just do it in your head. Some of us are trying to eat."

Gene Stapleton, Poppy Ainsworth and Millar Watt sat in their gang hut, the spot they considered to be the centre of the island. As huts went, it was pretty impressive - designed to stand up to the biting Atlantic wind and rain. Roughly hexagonal and set in a protective hollow, it was made from nailed together chunks of driftwood, secured by strands of discarded rope. Buttresses gave the building added resilience; cracks in the structure were filled with dried mud and the whole edifice was topped by thatched sea grass.

Everyone on Kirkfallen, even the children, had mastered carpentry. Everyone on the island knew how to build.

Gene, Poppy and Millar were the oldest children on the island. On rare occasions they let Marcie Gold and Bob McCombie join them, but they were only thirteen and too immature to be a proper part of the gang.

"What's the matter?" Millar waved a hand in front of his friend's face. "You're off in a world of your own."

Millar Watt was a short, confident boy, permanently decked out in a felt trilby, oversized ex-army boots with a camouflaged jacket and matching combat trousers. Gene wasn't sure if these were the only clothes his friend owned or if he had a dozen pairs of identical outfits. Millar refused to confirm or deny either theory.

"I was thinking."

"Well, please stop," Poppy grumped. "It means I'm stuck talking to Millar."

"And I use too many big words for her to understand what I'm saying."

Poppy was a large girl. Not fat but broad-shouldered and as sturdy as any man on the island – solidity only enhanced by her rugby top and baggy jeans. Add thick black eyebrows, a square jaw and a bowl cut of black hair and Poppy looked less flowery than anyone Gene could imagine.

"Want to tell us what's eating you?" she said. "You look like you've swallowed a nettle."

Gene smiled awkwardly at his friends.

"I was out on Pittenhall Ridge on Sunday…"

"You're not allowed there," Poppy gasped, looking around, although nobody could possibly be listening.

"I just went to sketch birds."

His friends understood. Drawing was Gene's hobby and he was turning out to be a pretty good artist. Pittenhall's reputation meant their friend was guaranteed to be undisturbed out there and birds were a lot easier to draw when they stayed on the ground.

"I spotted the Orbisons while I was sketching. It must have been right before they died."

"Fantastic!" Millar said breathlessly. "Did you see them jump?"

Poppy thumped the boy on the shoulder, almost knocking him across the room.

"Don't be so insensitive, you moron." She turned consolingly to Gene. "Well? Did you?"

"No, I didn't." The boy chewed at his lip. "In fact, I saw the exact opposite."

"What do you mean?"

"I was lying in a patch of grass drawing a nesting tern when I spotted the Orbisons walking along Pittenhall Ridge. And they weren't suicidal. They were talking and laughing."

"Did they see you?"

"I didn't want to be disturbed, so I moved further down where I couldn't see them and they couldn't see me. I guess I must have dozed off. When I checked again, they were gone."

He rubbed his temple awkwardly.

"Point is, they seemed in a great mood. And they were heading *away* from the Ridge, back towards the village."

"Jesus, Gene. Why didn't you tell anyone this?"

"Are you kidding? I'd be grounded for months if my dad knew I was anywhere *near* the fence."

"So, what are you getting at?" Poppy scratched her neck with a thick finger. "Are you saying they didn't commit suicide?

"From what I saw, it doesn't seem likely."

"You think someone *forced* them over?"

"I can't come up with a good reason why two happy people heading away from a clifftop would suddenly turn around and jump off the edge."

Millar's eyes were like saucers.

"If you think they were *murdered,* then you *have* to tell someone."

"Tell who? It would take more than one person to drag a healthy couple to the edge of a cliff and throw them over. Might even take three or four."

"Maybe there was a boat and the sailors came ashore and…" Millar petered out as he realised how dumb he sounded.

"And they flew up a sheer cliff on jetpacks?"

"There's nobody on the island except the people in our village," Poppy said incredulously. "Folk we've known forever."

"Exactly. But I can't get it out of my head that the Orbisons were murdered." Gene shook his head sadly.

"And, if they were, the killers have to be from our community."

7

Gene, Poppy and Millar huddled in the hut, pondering their dilemma. Outside, wheeling gulls shrilled, fighting the wind that always seemed to blow angrily across the thatch. For the first time, the teenagers were acutely aware of their own isolation.

"I think we should tell our parents," Poppy volunteered. "We can't just keep this to ourselves."

"I don't." Millar objected. Despite his casual manner and weird attire, he was a boy of fierce intellect. He had read almost every book in the island's information hut, which was a considerable amount. And he remembered almost all the data he had absorbed.

"Why not?"

"Look at us," Millar held both hands out to his friends. "We trust each other, don't we?"

Poppy raised a bushy eyebrow.

"You pinned a sign on my back saying *I am a truck*."

"That was two years ago!"

"Of course we do." Gene interrupted. "We've all grown up together."

"Same with the rest of Fallen," Millar said. "We live together. Work together. We haven't got anyone else."

It was true. The inhabitants of Kirkfallen were completely isolated. And though they came from all over the world, their diverse backgrounds and cultures had been forgotten. The adults never talked about where they came from, even when the children asked. They were, by some unspoken agreement, people without a past.

"It wouldn't go down well if we start spreading rumours that there are murderers among us." Gene agreed. "It could tear Fallen apart."

"Less of the *we*," Millar snorted. "You're the only one who saw the Orbisons."

"And you believe me, don't you?"

"Of course."

"That's what I mean. Everyone on this island trusts each other. We can't mess that up unless we have some actual proof."

"So, what do we do? Hold a séance?"

"We find the proof ourselves," Gene said decisively.

"We figure out who did it."

8

1 9 8 0

Dan and Louise rode in the back of an old pickup until they reached the spot where Highway 58 crossed Highway 14. After a few minutes standing at the flat, dusty cross-roads, they caught another ride heading north towards El Paso. A few miles later, they came to a sign.

Welcome to Rattray. Population 769. Please Drive Slowly

Someone had scored out the R and V on the word *drive* so that it now read.

Please D i e Slowly

"Yup. It's that kinda place." Louise tapped the driver on the shoulder. "This here is fine, thanks. We appreciate the ride."

Rattray was the definition of a one-horse town. Two strips of sun-bleached stores lined the main drag. Behind that, a handful of back streets curved up a steep sandy hill before petering out when the gradient got too severe. Two of the stores had **FOR SALE** signs in the windows. There were no people around that they could see.

Dan gave a low whistle.

"What do you do for fun around here, Louise? Grow cactuses?"

"The plural is cacti." The woman unshouldered her rucksack and dropped it in the nearest trash can. Perspiration moulded the t-shirt to her ample curves. "And you'll be getting one shoved up your butt if you sass me again."

The boy pulled at her arm.

"Louise. Why *are* we the only two alive? Why aren't we dead like everyone else on the base? And where did all the *ants* come from?"

"I don't know, Dan. Not even sure I want to."

She pointed to a row of modest one-story cabins halfway up the hill.

"That's where my daughter and I live. Her name's Emily."

"What about your husband?"

"I said I was pregnant, honey. Didn't say nothin about a husband." Louise gave a wry grin. "Guess you were right. There ain't much to do for fun around here."

Dan coughed politely and looked at the ground.

"Don't worry about it, honey. I like kids more than I like attachments."

When the teenager looked back up, tears sparkled in his eyes.

"What's going to happen to *me* now?"

Louise took a deep breath.

"I'm betting we both seen too much for the army to let us walk away." She patted her stomach protectively. "Me, Emily and the egg, we need to disappear."

"You're not going to take me, are you?" Dan could hardly speak.

"I can't. I know what you did."

"But I need to explain. I…"

"No." The woman put a finger to his lips. "I don't want explanations. You're a kid. All you need is forgiveness."

She pulled the teenager to the side of the street and parked him on a bench.

"But I need to make it clear why I did what *I* did."

Dan hung his head again.

"No. No. We look at each other for this." She tilted his chin up. "I was hired at Sheridan base cause I'm a trained nurse and they were shorthanded. When I saw what they were doing, I went along with it anyhow. I stood by and let them experiment on these prisoners. I did it for the money."

She stared into the teenager's eyes.

"Woman with a young child living in these parts? There ain't a lot of work and this paid handsomely."

The boy nodded, which was hard to do because Louise was still holding tightly onto his jaw.

"That was a mighty long speech for me, by the way."

"I understand," Dan whispered. Louise let go of his chin and pointed up the hill, her voice hardening.

"My ten-year-old daughter is there. She's my world and I can't have anything happen to her. I saved you. I reckon that makes us even. Can't do no more."

She reached into her pocket and pulled out a wad of notes.

"I got about a hundred dollars here. There's a Greyhound bus you can flag down in half an hour, heading for El Paso. Then you're on your own."

"I'm scared, Louise."

"Me too, son. But neither of us can go to the police. We've both done too much wrong."

She stuck out her hand and Dan gingerly took it.

"Good luck, honey."

"Same to you, Louise." The teenager choked back a sob.

The woman turned and marched determinedly up the hill, face red with shame, leaving Dan sitting alone on the deserted street.

Naish slunk back into the living quarter, dark rings under her eyes. Dr Kelty had fallen asleep at the desk, breathing softly, head lodged in his hands. The assistant watched him for a few moments. Then she reached out and pulled one elbow away. Kelty's head shot down, his chin slamming onto the hard wood.

"Eh? What? I wasn't asleep!"

"Course not, Sir," Naish nodded agreeably. "But choppers just found a jeep on the edge of the desert, about fifty miles north. Two dead soldiers inside. Looks like they killed each other."

"Sure." Kelty straightened up and placed two hands on his back, cracking it with a series of loud pops. "They escaped this carnage and drove fifty miles in the dark. *Then* they decided to kill each other."

"Maybe they fell out over who was gonna pay for gas."

"Don't be flippant, Naish." Kelty swung his head from side to side, creating more crunching noises. The woman winced.

"I'm betting there's only one jeep missing from the compound."

"Correct."

"Then there were *four* people in it." Kelty twisted a pen between his thin fingers, staring into space. "Odd that any fugitives would head north, though, don't you think?"

"There are far more towns to the west," his assistant agreed. "It would be easier to disappear if they headed in *that* direction."

"Narrow the search, Naish. Concentrate on any unidentified personnel who were bussed in from north of Sheridan base. And, when we find them, I don't want them killed anymore."

"That's mighty big of you."

"The two who escaped can't be a threat, or we'd know all about it by now." Kelty tapped the pen on his teeth. "My God. Those survivors might be the most important people on earth and they don't even know it."

"Without wanting to burst your bubble, Sir. There's a distinct possibility we *won't* locate them. They have quite a lead on us and it's pretty certain our funding will be pulled when Top Brass realise your experiment wiped out an entire research facility."

"I certainly have some fast talking to do." To Naish's horror, Kelty gave a broad smile. "But we'll find them."

He took the clipboard from his assistant and snapped it shut.

"Sooner or later. We *will* find them."

9

"We need to pool our resources." Millar Watt stroked his chin dramatically. "I'll figure out who killed the Orbisons and Poppy can sit on them until help arrives."

Poppy was used to comments like this and didn't even blink.

"What'll *I* do?" Gene said sarcastically. "Find you a pipe and deerstalker hat?"

"Can't look worse than the one he's wearing."

"Nothing wrong with Sherlock Holmes, my dear Popson." Millar removed the battered headgear and stroked it affectionately. "How often have I said, when you have eliminated the impossible, whatever remains, however improbable, must be the truth?"

"How about never?"

"It's a quote," Millar sighed. "From *The Sign of Four* by Arthur Conan Doyle."

"Is there a book in the information hut you've not read?"

51

"There's a history of the English Civil War I haven't got around to yet. Poppy's using it to block up a draught under her bedroom door."

Poppy shrugged. She wasn't interested in reading. The information hut had a battered television with a VCR and, though the only films were old black and white movies, Poppy had watched them dozens of times. Her ambition was to get to America someday and be a movie star – a notion Millar ridiculed every time he got the chance. But, no matter how much fun he made of her looks and size, Poppy was unshakeable in the belief she would eventually be a star.

"We should start with the facts we have." Gene fished around in the large tea chest where they kept their belongings. He eventually brought out a pad and paper.

"You want to take notes, Poppy?"

"Do I look like a secretary?"

"It's easy," Millar leered. "Just write with the sharp end of the pencil."

"I saw the Orbisons on Sunday at about one in the afternoon." Gene cut off the budding slanging match. "They must have died soon after."

On the paper, he wrote.

Time of death. Roughly 1.00 pm on Sunday.

"When were the bodies found?"

"A couple of hours later. Fred Wolper came across them."

"What would he be doing at the bottom of Pittenhall rocks?" Poppy wondered.

"Very good, Watson," Millar stroked his chin again. "Odd place for anyone to be."

"He was at the *top*, you idiots." Gene interrupted. "He'd been moving sheep to a new pasture and was missing a couple. He looked over the edge to see if they'd fallen and spotted the bodies."

"Put him down as a suspect."

"Is that what Sherlock Holmes would do?"

Millar shrugged.

"He's the only suspect we've got."

Gene dutifully wrote his name down.

Suspect 1. Fred Wolper. Shepherd.

"He couldn't have forced them both over himself," Poppy argued. "Guy's too small."

"That's right," Millar agreed. "Where were you at eleven on Sunday?"

"I was milking the cows."

"Excellent. So we can eliminate *them* as suspects."

"I remember seeing the McCombies walking past." Poppy thought for a moment. "I talked to Marcie Gold and she was with her parents."

"It's a start." Millar rubbed his hands. "Gene, can you write a list of everyone on the island? Then we can cross off anyone with an alibi."

"There must be fifty people on Fallen," Gene moaned. But he set out writing them all down. In the end, he counted 70, including the children.

"So? Who else couldn't have done it?"

"My parents," Poppy said with obvious relief. "They were in our croft."

"What about yours, Millar?"

"Having brunch with the Duke of Windsor, for all I know," the teenager retorted. "They sure as hell weren't *killing* anyone."

"I'll cross off your mom and dad, Poppy." Gene scored a pen through the Ainsworth's name. "And all the kids. They're too young to have done it."

"That still leaves 44 adults." Millar screwed up his face. "Including my parents and Gene's."

"Hey. We better get going." Poppy parted a nailed up sheet and looked out the small slit that served for a window. "It's pretty dark outside."

She picked up the kerosene lamp they used for illumination and the trio made their way back to Kirkfallen village. The ground had turned to ink but the teenagers knew their way so well they could have made it home with their eyes closed.

"See you tomorrow, guys." Millar broke off and headed towards his parents' croft. "The chase is afoot!"

"Well, you're sure to creep up on it in your big stupid camouflaged pants." Poppy moved off in the opposite direction. "Night, Gene."

"Night Poppy. Glad your parents aren't murderers."

He tucked the notebook inside his jersey and entered his own home.

Edward Stapleton was sitting by the roaring fire, reading a book. He glanced up as his son entered.

"You're late tonight."

"Sorry, dad."

"So long as you get up for school tomorrow."

"I will." Gene hesitated before going into his bedroom. "Dad?"

"Yes?"

"Do you like it here?"

His father waited much longer to reply than Gene expected.

"It's my home."

"Don't you miss all the stuff out there in the world?"

"I never wanted to work in some office wearing a suit and tie. And then what? An evening sitting on my ass watching TV?"

"No one has ever left the island, have they?" Gene persisted. "Does everyone feel the same?"

"I suppose. Here, we're in control of our own destiny. That's a great thing. Underappreciated, if you ask me."

He slammed shut the book, folded large hands across it and studied his son.

"Don't worry. You'll get a chance to travel when you're old enough. I don't expect you to stay here forever."

"I know. Night dad."

"Night, son." Edward gave him a half salute before dropping the hand back to the book on his lap. "I love you."

Gene paused on his way to the bedroom. His father was a good man, but emotional declarations were not something he was prone to.

"I love you too, dad."

Once Gene had closed his bedroom door, Edward Stapleton slowly opened his book and frowned.

Crushed between the pages were half a dozen ants.

Lying in bed that night, Gene found he was unable to sleep. Instead, he kept thinking about the list he had made of the islanders.

There was something odd about it. Nothing to do with murder suspects. He was sure of that.

No.

There was something strange about the list itself.

The Houdini Killer

All depends on me

As long as I live, I shall think only of victory

I shall annihilate everyone who is opposed to me

Adolph Hitler

10

The sky was slate grey when Gene left for school. It was hard to tell if the island was sheltering under one unending cloud, as usual, or if the firmament had simply abandoned colour for the duration of the day.

Gene's father was digging the frosty ground on the hill above their croft, sleeves rolled up over his burly arms, despite the cold. It was a sight Gene had witnessed on many mornings but, for the first time, the lone silhouette seemed dwarfed by the monochrome majesty of the island.

Gene had always been a curious type, yet that curiosity had always been focused on the great unknown – the world outside Kirkfallen. It occurred to him that he rarely asked any questions about the island itself.

Now he had begun, he was finding it hard to stop.

In the prefabricated school hut, he daydreamed through morning lessons. The Kirkfallen children were all taught together, with the elder children helping to educate the younger ones. This system had an advantage for the older kids as they were only required to attend school in the mornings. In the afternoons, they were supposed to study by themselves, using the considerable resources of the information hut. Sometimes they did – Millar especially. Sometimes they were needed to help their parents tend to the land or do repairs. Occasionally they played truant.

Today, Gene practically dragged Poppy and Millar to the information hut. He shut the door behind them and turned on the single barred electric fire.

"This is going to be a different kind of lesson," he said enigmatically. "What do we usually study when we're in here?"

"All sorts of stuff," Poppy said. "Maths. Spelling. Whatever we're set on our worksheets."

"What about books?" Gene turned instinctively to Millar. "What do you read about?"

"A lot of novels. Science. History."

"What about Fallen's history? When do we learn about that?"

"It doesn't have one." Poppy gave a dismissive shrug. "There used to be some kind of naval base here but it was abandoned years ago. The place was uninhabited when our families arrived."

She sounded like she was reciting a set text - which, in fact, she was.

"So, where are our relatives?" Gene persisted. "Our aunts and uncles?"

Again, Poppy reeled off the answer she had always been given.

"The families who come here are carefully chosen. We haven't got any close relatives. Otherwise, it would be too hard for everybody concerned to commit themselves to such an isolated place."

"We've got grandparents, though." Gene had spent most of the night pondering life on the island and now his misgivings came pouring out. "Mine are both dead but surely some of the adults have parents who want to visit?"

"My grandparents are dead too," Poppy said.

"And mine," Millar added slowly, doubt creasing his face.

"I tell you something else." Gene unfolded a piece of paper. "I made a new list of everyone who lives here. This time, I put in the children and their ages."

He spread the sheet on the large table where they studied.

Kirkfallen Residents.

The Stapletons plus Gene (14)
The Watts plus Millar (14)
The Ainsworths plus Poppy (14)
The Golds plus Marcie (12)
The Ng's plus Mona (12)

The McCombies plus Bob (12)
The Hayashidas plus Noriko (12)
The Nhols plus Talasa (10)
The Abrahms plus Ben (10)
The Cutters plus Liam (10)
The Wolpers plus Gemma (10)
The De Guglielmos plus Megan (8)
The Hamdallahs plus Faisal (8)
The Henrys plus Sarah (8)
The Luptiks plus Jakub (8)
The Nevilles plus Kyle (6)
The McMillans plus Ruairidh (6)
The Kitts plus Jordan (6)
The Von Speers plus Beth (6)
The Jodes plus Marius (4)
The Khadums plus Michael (4)
The Olsens plus Erin (4)
The Singhs plus Sagar (4)
The Orbisons (deceased)

"Reads like the debating chamber of the United Nations." Millar Watt was always ready to display knowledge of a world he had never seen.

"Twenty-three families, each with one child." Gene tapped the piece of paper. "But the children's ages are all in bunches of four, with a two-year gap between each group. What's more, the birthdays in each age bracket are all roughly four months apart, with no exceptions."

He checked the paper again to make sure his calculations were correct, even though he'd studied it a dozen times already.

"Don't you think it's kind of a weird coincidence?"

"Yeah. But that's probably all it is. After all, the Orbisons didn't have kids."

"I think being dead pretty much rules the Orbisons out as inhabitants." Gene wouldn't give in. "But one child each? How come nobody had another once they got to the island?"

"You're overreacting," Millar said. "You need a good spread of ages to have a thriving community. So our parents only allow groups of families with one child onto the island and they don't have another. Think of what a burden that would be!"

"Imagining two of you, it suddenly makes perfect sense," Poppy chimed in.

"And whose rules are they following?" Gene said. "Your parents? My parents? You notice we don't seem to have any leaders in this community. No kind of government. I mean, who really *runs* this place?"

"There's a book on one of these shelves about conspiracy theories and the weirdos who believe in them." Millar waved an arm at the bookshelf. "You want to have a read of that, nutty boy."

And it hit Gene. A simple, ridiculous fact.

"Why does an island in the middle of nowhere, with limited shelf space in its library, have a book making fun of conspiracy theories?"

Millar opened his mouth to make a smart retort. Then he shook his head.

"I don't know."

"I'm proposing a new kind of homework."

Gene looked at the books lining the shelves, wishing now that he had been as diligent in acquiring knowledge as Millar. It struck him that he didn't know nearly enough about anything.

"I want you to have a real think about what's always been right under our noses. This island and the people on it."

"Better than maths, I guess."

"Think about what?" Poppy still sounded unsure.

"Anything odd about this place. Anything that ever niggled at you."

"I thought we were supposed to be solving a murder?" Millar tilted his chair back and put his hands behind his head. "Unless you think it was a CIA plot to cover up some UFO hidden at Jackson Head."

"Could you pack more initials into one sentence, brainbox?"

"It's just a feeling," Gene said. "This is the right way to go about it."

"Sure." Millar tilted his hat back and grinned. "It's all a plot by Agatha Christie."

"Who's Agatha Christie?" Poppy asked innocently.

"She invented the atomic bomb."

"Cool! That's one in the eye for anyone who thinks women are dumb." The girl wafted a hand theatrically at Gene's list. "And I'm smart enough to have spotted something *you* didn't. Our birthdays are much closer together than the other groups of kids."

She thought for a moment.

"Oh! And there's only *three* of us."

"Maybe one family left."

"Don't think so." Millar had obviously appointed himself Devil's Advocate in the discussion. "My dad says nobody's *ever* left the island."

"Mine too." Gene folded up the list and stuck it in his pocket.

"But the Orbisons certainly did."

11

At dinner, Gene wasted no time with his awkward mealtime question. Over the years, it had become a ritual in the Stapleton household and his parents expected it.

"Dad. What would happen if you and mom got divorced?"

His father's egg covered fork paused halfway to his lips. Annie Stapleton gave a small cough.

"Why? Do we look like we're going to get divorced?"

"No. But what would happen? Would you leave the island?"

"Not at all," his father replied calmly. "I'd build another croft next door and you could spend the weekends there."

"No need to make fun." Gene bit into his toast, plotting his next move. "Don't people out in the world get divorced all the time?"

"Then I guess everyone is better off here."

"And why are there no boats?" The boy changed tack as quickly as any sailor. "Our staple diet is fish, so why do we always catch them from the shore? Wouldn't it be easier out on the ocean?"

"It would." Edward cut his toast into neat soldiers. "But we're terrible fishermen, Gene. That takes a lifetime to learn and the Atlantic Ocean is a treacherous place."

Gene's mother looked down at her plate and his father arranged the slices carefully in a circle.

"We had boats once," Annie Stapleton said softly.

"We did?"

Edward shot a look at his wife, then sighed and put down his fork.

"We did. The Kirkfallen community was founded using a government grant, as you know. It was a sort of... anthropological experiment. To see if a small group could sustain a village in the middle of nowhere by using alternative farming and fishing methods. Experimental fertilisers. New kinds of pesticides. Nets made of polymer fibres."

Gene nodded, although he had heard the story a dozen times.

"Funding dried up when the government administration changed, but we're still here," his father continued with a tinge of pride. "So, I guess you could say the project worked."

"There were only a few families when we began." Gene's mother carried on the original thread of the conversation. "Ourselves, the Ainsworths, the Watts and the Waltons."

"Who are the *Waltons*?" This was a part of the Kirkfallen story Gene had *never* heard. "There aren't any Waltons here."

"Not anymore." His father pushed the plate away, no longer hungry. "At the time, we were given what were thought essential to survive on a remote island. Including three small boats."

"To fish with," his mother added unnecessarily.

"One summer's day. A beautiful sunny day it was. The Waltons went out on the water. Just for a break from the toil. Nobody saw any harm in it…"

His father's story petered out and he motioned forlornly at his wife.

"It was a perfectly calm sea." Gene's mother folded her hands on her lap. "So they took their daughter with them."

"How come you never mentioned this before?"

"Not now, boy," his father cautioned.

"The currents off the west coast are deadly and a sudden squall sprang up." Annie's voice dried up and she took a sip of tea. "Nobody could have guessed."

"We found the wreckage of the boat on the other side of Pittenhall Ridge. Strewn across the rocks. That's where all the treacherous currents lead."

That's where the Orbisons died. Gene thought immediately. But he held his tongue. His father got up from the table and put on his jacket.

"They were our friends, Gene."

He patted his pockets, more for something to do than because he had to check his possessions. He didn't need anything on Kirkfallen. Not keys. Not money. Not identification.

"We're not sailors," he said gruffly. "We don't go out on the sea."

He ruffled the boy's hair and hurried out the door.

"The boats were taken away after that. Too many children around. Too much temptation."

His mother also rose and began clearing away the dishes despite the fact that her own meal was only half-finished.

"That's the problem with living in isolation." She seemed suddenly agitated, looking about for something else to wash. "When a storm comes, there's nothing you can do but ride it out."

Annie Stapleton plonked the dishes in the sink. Her back was to the boy and she wiped furiously at the greasy plates.

"But you never know who it will take."

A shiver ran up the teenager's spine.

Something in the way she spoke made the phrase sound more like a premonition than an observation.

12

Apathy Amazon Walton leaned her elbows on the sill of the living room window and traced her strange name on the dirty glass. Home was the seventh floor of a high-rise block on the outskirts of Edinburgh and the city's rooftops glistened like big, dirty cobbles stretching into the gloom.

On the coffee table lay a copy of the *Scotsman* newspaper. There was nothing good on TV, so she'd tried reading it while she waited for her mother to come home. But every page seemed to hold something depressing.

Freak Accident Kills Aberdeen Family

A suspected gas leak killed a family while they slept in the early hours of Wednesday morning. Andrew Flintheart, 36, Aiki Flintheart, 30, and their daughter Elspeth, 15, were overcome by fumes from a broken gas pipe in their semi-detached bungalow.

Fire services responded to a call by an anonymous passer-by who smelt gas outside the suburban home at 32 Westmoreland Drive but were too late to save the family.

"An investigation has begun into the deaths," said a spokesman for Aberdeenshire police, "But all initial signs point to this being a tragic accident."

She heard the front door swing open and, seconds later, her mother barged into the living room, a straining Tesco's shopping bag hanging from each arm. A strand of hair had come loose from her tight bun and hung down over one eye.

Emily Walton looked tired. But then, she always looked tired. She kicked her daughter's foot in greeting and sniffed the air.

"You been smoking?"

"I don't smoke, mum."

"Yeah, but you turn sixteen tomorrow. That's when I started."

"You got me a present yet?" Apathy inspected the bags, looking for any recognisable bulge.

"Two packs of Marlboro Lights. It was, buy one, get one free."

Emily lugged the groceries into the kitchen and set them on the table. Apathy could hear her putting her purchases away, then the pop of a bottle being opened. When Emily returned, she held a large glass of wine in one hand. She sank down on the sofa next to her daughter and let out a heartfelt sigh.

"Hard day, mum?"

"No. I just love unjamming the photocopier after the boss has made multiple pictures of his bum."

Emily lifted the glass to her lips and drained it in one go. Apathy was a little taken aback. Her mother got up again and marched back into the kitchen. When she returned, she had two full glasses and a half-empty bottle wedged under one arm.

"Want to split this with me?"

This time her daughter couldn't conceal her astonishment.

"You getting me started young?"

"Don't say that." Emily handed her a glass anyway. Apathy took a tentative sip and screwed up her face.

"Yuk. Got a cigarette?"

"What?"

"I'm joking."

"Oh. Yeah." Emily laughed humourlessly. "Kids."

Apathy fidgeted uncomfortably. Her mother was a melancholy type but she rarely looked this disconsolate. Emily took another large gulp of wine and pulled a Marlboro from the packet on the coffee table. She lit it and flicked the match at the ashtray. It missed and landed on the floor, still smoking. Emily ignored it. She slapped her palms on her knees several times and took a deep breath.

"We need to have a talk."

"Whatever it was, I didn't do it. And a dog ate my homework."

Apathy's mother fidgeted with her wine glass.

"What is it, mum?"

"You never wonder why I called you Apathy?" Emily said suddenly.

"Eh? I *know* why." The teenager replied, mystified. "You thought it sounded pretty and you didn't know what it meant at the time."

"You really think I'm *that* dumb?"

"It's what you've always told me. And Amazon is after my grandmother because she terrified people."

Emily Walton took another drink and screwed her eyes shut. She rubbed her temple. Tucked the loose strand of hair behind her ear. Her daughter waited.

"I don't know what to say except... none of that's true. I called you Apathy Amazon because of a joke your father made."

"What?" Where had *this* revelation come from? Emily Walton *never* talked about Apathy's father. Apart from his name, she knew virtually nothing about her dad. A dozen questions formed in the teenager's mind. Of course, the dumbest one came out first.

"You named me after a *joke*? You know how much crap I get at school about what I'm called?"

"Not very funny, huh?" Emily took another swig of wine. Her glass was nearly empty again. "I thought

I had a good reason at the time. I've had years to dwell on *that* particular mistake."

"Eh... You're rambling a bit."

"I called you Apathy to make it easier for your dad to find you." Emily's voice was almost a whisper. "Can't be two people in the world with *that* handle."

"Mum. He ran out on you when you were pregnant and you haven't seen him since." Despite the taste, Apathy took another sip of wine. "If he hasn't turned up by now, I don't see that he ever will."

"I used to pray that he would." Emily stubbed her cigarette out with an angry jab.

"But now that thought scares the shit out of me."

13

A white van drew up outside the tower block where Apathy lived. On either side, in bright orange letters, it bore the logo.

BuG: Pest Control

The driver got out and stared up at the multi-storey. Night was falling and yellow squares had begun to stud the concrete façade as people arrived home from work.

A short man climbed from the back of the van, pulling on a baseball cap as he alighted. On his back was a tank with a hose and nozzle attached. He lit a cigarette, the glow of the struck match illuminating a round, jolly face that matched his physique. He stared up at the tower block.

"Bit of a crappy place to live, Mr Bundy."

The van driver did a double-take.

"Take off the fake beard, Mr Gacy," he sighed.

"Have you seen how many CCTV cameras are in this area?"

"The caps will hide our faces."

"Plenty people about too."

"We're wearing overalls and driving a van." Mr Bundy tilted his own cap over his eyes. "Nobody is going to look twice."

He was right. People were scurrying home without glancing left or right, carrying shopping bags or bent almost double to combat the biting wind. Even so, Mr Gacy put on a pronounced limp to throw any observers off track.

"They're not going to notice your face," Mr Bundy said pointedly as they headed towards the multi-story. "But they'll sure as hell look twice at someone who walks like Long John Silver."

"Right. And calling ourselves by the surnames of two famous serial killers isn't conspicuous?"

"I thought it was funny."

Mr Bundy switched on a flashlight and played it in front of him. They began to circle the building, Mr Bundy lighting the ground while Mr Gacy squirted the grass with a foul-smelling liquid from the tank on his back.

"How did it go up in Aberdeen, by the way?" Mr Bundy asked.

"Fine," Mr Gacy replied curtly. "Did my psychic mumbo jumbo. Got a couple of hundred quid."

"That's a long way to travel for a small job."

"I like the sea air." Mr Gacy gave the ground another squirt, shuddering with revulsion. "Crap! There are ants everywhere, Mr Bundy. I *hate* ants."

"This stuff'll make short work of them." Mr Bundy wiped both hands on his coveralls and sniffed his fingers in distaste. "That tank's leaking, though. Bet it's all over the back of the van."

"Don't worry." Mr Gacy switched off the bug spray. "I mopped it up with your newspaper."

"Hey. I hadn't read it yet."

"What are you two *doing*?"

The pair spun round. A woman in a quilted jacket was standing behind them. Underneath, she wore tracksuit bottoms and slippers.

"Hey there, love," Mr Bundy replied cheerily. "You the caretaker?"

"He's not here. I'm his wife."

"Good enough for me, darling." Mr Bundy waved a blue form at her. "Pest control. Council sent us over. Some of the residents been complaining about an ant manifestation."

He indicated the ground.

"Right enough, they're all over the shop."

"That was quick." The woman sounded uncertain. "They only started appearing a couple of days ago."

Mr Gacy and Mr Bundy glanced at each other.

"And I didn't know the council worked at night." The woman narrowed her eyes.

"Contracted the job out to us." Mr Bundy patted the tank on his companion's back. "We don't want to be spraying this nasty stuff around when there are kids out playing."

"Can you do the laundry room too?" The woman pulled her coat tighter and shivered. "Place is full of the little buggers."

"Sure thing." Bundy thrust the form out. "Sign here? Show that we've been?"

The caretaker's wife scribbled her signature at the bottom of the paper and hurried back inside.

"Ants everywhere." Mr Gacy shook his head in admiration. "You were right."

"Ain't I always?" Mr Bundy crumpled up the form and threw it away.

"I just wish to God that, this time, I'd been wrong."

14

Emily Walton got up and went to the window. It was night outside now and spatters of rain began to click against the pane and slalom down the dark surface.

"We're having this conversation because I made a promise to myself," she said without looking round. "I swore I'd tell you about your father when you reached sixteen. Against my better judgement, I'll admit."

She peered into the darkness again.

"But it's kind of a tradition in my family to drop bombshells on their offspring at that age."

Apathy held her breath. Her mother had always refused to talk about her dad and, eventually, the teenager had given up asking. But that didn't mean she didn't want to know what he was like. She very much wanted to know.

"I'll make a deal with you." Emily was still staring into the sodden night. "I'll tell you as much as I know and I'll answer your questions as best I can. But you have to accept that you might not like what you hear."

She clutched at the sill, head bowed.

"That includes what I'm about to tell you about myself."

"Oh, I'm sure I'll still love you." Apathy leaned over the back of the couch. "Unless you didn't get the Nikes I wanted for my birthday."

Emily pulled the curtains shut and came back to the couch, resting her work-worn hands on either side of her daughter's upturned face.

"Just remember. Your dad's part of my past. For me, that's where he stays."

Apathy put her hand gently over her mother's.

"You know, you don't have to tell me if it's too painful."

But she didn't mean what she said and Emily knew it.

"God, I need more wine." The woman pulled her hand away and darted into the kitchen, emerging with another opened bottle. Apathy looked uneasily at her.

"You're drinking awful fast."

"I know. And I had a couple of vodkas before I got home." Emily gave a lopsided smile that turned into a flinch. "I just... I just..."

"Do you hate my dad because he stuck you with me?"

"No, honey!" Apathy's mother sounded shocked. "I can't dislike him for *that*."

"No. You'd rather forget him for it."

Emily set the bottle determinedly on the coffee table and blurted out the next sentence before she had another chance to reconsider.

"I've always said your father was called Alan Parker and that he was a computer programmer I met when I was living in Manchester." The words tumbled over each other.

"I know all that. You fell in love. You got pregnant. He dumped you. You moved and never saw him again."

Emily poured herself more wine. Her hands were shaking so badly now that most of it splashed across the table.

"Mum, this is embarrassing." Apathy rose to fetch a cloth from the kitchen. Emily grabbed her t-shirt and pulled her daughter back onto the couch.

"Let me tell the truth. While I still have the nerve."

Apathy nodded silently, not daring to move.

"I made up the story about Alan Parker." Her mother licked her lips uncertainly. "Your father was actually called Daniel Boone Salty."

"And I thought *I* had a daft name." It was an inane comment but Apathy was too shocked to come up with a witty rejoinder.

"We grew up together. When I met him, I was living in a little town called Rattray. In New Mexico."

"New Mexico? But that's in the United States."

"Yes, it is."

"I didn't know you'd even *been* to America."

"I lived there all my life... until just before you were born, that is."

"But... you're not American." Apathy tried to get her mind around this next revelation. "You've got a Scottish *accent*."

"It's fake." Emily reached out and gently touched her daughter's face. "Baby, everything about me is fake."

"Mum, what are you *telling* me?"

"Oh God, this was a mistake." To Apathy's horror, her mother began to cry. "I can't do this, honey. I thought I could, but I can't."

She struggled up from the couch and wine sloshed over the rim of her glass, dribbling down her hand.

"You're scaring me!" the girl pleaded. "What are you trying to say?"

"I should have done this sober."

Emily set the wine glass down on the bookcase beside a picture of her infant daughter, misjudging the distance and knocking it over.

"Dammit all to hell! Dammit, dammit!"

"Just *talk* to me."

"I need to take a shower. Clear my head."

Emily paced up and down the living room, a lost look on her face. Tears ran down her cheeks, streaking them with mascara.

"Just give me a few minutes. Please?"

"OK. All right, mum." Apathy was genuinely frightened now.

"Ten minutes." Emily Walton whirled and almost ran into the bathroom. "And don't answer the door if anyone knocks."

Apathy sat rigid on the couch, trying to make sense of what she had heard. Surely this had to be a cruel joke? Only she knew her mother - and Emily wouldn't do that. Not the night before her birthday.

And, despite the turmoil in her heart, something about the name Daniel Salty nagged at her.

She had heard it before.

Apathy waited until she heard the hiss of the shower then got up, padded quietly into her bedroom and switched on the computer. Connecting with the internet, she Googled the name *Daniel Boone Salty*. A whole scree of entries came up.

She clicked on the first one and began to read.

Her face drained of all colour and her throat went dry.

The Houdini Killer

D.B. Salty is one of America's most notorious mass murderers. In 1978, at the age of 13, he butch-ered his mother and father - Alex and Wilma Salty. He killed his mother in the kitchen of their suburban home in Granby, Colorado with a carving knife. Witnesses then saw him chase his father into the street and blast the man in the back with a shotgun. Though police responded within minutes, the teenager was never caught.

In 1995, now aged 30, Salty was identified as the perpetrator of the infamous 'Diamondback Massacre'. He used a semi-automatic rifle to kill all thirteen inhabitants of the Diamondback trailer park in New York State's Adirondack Mountains – including the family he had been living with. Despite a massive manhunt, he, once again, vanished without trace.

These miraculous escapes earned him the nickname the 'Houdini Killer.'

He is still at large to this day.

15

Apathy sat on the couch, hardly knowing where she was. Finding out her mother had lied about her past was a big enough blow. Discovering her dad was a mass killer. Now, *that* was a bit much.

She looked up several other web pages before she heard the shower stop and Emily pad into her own bedroom. All the entries told more or less the same story. Then she dashed back to the living room before her mother realised what she was up to.

Emily Walton emerged from her room, transformed. She had put on a plain black dress, reapplied her makeup and tied her hair back. Under one arm, she carried a small wooden box. She looked beautiful.

Apathy was ready to let fly with a torrent of angry accusations, but the expression on her mother's face stopped her. Emily wore a look of sorrowful resignation that both alarmed and moved her daughter.

The teenager held her tongue. Her mother had begun this. She would give her a chance to finish.

"I have a story to tell you," Emily sat down next to her daughter, curling up bare legs. "It's a terrible story."

She opened the box and took out a small, square Polaroid.

"This is *my* mother. Her name was Louise."

The picture showed a pretty, broad-faced woman with thick black hair streaked with grey and a gap between her front teeth. She was standing in front of a trailer, one arm leaning casually against the door. There was a rifle on the ground beside her.

"It's the only picture she ever let me take of her. She even put the gun down for it."

"That was good of her."

Apathy didn't know what else to say. She had never seen her gran before. Louise had died before Apathy was born and her mother had claimed not to have any images of the woman.

Emily reluctantly handed over the picture, as if she couldn't bear to part from it, after having hidden it for so long.

"How come she only let you take one snapshot? She's pretty enough."

"Photographs were... eh... discouraged in our family."

Apathy nodded. It was a secretive trait Emily had continued. And she had never seen a photograph of her mother. Emily absolutely would not allow her picture to be taken.

"What's that behind her?"

Apathy pointed to a dark smudge by the door of the trailer. The mark was too blurred to identify, but its shape reminded the girl of a crouching figure.

"It looks like someone watching her."

"It's just a flaw in the developing." Emily quickly took another photograph from the box and handed it over. This picture was of a group of people enjoying a barbecue. On the far right was a pretty young woman, half-turned towards the camera.

"Yeah, it's me." Apathy's mother gave a bashful smile. "From when your dad and I lived in Texas. Didn't know the picture was going to be taken. Then I couldn't bring myself to destroy it cause he was in it too."

She pointed to a young man at the front of the group, looking somewhat startled at being caught by the camera. He had a thin, good looking face and a mass of wavy hair. Despite his solemn countenance, his eyes were wide and expressive.

"That's D.B. Salty. The only photograph I have of him. Probably the only photograph *anyone* has of him." Her mother reached out to take the picture, then hesitantly drew her hand back.

"I was ten years old the day I met him," she said.

"First thing he did was save my life."

16

1 9 8 0

Ten-year-old Emily Martin stood by the unlit stove, confused and afraid. The kitchen was a place for sandy
footprints, lemonade and the hot smell of nearly ready
meals. Now the cupboards were open wide, her mother was
loading provisions into a cardboard box and a hunting rifle
was propped against the fridge. Two hastily packed suit-
cases were already in the back of their old Buick Station
wagon.

"No sense in letting good food go to waste." Her mother
dropped five tins of refried beans into the box.

"Why did you pull me out of school?" Emily demanded
for the third time. "Where are we going?"

Louise wished she knew.

"On a trip, babe! I told you." She tried to sound like it
was going to be some big adventure, but the girl could de-

tect a nervy tremor in her mom's voice. "It won't be for long."

"But I was supposed to stay at Alice's house tonight."

Alice was a neighbour who looked after Emily when her mother was away, working three-day shifts.

"She doesn't even know you're home."

"We'll call when we get to where we're going," Louise said gaily, hating herself for the lie. Her daughter was never going to see her friends and neighbours again.

"I'll fetch our coats. You put this box in the car."

She gave Emily a kiss on the head and went upstairs. She pulled weatherproof jackets for them both from the closet and was looking around for anything sentimental she'd forgotten when she heard a car draw up outside.

Louise dashed to the window and looked out.

Four soldiers in a jeep were parked next to her daughter. One was staring straight up at the window. She saw him glance down at a sheaf of papers in his hand and immediately guessed it was her security file.

She jerked back from the window, too late. The man motioned to his companions and one jumped down and accompanied his superior to the front door.

Louise raced downstairs and into the kitchen, scooping up the hunting rifle and clicking a round into the chamber. There was a knock at the door. She slid into a crouch below the sightline of the kitchen window.

"We saw you, Miss Martin," a voice shouted. "My name is Sergeant Sommers and I have orders to escort you back to Sheridan base."

Louise stayed silent, rifle clutched against her chest.

"We've got your daughter out here and she's pretty scared," the voice continued. "I promise neither of you will be harmed, but you do have to come with me."

Then, after a few seconds

"Louise. You really don't have a choice."

With a silent curse, the woman put down the rifle and went to the door.

Emily was already seated in the back of the army jeep, flanked by two soldiers. She was crying. Sergeant Sommers and his companion took one arm each and escorted Louise towards the vehicle.

"You can't do this," the woman protested. "My daughter and I are civilians."

"I'm sure the matter will be sorted out quickly." The sergeant's expression was impassive. "But we need to talk to you back at Sheridan."

"What the hell is *he* up to?" Sommer's companion indicated uphill.

At the top of the incline, a youth was zig-zagging back and forth across the street, from house to house. Each time he reached a residence, he picked up a rock and launched it through the largest window of the dwelling.

"What the hell?" Sergeant Sommers unslung his rifle and stepped away from Louise.

"Hey, you!" he bellowed up the hill. "Stop that right now!"

Dan Salty ignored the warning, still speeding across the narrow road and back, launching missiles through windows.

People began to run into the street, shouting angrily at the young vandal.

"Get into the jeep, Ma'am," the sergeant urged. "This minute."

"Make me." Louise tried to pull away from her captors.

"Private Buckmaster, get her into the vehicle."

Buckmaster twisted Louise's arm roughly behind her back and frog marched her towards the jeep. Emily saw what was happening and began to scream. The nearest soldier clasped a hand over the girl's mouth.

"They're not real troops!" Dan Salty yelled. "They're kidnapping Louise Martin!"

All eyes turned towards the intruders. Louise's neighbour, Bill Hahn, emerged from the house opposite, blinking in the bright sunlight. His wife bobbed around in the open doorway, clutching her apron.

"What the hell's all the noise about?" Hahn spotted the soldiers and his eyes widened. "What's going on, Louise?"

Louise Martin took a deep breath.

"Help!" she shouted, taking Dan Salty's tack. "They're kidnapping me!"

Private Buckmaster yanked her arm so hard, the shout turned into a groan. The crowd gathering on the hill stopped suddenly, their attention now focused completely on the disturbance below. Bill Hahn turned and darted back into the house, sweeping his wife out of the way.

"They're not real soldiers," Dan Salty yelled again. "They're taking her. Do something!"

"That's gotta be the other fugitive," Sergeant Sommers grunted. "Anderson. Jordan. Get up there and apprehend him."

The soldiers leapt from the vehicle and started up the incline, leaving Emily in the back, too afraid to move. The crowd surged down to meet them, bunching behind the boy.

The residents of Rattray had never seen Dan Salty or the uniformed men before, but they knew Louise Martin. She was a good neighbour with a lovely daughter. And because of the secrecy surrounding Sheridan base, the town had no idea she worked there, for she was picked up each day in an unmarked van. They believed she was a nurse in El Paso.

Now, armed men were trying to bundle her away. That couldn't be right.

Bill Hahn emerged from his house, holding a shotgun. He pointed it at Sergeant Sommers.

"You let that woman go," he stammered.

"You are interfering with the operations of the United States Army!" Sergeant Sommers roared back. "Lower that weapon right now, mister!"

The barrel of Bill Hahn's gun trembled but he kept it pointed at the sergeant.

"How do I know who you are? Since when did the U.S. military pull women and kids outta their houses?"

Seeing Hahn's defiance, the crowd began to move forward again. The soldiers running to meet them stopped and looked back uncertainly.

Sergeant Sommers pulled Louise in front of him and swung up his weapon. He fired a long burst over Bill Hahn's head, shattering the upper windows of his home and tearing chunks out of the guttering. Hahn's wife gave a squeal and disappeared inside. The crowd on the hill shrank away, some of the women shrieking.

Dan Salty darted sideways, vaulted a garden fence and vanished between two houses. Private Jordan sprinted after him. Private Anderson was about to follow, but the crowd had begun moving downhill again in a menacing huddle. Some had picked up rocks from the dusty road. More doors were opening, below them this time, the occupants drawn from their houses by the sound of gunfire.

"Drop the weapon and go back inside!" the sergeant screamed, sweat breaking out on his forehead.

After a few seconds, Bill Hahn let the shotgun fall and backed slowly into his house, hands above his head.

"Where are all these people *coming* from?" Private Buckmaster grunted. "Don't anyone have jobs around here?"

"It's that kinda town," Louise smirked. "Lotta hunters, though. Lotta guns."

She was right. At least a half dozen of the men, up and down the hill had darted back into their dwellings and emerged with rifles. A couple of them even held handguns.

The mass of people uphill had almost reached Private Anderson. The soldier had unslung his own rifle and was holding it in front of him, unsure what to do next. Sergeant

Sommers fired another burst into the air. This time, the throng only moved back a few feet.

"This aint a crowd," Buckmaster said apprehensively. "It's a damned lynch mob."

He wrenched Louise towards the jeep, but the woman caught her foot and fell forwards on her hands and knees.

"Anderson, fetch Jordan and get back to the vehicle!" Sommers bellowed up the hill. "We'll come back for the boy."

"Boy's already here."

The sergeant swung round.

Dan Salty was standing in front of Bill Hahn's house, the discarded shotgun in his hands.

"I'm quite capable of using this." He stepped calmly out of the shadows and onto the sidewalk. "As you probably know."

Ten-year-old Emily Walton goggled at the teenager, facing down the soldiers like some old-time gunslinger. The sergeant was less impressed.

"Don't be stupid, kid. There's four of us and we don't *have* to take you alive."

As if on cue, Private Jordan sprinted round the corner of Hahn's house, skidding to a halt as he took in the unfolding situation.

Dan Salty kept walking towards the jeep. Behind him, Jordan raised his rifle and sighted on the boy's back.

A sharp crack echoed in the dusty air. Jordan dropped the weapon and staggered back, clutching his hand. Uphill, a wisp of smoke drifted from the barrel of a rifle held by a kneeling man in a red checked shirt. He had already snapped another shell in the breech and was squinting through the sights again. Two or three other townspeople had taken up similar stances and the crowd parted to give them a better shot.

"You idiot," Louise hissed at the sergeant. "Half the people in this town can fell a deer at three hundred yards. Lower your weapons before they kill you."

The soldiers looked at their Commander, realising for the first time just how precarious their position had become.

"Dumb, fucking rednecks." The sergeant dropped the gun and raised his hands. "Got no respect for authority." After a pause, his men followed suit.

"Not your sort, anyhow." Louise picked up the fallen rifle.

"It's all right," she shouted to her neighbours. "Everything's ok now!"

The mob stared at her, waiting for an explanation. Nobody seemed inclined to go back indoors.

"It really is OK!" Dan Salty lowered his shotgun. "Did anyone call the police?"

"I did." Bill Hahn emerged from his house. "Nearest station's in Hurricane, though, bout thirty miles from here. Take em a while to reach us."

"Then can I get a couple of volunteers to tie these guys up?"

There was no shortage of offers.

Ten minutes later, Louise and her daughter stood beside Bill Hahn's Ford Pickup, their belongings stored in the rear. The rest of the residents of Rattray had quietly dispersed, unwilling to act as witnesses when the police came. It was that kind of town.

"You positive about this Bill?" Louise asked.

"Police will be here soon," the bearded man motioned to the soldiers tied up and blindfolded in the jeep. "I'm guessing they're gonna find out that those are real military, ain't they?"

Louise hesitated.

"They are."

"That's why you're taking my car," Hahn whispered. "To get a head start. We'll all keep quiet about it."

He regarded the empty street.

"You were always well-liked here."

The woman looked her neighbour in the eye. "Ain't you gonna ask what I've done?"

"You're a damned fine gal, Louise. That's all I need to know."

Louise turned to Dan Salty, standing silently beside her daughter. The girl was looking at her saviour in awe.

"Where *are* we going, mom?" she asked plaintively.

"Well. I'm not sure." The woman swallowed hard and then made a supreme effort to be positive. "But wherever we go, it won't be so bad. We'll need to find somewhere out of the way. We'll be like the Waltons on that old TV programme. Living in the middle of nowhere and trusting each other and growing cactus."

"Cacti, Louise."

The woman walked over and put her hands on Dan's shoulders.

"So? You gonna come along?"

"Really?"

"You risked your life to save us, honey. Even though I was gonna leave you behind."

"Seemed like the right thing to do."

"They say everyone deserves a second chance." Louise steered the teenager away. "So, here's yours."

She lowered her voice to a whisper.

"My daughter is my life. You gotta promise me you'll never do anything to harm her. In fact, you promise that you'll keep her safe." She leaned in close to his ear. "Whatever that may take."

"I promise, Louise." The teenager had tears of gratitude in his eyes.

"A man's promise is the measure of his worth, son." Her grip tightened on Dan's shoulder until the teenager flinched. "You want to be the man in our family, you gotta hold that sacred. If you give your word to us, you *never* break it."

"I'll never break it. I swear."

"Then get in the truck."

Dan Salty took Emily's hand and they climbed into the Ford.

Louise turned to Bill Hahn.

"I love you for what you're doing, Bill."

"I love you too, Louise. Whatever *you've* done."

The woman put her arms around Bill Hahn and kissed him on the lips. Bill turned to see if his wife had witnessed the moment, but she was upstairs surveying the damage Sergeant Sommers had done to her house. He walked to the truck and smiled at Emily through the streaked glass.

"Bye, baby."

Louise climbed into the driver's seat of Hahn's car and drove away, tears streaming down her face.

Emily Walton sat back on the couch and took a deep drag on her cigarette.

"I fell in love with Dan Salty the first moment I met him," she said. "So busy looking at him I didn't even wave goodbye to Bill Hahn."

She exhaled slowly, a thin grey cloud enveloping her head.

"Mom didn't tell me, not until years later, that Hahn was my father."

The Diamondback Massacre

According to the United Nations' Millennium Ecosystem Assessment of 2005, another mass extinction is underway - the worst loss of species since the dinosaurs died out 65 million years ago

17

1985

Diamondback trailer park occupied an untidy forest clearing in the Adirondack Mountains, four thousand feet above sea level. Behind haphazard stacks of logs, a barely visible dirt track dropped dizzily through the trees to join Interstate 40, but the closest concentration of people was the small town of Port Henry on the shore of Lake Champlain, a good twenty miles south.

The thirteen residents of the makeshift trailer park didn't mind the seclusion. They preferred it that way. They were an odd mixture of social outcasts, for Diamondback was a place people went to forget their past and where they hoped others would forget them.

The 'Waltons' had lived in a nearby log cabin for almost four years. Louise Walton tended bar in the Red Creek Saloon in Port Henry. Her son, Dan, did odd jobs - carpentry, wood chopping, painting – whatever needed seeing to. Louise's youngest, Colin, was only a toddler and usually looked after by his sister, Emily.

Tonight, however, the family were celebrating - the next day was Emily's sixteenth birthday. Since Dan had to work in the morning, they were having the party early.

Once the little one had been put to bed, Louise and Dan opened bottles of Coors and relaxed on the couch. Emily sat on the floor in front of the log fire, an untouched piece of birthday cake on her lap.

"So, honey," Louise took a sip of her beer. "What's your birthday wish?"

"Some new faces would be nice."

"I could grow a moustache." Dan Walton grinned at Louise, but the woman seemed engrossed in her beer.

"You know what I want, mom," Emily said pensively.

"I haven't forgotten."

"What's this, then?" Dan dragged a bowl of Cheezits on-to his lap. "You girls conspiring?"

"Sort of."

"Where is everybody, anyhow?" Dan looked at his watch. "Where's Billy and Kirby? Why isn't Veronica here?" He stuffed a handful of bright yellow squares into his mouth. "I even invited those butch women with the leather jackets that live in the green trailer."

"They're not coming."

"What? None of them?" There was a prolonged silence while Dan chewed and swallowed. "Am I missing something here?"

"I uninvited everyone," Louise said simply.

"That's not very fair on the kid."

"Don't call me a kid," Emily said. "I knew they weren't coming."

Dan raised his eyebrows. "You did?"

"When we first came here, mom promised to tell me everything," Emily stirred the chocolate round the plate with her fork. She was too nervous to eat. "When I turned sixteen. It was a deal."

"Everything?" Dan looked troubled.

"Figured you wouldn't want an audience for that, honey." Louise gave a half-hearted smile. "Guess I never really believed my little girl would grow up. But she's old enough to trust with the truth, I reckon."

"Mom said she'd tell me why we're living in the middle of nowhere. Why we changed our name from Martin to Walton. Why I was taught at home rather than going to school."

"Jeez," Dan whistled. "You sure did make a lot of promises, Louise."

"None I don't intend to keep." The woman curled her dark hair, now streaked with grey, uneasily around one finger. "And the girl's been superhumanly patient, you have to admit."

"She even promised to tell me why *you* appeared in our lives." Emily pointed her muddy fork at Dan.

Dan blinked rapidly. Louise kept her head down.

"You don't like me in your life?" He sounded genuinely hurt.

"Course I do." The teenager flushed. "Even though we don't hang out anymore – what with you out on jobs all the time." She looked around disdainfully at the well-worn furniture. "Not that we actually spend any cash on this place."

"I'm saving for your future, honey."

"I know. And you both work real hard." The girl stuck the fork dispiritedly back into her slice of chocolate cake. "It just don't look like I have much of a future here."

"That's true." Louise sipped thoughtfully at her drink. "But you'll be free to leave soon enough."

"Mom!" The girl looked horrified. "That's not what I meant."

"I mean, you'll have a choice." Louise set the bottle down and stood up. "But you have to know the facts first." She glanced sideways at Dan.

"Whatever you say, Louise."

"Dan and I are in hiding." Louise looked straight at her daughter. "You know that much."

"I didn't think we moved here for the skiing."

"We were both at a research facility called Sheridan Base in the Mohave Desert a few years ago." Louise lit a cigarette and took a long drag. "I'm still not sure what kind of experiments they were doing, but one went terribly wrong."

Emily held her breath.

"Everyone went crazy. Don't ask me why, because I still got no idea. It was a mass frenzy... and..." the woman faltered.

"They began killing each other," Dan finished her sentence.

"What?"

"The whole base turned homicidal." Louise stared out of the window. Silver birch surrounded the cabin, filtering the moonlight. "Only, for some reason, Dan and I weren't affected."

She rubbed her hands nervously on her legs.

"I killed, baby. In self-defence, admittedly, but I killed. And that's why we're hiding. Partly because I killed people and partly because the army are probably dying to know why Dan and I were the only two people on that whole base who walked away unscathed."

Emily dropped the fork onto the carpet and bits of chocolate spattered on the threadbare rug. She looked at Dan.

"I killed too," he said. "But I did it in...."

"Enough of that. I have an early present for you." Louise opened a drawer in the pine dresser below the window, pulled out a shoebox and handed it to Emily. "I warn you now, it's not the training shoes you were hoping for."

The girl opened the box. Inside were two passports. One was inscribed with the name Emily Walton, one with Dan Walton.

"I've also got you fake social security numbers and a bank account in your new names with a few thousand dollars in it," Louise said. "That's where most of the money's gone."

Emily handed Dan's passport to him. The young man opened and shut it again quickly.

"This is crazy, Louise."

"When you're old enough, you can use it, Emily. Have a bit of an adventure. You always said you wanted to see Scotland, huh? That's where our ancestors came from, Dan. You didn't know that, did you?"

"Mom." Emily cut into her mother's rambling. "Have you got a passport too?"

Louise took a deep breath.

"I ain't leaving. Got to quite like it here. It's peaceful. That's what I want."

Dan slid across the couch and put his arm around the woman's shoulders.

"I'm not deserting you, Louise," he said, fighting to get the words past the lump in his throat. "You saved my life. You brought me up."

He patted her leg.

"You're my mother."

Louise smiled gratefully. Emily scooted over, wedging herself between her mother's knees.

"I'm not going anywhere either. I love you more than I can say."

Louise put her arms around her children.

"But, at least you have the choice. Now, I need to go powder my nose." Prying herself loose, she went to the bathroom and locked the door.

"Holy Mother of God," Dan whispered. "This is some birthday."

"Best I ever had," Emily said, squeezing his hand. "Best birthday ever."

Inside the bathroom, Louise silently sobbed, a hand clasped over her mouth. She hadn't told her daughter, but she had an inkling of what really happened at Sheridan base.

Emily and Dan would *have* to leave Diamondback someday.

She and her little son could not.

"I stayed another couple of years." Apathy's mother ran a finger around the rim of her glass. "I didn't want to abandon my mum and my little brother, but there was a big world out there and I'd never seen it. Dan came too, of course. He'd promised Louise he would always look after me and he didn't intend to break that promise. He *never* broke a promise."

She licked wine from her finger and held it up, letting the liquid evaporate.

"I didn't know it at the time, but his word was the only real moral compass he had."

It was late now. A small desk lamp lit one corner of the room but mother and daughter were wrapped in soft-skinned shadows on the couch. Apathy could not take her eyes off Emily's face. In the dim light, she looked so much younger. For the first time, the girl was getting a glimpse of the person her mum had once been.

"My dad doesn't sound like such a bad guy," she ventured.

"He was fun," Emily admitted. "And smart. And that's about all he would let people see. He believed that a problem shared was a problem doubled."

She opened the box once more and gently touched the photographs.

"Me and Dan eventually settled in a little condo in Austin, Texas. Dan got a job in a Farmer's Market and I worked at an auto insurance company and we tried to pretend we were normal. Even our romance, when it finally happened, was accidental. Since we had the same name, people assumed we were married and we didn't correct them. Then, after a while, that was exactly what happened. Mum was delighted when I wrote and told her we were a couple. She loved your father."

She moved Louise's picture to the side so that Dan's image appeared underneath.

"God help me, so did I."

18

1995

The door burst open and Dan elbowed his way into the condo, a Circle K bag dangling from one arm. Emily was sprawled across the couch, still in her office clothes, her stockinged feet resting on the coffee table. She shot him a tired glance and pushed greasy hair back from her face. Dan removed his wallet from the leather jacket he always insisted on wearing, despite the Texas heat.

"I'm from the Fashion Police, Ma'am," he said sternly, flipping it open. "We've had reports of an abnormally high polyester content in your outfit. One sneeze and you could start a flash fire."

He opened the carrier bag, pulled out a bottle and began struggling with the cork.

"Never mind, this has twice the range of a fire extinguisher if you shake it hard enough."

"You bought champagne?" Emily struggled upright on the couch. "Can we afford it?"

"Absolutely not. This is fizzy wine. And it was on sale."

Emily smiled despite her exhaustion.

"I got you a rose too." Dan pulled a tattered stalk from up his sleeve. "But the petals fell off when I was climbing out of the neighbour's yard."

"Thank you." Emily got to her feet, grinning. "I'll fetch a vase."

"Yeah. And grab some glasses." Dan was still struggling with the cork. "The dusty ones with the decorative soap rings."

Emily stopped on her way to the tiny kitchen and put her arms around Dan's neck.

"Thank you, D.B." She kissed him on the lips. The bottle gave a loud pop and the cork shot into the air and bounced off the low ceiling. Emily vanished into the kitchen and returned with a couple of plastic tumblers. She set them on the coffee table, brushing away a sprinkling of crumbs onto the floor.

"Sorry about the mess."

"Don't worry." Dan poured wine into each tumbler. "The mice will get it."

Emily sipped the sparkling liquid and wrinkled her nose.

"This is nice." She leaned back and stretched wearily. "God, I'm pooped. Put up the Christmas tree, though. She nodded towards the window where a tiny sapling decorated with a few haphazard baubles rested dispiritedly on the sill.

"You think Santa will spot that without a telescope?"

"Hard to get into the Christmas spirit when it's ninety degrees outside."

Emily raised her glass and clinked it against Dan's.

"We should be with mom in New York State. Christmas is a time for snow and families."

She felt awkward as soon as the words were out of her mouth. Dan's real parents had died when he was young – something he refused to talk about. Louise, when questioned by her daughter, had been equally tight-lipped.

You know Dan she had told Emily. *If he doesn't want to dredge up the past, that's his decision.*

"Sorry. That was insensitive," Emily said.

"S'all right." Dan tapped the rim of the glass on his teeth and grinned. "I never listen to you anyhow."

Emily hesitated.

"Would you *like* a real family?"

"Eh? I already have one. You and Louise."

"No." Emily took a long swig of wine to fortify herself. "I mean a *real* family."

Dan tilted his head to one side. "You saying what I think you're saying?"

"Do I have to wave a flag? I'm three months pregnant."

Her partner's mouth opened but no sound came out. Emily held her breath. Then Dan gave the biggest, brightest smile she had ever seen on his face.

"We'll call him Norman D. Landing Walton," he enthused. "Norm for short!"

"What if it's a girl?"

"Eh... Apathy Amazon! I don't care!"

And Emily knew things were going to be OK.

Tears had begun to run down Emily Walton's face again. She sniffed and wiped them away with the back of her hand.

"Glad I put on waterproof mascara this time."

"What happened, mum? What went wrong?"

"My mother called a few days later. We were both out and she left a message on the answering machine. Not for me. For Dan. It was just two sentences."

Dan, you have to come back. The ants are gathering.

"He took a plane that night. He wouldn't explain and he made me solemnly promise to stay in Texas till he got back." She gave a thin smile. "Well, you know me."

"You followed him?" Apathy did indeed know her mother.

"Couldn't afford a plane fare, so I took the car." Emily lit a cigarette and puffed a swirling spiral towards the ceiling. "It was a three-day drive." Her voice became flat and cold. "I arrived at Diamondback in time to catch him red-handed. Literally."

Apathy took another sip of wine and let her mother continue.

"He was in the middle of a bloodbath."

19

The car made sputtering noises as it wound its way up Scharges Pass and levelled out at the top. Mountain summits, ringing the forest like open jaws, were covered in pristine snow - but here it was heaped in dirty grey banks on either side of the road.

Emily turned onto the dirt track that led to Diamondback trailer park and the vehicle shuddered its way up the incline. The whole landscape was frosted, the branches of the pines laden with snow - a living Christmas card.

A few hundred yards from her destination, she heard the crackle of gunfire. Living a large part of her life surrounded by hunters, it was a sound the young woman could not mistake. But this noise was staccato like a typewriter.

Someone was using a semi-automatic.

With a gasp of dread, she put her foot on the gas and the car leapt forward. She could make out the sound of more than one weapon now.

The car crested the rise leading to the trailer park and Emily let out a shriek as it thumped over a body lying in the middle of the road. She glanced into the rear-view mirror in time to see the corpse settle back into the snow, one broken leg sticking in the air. She spotted at least three more bodies littering the park.

Dan was crouched behind a log pile, shooting at the ring of trailers. Puffs of smoke from under one of the vehicles betrayed the position of the person returning fire. Dan jerked round and saw Emily sitting, rigid with shock, behind the wheel.

"Get out of the car!" he screamed, waving his arms at her. There was a burst of fire from the trailer and pock marks sprouted across the hood.

Dan stood up, still shooting, giving the assailant a better target, trying to draw fire away from Emily. She didn't need a second warning. Tearing loose her seat belt, she launched herself across the passenger seat and flung open the door. As bullets thudded into the driver's side, she slid out of the car and collapsed in the snow.

Dan ducked down again and pulled a pistol from his belt.

"Stay there! Stay down!" He tossed the weapon to Emily. It landed between her outstretched arms and she pulled it to her chest. Using the wheel as shelter, she cocked the weapon, rolled under the car and began firing at the underside of the trailer. Emily had grown up handling weapons and instinct took over before she had time to question her own actions. Someone was firing at Dan and that filled her with a sudden, overpowering rage. She noticed, with detached horror, that the snow was speckled with little black dots. They were ants. Writhing in their thousands, dying in the cold.

"Fire at the propane tanks!" Dan shouted. "They're out of my line of sight. I'm pinned down."

Gobs of snow bounced into the air in front of Emily as the assailant targeted her again. She took careful aim at the large blue tanks that fuelled the trailers and squeezed the trigger three times.

The propane tank exploded in a ball of blue flame. Seconds later, the trailer went with it. Emily curled into a ball, hands covering her head, debris raining around her. Plumes of fire shot into the air, heat from the blast scorching her exposed hands. All around her, ants shrivelled into black ash.

Dan sprinted from his cover towards the car, threw himself headlong to the ground and rolled underneath. He wrapped his arms around Emily and held on until the flames began to subside. Eventually, he slid back out, pulling her with him.

The trailer was a blazing hulk, oily smoke ballooning up from the wreckage and curling over the surrounding trees. There was no sign of life in or around the inferno. Nobody could have survived.

"You all right?" Dan checked Emily for injuries, recoiling when he saw her hands. "My God, why are you here?"

"What in Christ's name is happening?"

"You have to go!" Dan began pushing her towards the driver's side of the car. Emily shook him off, staggering back.

"D.B.! There are dead people everywhere! Did you do this?"

"I haven't time to explain." Dan scooped up a handful of snow and rubbed it into her scalded hands. "Please get in the car! You have to *leave!*"

"What do you mean?" Emily was shaking all over. "Why are people *shooting* at you?"

"You have to trust me. I know how this looks, but you have to believe I was doing the right thing!" Dan's words tripped over themselves in his urgency to get his message across. He patted the snow from Emily's body, dead ants still stuck to the white patches. "You've *got* to leave!"

"Where's mom?"

"These people. It's like they're *possessed!*" He dragged her around the car by the shoulder and hauled open the driver's door. "I'm immune. You're *not*. Get *out* of here!"

"Possessed by *what*? Where's my mom and my brother?"

"I'll find them. But you have our baby to think about." He put a hand on either side of Emily's face and stared into her eyes.

"This is what your mother and I have been afraid of for years. No, *look* at me!"

His fingers curled into her hair, forcing Emily to keep her face inches from his own.

"The people we were running from have been waiting as well! They'll know what this means and they'll come here, looking for survivors – just like they did sixteen years ago. Go back to Austin and destroy anything that links us to the place. Then you have to move immediately. Withdraw all our money and use your fake passport while you still can."

"I'm not leaving you!"

"I'll find you. I promise! Do you hear? But you have to stay under the radar. Not let anyone know you're connected to me."

"Are you *crazy*?"

"Emily." Dan let go and swept his hand in a savage arc. There were bodies everywhere and great curtains of acrid smoke hung over the trees. "I can't explain right now. You can see that. I should have done it a long time ago, but I hoped this day would never come."

He pushed the woman, still resisting, into the driver's seat.

"When we're together again, I'll tell you everything. And I mean *everything*! But, if you don't disappear completely, they *will* find you. They'll make you vanish. They'll take your baby from you and you'll never see it again."

"When will I see *you*?"

"I don't know, but I'll find you, I promise. You know I always keep my promises!"

He kissed her gently on the lips and she tasted smoke and gunpowder.

"Now go. Hurry before it's too late."

"I don't understand!"

"Then you have to *trust* me!"

"I love you D.B." Emily touched his cheek gently.

"I love you too." Dan whirled round and marched back to collect his gun.

Emily started the car. She reversed, spun the vehicle around and looked through the rear-view mirror. Dan was leaning on the rifle, sorrow and exhaustion etched into his face and posture. He waved at her with one hand.

Go!

With a sob, she crunched the car into gear and roared off down the hill.

"And that was it." Emily stubbed out her cigarette in the ashtray and rested her head on her daughter's shoulder.

"I never saw your father again."

20

"I had to drive at nights to get back to Texas. There were bullet holes all over the car." Emily looked at her watch.

"Christ, it's three o'clock in the morning," she said, astonished. "Honey, we *have* to go to bed."

"What? But you haven't told me anything! What was this possession dad was talking about? What happened to him?"

"I think you already know. I'm betting you were on the internet while I was in the shower. I could hear the click of the keys when I came out."

Apathy tried to hide a look of guilt.

"You're smart like your father and curious like your mother."

Emily didn't seem angry, just exhausted.

"Now you know as much as I do. The police found Dan's fingerprints all over the place. They ran them through the national database and got his real name -

D.B. Salty. He murdered his parents when he was thirteen."

"I know," Apathy admitted. "I Googled him,"

"Yeah," Emily couldn't conceal her scorn. "That was something he'd neglected to mention in the years I knew him."

"What happened to Louise?"

"The police found two bodies in their cabin near Diamondback. Louise's best friend in Port Henry identified them as my mother and my brother, Colin."

"That doesn't mean my dad killed them," Apathy protested, unsure why she was defending a man she'd never met.

"I didn't want to believe it either." Emily took a final cigarette from her packet and lit it. "Then I remembered Dan saying he would go to the cabin and find Louise."

"Maybe he did."

"He'd already been there," Emily shook her head vehemently. "In all the confusion, it didn't even register what I was looking at. The rifle and handgun D.B. was using belonged to my mother. She *never* let them out of the cabin."

"What if she gave the guns to Dan... I mean, dad?"

"No. She would have been by his side, using them herself. She was a much better shot than your father. Apathy, he used my mom's own gun to kill her. Police forensics proved it."

Emily looked at her watch again.

"We have to go to bed, baby. I'm falling apart." Her shoulders sagged. "I can't begin to guess what *you* feel."

"I feel like I *do* want a cigarette."

"Doesn't help."

"Do I remind you of my father?" Apathy wasn't sure she wanted to know the answer. She was suddenly acutely aware that she was the daughter of a mass murderer.

"At times like these, I'm painfully reminded. Then again, I loved him with all my heart."

"You must have. Giving me this dumb name just because he made a joke about it."

"Caused quite a few laughs at the registry office, I can tell you."

"You thought he might remember what he'd said, didn't you? Start looking for a kid with that name."

"It was a pretty long shot. He couldn't have had a clue where we'd gone. But I was *sure* he'd find us and he'd be able to explain. He *never* broke a promise."

Emily gave a quick smile.

"I was *that* naïve. Then, as the years passed, I realised it was just wishful thinking."

She bowed her head and teardrops splashed into the ashtray.

"I hate to admit it, Apathy, but your father was a delusional psychopath. Now I hope to God he never catches up with us."

"That's why you've never settled in one place." Apathy watched the spreading tears turn the ash to ink. "Couldn't we just have changed our names again?"

"All our lives, we've been changing towns, changing jobs, changing schools." Emily wiped the tears angrily away. "But my mother gave me this name and I'm keeping it."

"It's been a long time," Apathy said hopefully. "Maybe there's nobody after you anymore."

"I'd like to think so. But mom told me the guy in charge of Sheridan base was the type who never gives up."

Emily put the lid back on her shoebox, defeated.

"His name was Dr Markus Kelty."

21

1996

Dr Kelty sat in front of his computer, staring at the screen. On the desk in front of him were two newspaper clippings dated a month earlier. Both were taken from the *Adirondack Mountain Times.*

The first read

Trailer Park Massacre in New York State 13 Bodies Found

The second was the next week's edition.

Fingerprints Point to Teenage Murderer D. B. Salty as the Diamondback Killer

"Told you we'd find you someday," Kelty muttered. "Just didn't expect it to take more than a decade."

On the computer screen, a red warning rectangle was flashing.

ARE YOU SURE YOU WANT TO DELETE?

Kelty's finger hovered over the keyboard.

"If only things were that simple."

The door opened and Dr McMurphy, the head technician, entered. With him was Captain Hammill, head of base security. Both stood respectfully in front of Kelty's desk until the doctor finally acknowledged them.

"You've tested the subjects again?"

"This is the third time, Sir," McMurphy answered, though he knew Kelty was well aware of that fact. He placed a manila folder on the desk.

"Top Brass won't stand for another hold-up in our report," Hammill added. "They're calling for results almost daily. Don't know why they're suddenly so insistent."

Kelty knew. He glanced at the newspaper clippings again.

"And I was going to cure cancer this afternoon." He picked up the folder and leafed through it, feigning interest. He had delayed sending his findings for weeks now. What McMurphy and Hammill didn't know was that he had been falsifying the reports for the last two months.

"Very well, Captain. I want you to assemble everyone in the canteen. Your men and McMurphy's team also." Kelty shut the folder. "I'm going to address the whole base personally."

"Right now?"

"Why? You got a facial booked?"

"As you wish, Colonel." Hammill saluted and strode out of the room. Kelty went back to staring at the screen.

"Can I speak frankly?" McMurphy asked.

"As far as I'm aware, that's the only method you know." Kelty sighed. He missed Naish, but she had her own posting now, back in the States. He hadn't heard from her in years.

"I don't see why we're so cagey about what we've found. The evidence that we're back on track is compelling." McMurphy clasped his hands together excitedly. "These are *very* positive results."

"Depends on how you look at it," the doctor said sourly. "To the Nazis, for instance, the genocide of an entire race was a *positive* result."

He withdrew his hand from the drawer. In his fist was a small pistol with a silencer attached. Kelty raised the gun and shot McMurphy between the eyes.

As the head technician crumpled to the floor, the doctor glanced at the wall clock. It would take about fifteen minutes for Hammill to fill the mess hall. Five minutes after that, the incendiary devices Kelty had hidden in the roof panels would go off.

He looked at the flashing screen one last time. It was filled with complex formulas that only he understood.

ARE YOU SURE YOU WANT TO DELETE?

"No, I'm damned well not. But If I don't do it now, I never will."

He hit the button.

Kelty fetched an automatic rifle from his arms cupboard. He now had ten minutes to complete his task before the bombs went off. He switched off the computer and headed for the exit.

By the time the incendiary devices exploded, Kelty had killed the guards on the door and trudged up to a hillock overlooking the entrance to the complex. He lay down in the snow and put the rifle to his shoulder as the interior of MacLellan base was enveloped by flames.

Most of the facility was underground and few of the base personnel made it out of the burning complex. As the survivors ran in panic from the building, Kelty picked them off one by one.

Scurrying through the melting snow, they looked just like ants.

Kelty made his way down Pittenhall Ridge to a launch. He waded through the surf, climbed in and started the motor.

As the boat plunged into the swells, lurching over each cresting wave, the doctor glanced back at Kirkfallen. Smoke spread out across the top of Jackson Ridge and there was an orange tinge to the darkening sky.

Kelty raised a hand to his eyes.

A hulking figure, black against the fiery glow, stood watching the boat from the cliff top at Jackson Head.

The Kidnapping

The scientist James Lovelock has predicted a looming human catastrophe, with wars over fuel, water and land - and a population crash that could leave just 500 million survivors of the current population of 6.6 billion

22

Apathy packed her rucksack and left the flat for school. She was worn out from the late night and emotionally drained by the revelations she had heard. And, as expected, there hadn't been any birthday cards on the mat when she went to check.

She didn't notice the figure lurking one flight up. As soon as the teenager was out of sight, it hurried down the stairs and sidled over to her front door. The figure expertly picked the lock and, with a few practised twists of the wrist, clicked it open and slunk into the flat.

Apathy walked to school alone. No other pupils spoke to her. Nobody said hello or engaged in conversation, for Apathy wasn't popular. In fact, she had never been well-liked at any school and it left her angry and bitter. She tried her best to be friendly, whenever she and her mother moved to a new area, but it never seemed to work. Sometimes Apathy acted confident. Sometimes she acted shy. It didn't make any difference – she just seemed to bring out the worst in people. She'd lost count of the number of fights she'd gotten into without even grasping what had caused it.

Apathy walked along Merchiston Avenue, a tree-lined suburban street filled with houses much grander than her mother would ever be able to afford. Deep in thought, she didn't notice the white van cruising behind her adorned with a large black logo.

G.B. Paranormal.
Psychic Investigators

Apathy didn't hear the vehicle's side panel slide open. Didn't see the short man leap out.

Then, suddenly, there were arms around her waist and she was being dragged backwards into the rear of the van. Before she had time to scream, a wad of cloth was clamped over her mouth, soaked with a liquid that made her head swim. Seconds later, she was unconscious.

The door slid shut, and the vehicle moved off. The driver glanced over his shoulder.

"She OK, Mr Gacy?"

"She's out cold, Mr Bundy." The man in the back checked the girl's pulse. "Now, I suggest we get to the motorway and drive like the demons of hell are after us."

The driver shifted gears and picked up speed.

"I wouldn't find that hard to believe," he said morosely.

23

"Today's lecture will be by Millar Watt. All-round fancy pants and genius in residence." Millar took a small bow and waved Gene and Poppy towards two empty chairs. The morning lessons were over and the children were alone in the information hut.

"Today's topic will be Kirkfallen Island."

"Nice to see you're taking this seriously."

"I wasn't to start with." Millar straddled his own chair. "But you asked me to think about Fallen and I said I would."

He opened a notebook on the table in front of him.

"Much as it pains me to admit it, you're right. A lot of things about this place don't add up when you look at them closely enough."

He leaned over his notes. Poppy and Gene exchanged puzzled glances.

"Point one. We get a mass of supplies dropped off twice a year by the guys at the U.S. Naval base in the Hebrides. Plus, a doctor lands and gives everyone a

139

health check. We're given books, batteries, fuel, cigarettes... the works."

He waggled bushy black eyebrows.

"How do we pay for it?"

"That's easy." Poppy broke in. "We get a government grant."

"No, we don't," Gene countered. "My dad says the funding was stopped years ago."

"Then we trade." Poppy wasn't put off. "Vegetables and crafts and things like that."

"Unless there's a gold mine hidden on the island somewhere, that just won't wash." Millar shook his finger like a condescending schoolmaster. "How many turnips do *you* think it would take to trade for a land buggy?"

"We couldn't possibly produce enough things of value to barter for what we get, is what you're saying."

"Not a chance. And why would we be trading with a U.S. Naval base rather than boats from the mainland? It doesn't make sense."

The children pondered this. Even Poppy was stuck for an answer.

"Which brings me neatly to point two." Millar was obviously enjoying the attention paid to his genius. "Have we ever had a ship moor on this island that you can remember? A pleasure boat or even a fishing trawler."

"That's easy. We're using experimental crops and fertilisers. We can't risk outside contamination."

"And what about the twice-yearly inspection from the naval base? They don't come here wearing protective suits, do they? So why are those visits acceptable?"

"I don't know. But I bet you have some crazy theory, or else you wouldn't have brought it up."

"Jackson Head," Millar shot back without hesitation. "Nobody knows what's up there. Nobody's allowed to go there. What if it's *still* owned by the U.S. Navy?"

"So what?"

"If Jackson Head is still military property, then why not the whole island? What if Fallen is off-limits to everyone except the armed forces?"

"That's pretty farfetched."

"Is it?" Millar spread his hands. "Why didn't any police come to investigate the Orbison's deaths? Why was it a U.S. army helicopter that took away the bodies?"

"Then why are *we* allowed to live here?" Gene protested.

"I don't have the answer to everything." Millar consulted his notes again. "But I think I have a clue." He gave a shrug. "Only I don't know what it means."

"It probably means you aren't as darned smart as you think."

"The clue is in what you just said," Millar replied enigmatically. "Point three. I refer you to Jane Austen, Charles Dickens and George Orwell."

He pointed to a shelf filled with classic novels.

"There are also books by Scott Fitzgerald, Raymond Chandler and John Grissom. You see what I'm getting at?"

"Not in any way, shape or form,"

"And you know I haven't read any of them," Poppy added proudly.

"Our parents told us they came from all over the place to form a community, haven't they?"

"Yeah. That's right."

"If you'd bothered to read these books, you'd notice a big discrepancy in the way they're written." Millar picked his words carefully, leading his companions through his thought process. "The first three writers I mentioned are British. The second three are American."

"Losing us again."

"British writers say things like rubbish, mum, football and bloody. Americans say garbage, mom, soccer and darned."

"I say darned all the time..." Poppy stopped in mid-sentence.

"Exactly." Millar raised his eyebrows. "Everyone on this island speaks English, which is understandable – Fallen wouldn't be able to function otherwise. But they all use *American* lingo. They may have different accents but how would you recognise a real Chinese or German accent if you heard one?"

"We got a VCR."

"And a few dozen old films. All of which are American."

"*King Kong* has foreigners in it!"

"All they do is grunt, Poppy."

"What are you trying to say?" Gene rubbed his hands anxiously. He hadn't expected his friend to put this much thought into the investigation, but the results were certainly intriguing.

"I can believe that there's no television signal reaching this island." Millar lowered his voice. "But there aren't any *radios* on Fallen. How can there be no radios?"

"To stop us finding out what's going on in the world?"

"No. I think it's to stop us realising what's staring us in the face. That our parents don't come from all over the place at all."

Millar shut his notebook.

"Here's my theory. This island is owned by the United States, supplied and funded by its armed forces and everyone on it is an American citizen. African Americans, Chinese Americans, Asian Americans. But all American, nevertheless."

He tucked the notebook into his pocket.

"So why is that? And why are our parents lying about it?"

24

Gene Stapleton and his father sat opposite each other at the table, eating dinner. Annie was out delivering eggs to the families of Kirkfallen.

"Well?" Edward Stapleton asked amiably. "Where's this mealtime's awkward question?"

Gene stirred his soup, saying nothing, while his father buttered toast.

"Shame." Edward bit hungrily into a golden square. "It's the highlight of my day."

"Why aren't we allowed to go near Pittenhall Ridge?"

"That's easy. It's dangerous."

"No, it isn't. Jackson Head is dangerous. But you can't get to it from Pittenhall. Not with that damned fence in the way."

"Watch your language, son."

Gene stayed quiet, stirring his soup. Edward leaned back, mouth working silently. Watching. Waiting.

"Dad," his son said urgently. "What's *wrong* with Kirkfallen Island?"

Edward Stapleton was still staring. Gene held the look for as long as he could but, eventually, his gaze dropped to the table.

"Remind me," Edward put down his toast. "When is your sixteenth birthday?"

"In a week."

"Fallen isn't like the rest of the world." Edward got up and carried his coffee to the window. "It's a place of secrets. Though I hate to admit it, they're secrets we've kept from you and the other kids."

The teenager was genuinely astonished. It was the last thing he expected his father to say - but the response only fuelled his own doubts.

"Dad? Did the Orbisons die because they went to Pittenhall?"

He wondered if he had crossed some unspoken line, but his father didn't seem angry. The man peered through the window, one burly forearm leaning against the cool glass.

"Your mother and I wanted you to have a happy life, Gene. That meant keeping quiet about certain... things."

"I don't like the way you used 'happy' in the past tense."

"You're a smart cookie, for sure." Edward wiped condensation from the pane and peered outside. "But your mother has the final say on what I tell you and I won't go against her."

"That's not fair!"

"Don't whine." His father drained his coffee. "Here she comes now. So don't be bothering her with these kinds of questions. Not until I've spoken with her, all right?" His gaze fastened on his son again and there was a steely glint in his eyes.

"All *right*?"

"OK, dad."

"In fact, you don't tell anyone what I just said." Edward's eyes narrowed. "Don't you cross me on this, boy."

"I won't."

Gene's father opened the door and waved.

"Hi, honey! Coffee's on."

25

Gene stared at the wall of the gang hut, lost in thought. Poppy and Millar were playing chess on a tatty wooden board laid across the tea chest.

"Checkmate," Poppy crowed. "Maybe you'd have better luck if you camouflaged the pieces. Gave them funny hats like yours."

"You lulled me into a sense of false security by looking like you had an IQ of 70."

"Actresses are supposed to look dumb." Poppy patted her bob daintily. "Just like Marilyn Monroe."

"Yeah. She also looked pretty."

"That's just *acting*."

Millar gave up and tipped over his king. "You want a game, Gene?"

"Jackson Head," Gene said. "The answers to all our questions are in that abandoned base on Jackson Head. I just know it."

"Unless you've taken up pole vaulting, that's where they'll have to stay."

149

"No. I'm going there." Gene slapped a hand on his knee. "Who's coming with me?"

"Are you out of your mind?"

"Don't you want to know what's going on? Don't you want answers?"

"Not enough to be grounded forever."

"We've spent our whole lives on this little bit of land," Gene snarled. "We've never asked questions. We're so fucking... contented! So complacent!"

"I like the island." Poppy frowned. "What's got into you?"

"Something's not right!" Gene could hardly contain his anger. "Real teenagers are rebellious. They take chances!"

"There's a good chance of *this* teenager being grounded forever if he even goes near the fence."

"I've been thinking about your books, Millar. They're full of wars and arguments and exploration and discoveries. None of the adults here do anything like that. None of the kids either." Gene clenched his fists by his side.

"WE'RE NOT NORMAL!"

There was a stunned silence.

"Is that a bad thing?" Poppy asked tentatively. "I mean. We're happy."

"I'm not happy anymore," Gene said bitterly. "I got too many questions. And I'm going to Jackson Head to find out the answers, with or without the two of you."

A longer silence this time. Poppy quietly began setting up the chess pieces again.

"Well, since your happiness is obviously *my* prime concern," Millar sighed. "I better come with you."

"Really?"

"You're my friend. We watch out for each other. Always have."

They both looked at Poppy.

"Our parents told us Jackson Head was really dangerous."

"I can confidently say our parents haven't been telling the entire truth about this place." Gene gave a disarming smile. "But we've always done everything together. We gonna stop now?"

"Besides, Poppy," Millar chimed in. "We'll need you to lie at the bottom of the fence to use as a trampoline."

"Whatever. Find a way over that doesn't require me throwing Millar and I'll come along."

"We'll use a ladder," Gene said. "After all, what do we all know how to do?"

"Annoy you?"

"No." The boy smiled for the first time that day.

"We know how to build."

That night, Gene lay in his bed, wide awake despite the late hour. He could hear his parents talking softly in the next room. On impulse, he got up and crept to the door. It was open a crack.

He could see his parents sitting side by side at their narrow kitchen table, drinking from tin mugs. The fire crackled in the grate and red light and black shadow wrestled for dominance along the walls.

"What did you tell Gene?" Annie Stapleton whispered.

"Not much. But he's a smart kid. He's getting more and more inquisitive. He was asking about the Orbisons."

"I been thinking about that myself," she admitted. "Any word on when *they'll* be coming?" The mug trembled in her hand. "It must be soon."

"I imagine so." Her husband stirred his tea slowly and deliberately. "It's what we planned for."

"But so many things could go wrong."

"I don't need reminding of that."

"It keeps me awake at night, Eddie." The woman sounded exhausted. "Lying there wondering if we're not every bit as evil as the forces we're bringing down on Fallen."

"You think I don't?" Edward grunted. "This gamble doesn't pay off? We'll be sacrificing our own kids for nothing."

The large figure got up and pushed a poker into the fire, stirring the flames.

"But I haven't heard you come up with a better idea."

Orange lambency washed back and forth across his broad shoulders.

And Gene hurried back to his bed, all hope of sleep extinguished.

26

Apathy woke, lying on a strange bed. For a few seconds, she was confused. Then bewilderment gave way to terror as vague memories of the last few hours separated themselves from her dreams. She recalled a nightmare journey in a windowless van, drifting in and out of consciousness, the overpowering smell being held to her face every time she seemed to be waking.

The roof above the bed was low, with unpainted wooden beams striping its surface. Her head throbbed when she turned to look across the room. Under an attic window with bright yellow curtains was a small table with a salad and a can of Coke sitting on it.

She rolled over, wincing.

A man was sitting on a wicker chair on the other side of the room. Apathy slithered away, eyes wide, almost falling off the bed.

"Steady there." The stranger put out a hand, though he didn't attempt to rise from his seat. "You probably have a bad headache, but it'll pass."

"Who are you? Where am I?" Apathy struggled into a sitting position. "My mum will be looking for me!"

"I don't doubt it." The man reached out and switched on the bedside lamp. "I've been searching for you myself."

The shadows were obliterated and Apathy saw a broad, tight lipped face, framed by shoulder-length greying hair. Despite the age, she immediately recognised the features from her mother's photograph.

"Oh my God. It's you!"

"Hi there." The man waggled his fingers at her. "The notorious D.B. Salty. Also known as Dan Walton, Dan Bundy and a dozen other names. Including *dad*, I guess."

Apathy gripped the covers, her head spinning.

"You should eat something." Her father gestured towards the sparse meal on the table. "I assumed, since you've turned sixteen, that you're on some kind of diet."

"How long have I been here?" Apathy looked around for a clock. "My mum will be going crazy."

"She knows you're with me. My associate left her a note. She just doesn't know where you are."

"You kidnapped me!"

"I'm wanted by about every organisation under the sun," Dan said dismissively. "I can hardly get into more trouble."

"But you're my father." Apathy relaxed slightly, sensing that she was in no immediate danger. "Why didn't you just get in touch normally?"

"Couldn't exactly go strolling up to your door, could I?" Dan got up and went around the bed. The teenager watched him apprehensively but he merely picked up the tray of food and put it on the covers.

"It's been a long time. Wasn't sure of the reception I'd receive."

"Are you going to hurt me?"

Dan raised an eyebrow.

"No. We just need to talk."

"I want to leave." Apathy stuck out her chin. "You can't keep me here."

"Actually, I can. You are in an extremely grave situation."

"I can see that."

"I don't mean me." Her father sat on the edge of her bed. "I have a story I need to tell you. Then you're free to do whatever you decide is best."

"Does that include leaving?"

"We'll discuss that."

"My mum will be worried sick. What if she calls the police?"

"I don't think she will, but I'm prepared to take that chance. Right now, this is the safest place in the world for you."

Dan opened the can of Coke on the tray. It gave an evil fizz and frothed over the top of the tin.

"I won't harm you. You have to trust me on that."

"Trust you? I don't even know you."

"I'm the famous Houdini Killer." Dan grinned broadly, crossing to the door and opening it.

"If I had murder in mind, you'd already be dead."

As soon as her father was gone, Apathy tested the window, but it was locked. It was dark outside, with no house or streetlights deflating the void. Despite her dread, Apathy returned to the bed and ate the salad. She hadn't realised how hungry she was.

Once the teenager had finished, she tried the bedroom door. It opened and she stepped into a snug, sparsely decorated living room. There was a log fire burning in the grate and a dining table with a chequered tablecloth in the corner. Her father sat on a stool beside it, wrapping a present. On a chair by the fire was a short, overweight man. He was considerably younger than her dad, with a thick fringe of black hair and a pleasant, round face.

"Apathy Walton." He rose and held out a podgy hand. "A pleasure to finally meet you properly. Happy birthday, by the way."

Apathy kept her arms at her side.

"Who are you?" she asked rudely.

"I like her," the short man grinned. "She's feisty."

"This is Mr Gacy, aka Colin Walton." Dan lit a cigarette and waved it at his companion.

"Apathy, I'd like you to meet your uncle."

27

Colin and Dan sat by the fire, drinking wine and smoking cigarettes. Apathy perched on a stool next to the window, looking forlornly at her presents. Dan had presented her with a gleaming Swiss army knife and Colin had given her a silver heart on a chain. Despite the gifts, she hadn't spoken for half an hour. A glass of wine sat on the table in front of her, untouched.

The men didn't seem to mind. They were obviously used to each other's company and had become embroiled in a lively debate.

"You kidnap your own daughter and then you give her a knife as a present." Colin looked warily in the direction of his silent niece. "What if she stabs us in our beds?"

"It's a Swiss army knife, not a machete. If she wanted to kill us, there's a meat cleaver in the kitchen."

"Oh, *that's* a bit of information she sorely needed to know." Colin poured himself another glass. "I'll be sleeping in the shed tonight."

"She's not going to kill us, Colin. If she does, she'll never know the rest of the story."

"Maybe she's not a curious person."

"She's Emily's daughter. She'll want to find out."

"My mother never tried," Apathy said viciously. "She didn't even tell me about you till yesterday."

"That's because she was trying to protect you." Dan shook a cigarette from its packet and lit it. "Now it's our turn."

"Then why didn't you come back and do it sooner? Why wait fifteen years?"

"You and your mom haven't exactly been easy to find." Dan looked embarrassed. "It was Colin who finally tracked you down."

"Can't hide anything from a psychic investigator," Apathy's uncle gave a small bow.

"*Psychic investigator?*"

"One of our many side-lines," Colin said affably. "Actually, we're con men. There's a lot of cash to be made convincing gullible punters that we've got in touch with their dead granny."

"Oh, very nice." Apathy turned her back on them again.

"How *is* your mother these days?" Dan asked.

"None of your business."

Her father pursed his lips angrily but said nothing. He picked up the wine bottle. It was empty. He got up and went out to the van to get more.

"You're pretty uppity," Colin yawned. "Back chatting the notorious D.B. Salty."

"*You* don't seem scared of him."

"True." He stretched his arms, revealing a bulging midriff. "Well, well. As far as I can see, this parent and child relationship is going to be a bit of a sticky wicket."

"No kidding."

"Ever heard of J.B. Watson, father of the Behaviourist movement?" Colin looked at the ceiling, trying to remember correctly.

"I quote. *Children should be brought up by scientific method rather than an emotional basis, with no kissing cuddling or mollycoddling.* One of his sons committed suicide and the other became a psychoanalyst - much to Watson's annoyance."

"I have *no* idea what you're talking about."

"On the other hand, we have Dr Spock saying that parents should get all kissy-kissy with their little mites. His book, *Baby and Child Care* outsold every publication in America, except the Bible, of course. Then he admitted he didn't have a clue what he was talking about. He also won a gold medal for skiing in the 1924 Olympics, but that's beside the point."

"My mum will be going frantic."

"Dan Salty has spent his life trying to protect your mother." Colin's voice suddenly became hard and flat. "When that meant staying away, he stayed away. Now it means taking you here, so he took you here. It's how it has to be."

"Where *are* we?"

"We're on one of the islands in the Hebrides. As deserted as the moon and, judging by the way this party's going, it's got just as poisonous an atmosphere."

"And what are *you* doing here? My mum said D B Salty killed you."

"Maybe she lied. It wouldn't be the first time she lied to you, now would it?"

"Maybe you're the kind of uncle nobody likes to admit to."

"God, you're a firecracker." Colin gave a hearty laugh. "This is a family filled with secrets, Apathy. I got mine. Your mom has hers. But you'll probably get the truth out of Dan. All you have to do is make him promise. He never breaks a promise."

"Is he going to kill me?"

"Of course not." Colin looked shocked. "You're family."

"So were his mum and dad." Apathy gritted her teeth. "So was my grandmother."

The smile slid from her uncle's face.

The door swung open and a blast of icy air swept Dan into the cottage. He gave a heartfelt shiver and marched over to the fire, plonking two bottles of wine on the hearth. He threw himself down on the chair, unscrewed the top and poured himself a drink.

"I don't suppose you have a picture of your mom?"

"She would never let anyone take one." Apathy wasn't about to let the only photograph she had out of her possession.

"Clever girl." Dan sipped his wine thoughtfully. "Clever, clever girl."

"Do you know that she loved you?"

"I take back that last comment."

The room lapsed into silence. Colin looked at Dan and then at his niece.

"Tell her, D.B. She deserves to hear your side."

"I don't think she wants to hear anything I have to say."

"Yes, I do." Apathy retorted. "If you promise to tell me the truth."

Dan shot Colin a dirty look. The shorter man stared at the ceiling, twiddling his thumbs.

"All right, I promise. I'm… just not sure where to start."

"The beginning, dad."

Dan blinked rapidly. He opened his mouth and shut it again.

"You called me dad."

Apathy waited.

"This whole mess began on a summer's day. August 1978." Dan took a deep breath.

"That was the day I killed my father."

28

Dan heard his parents screaming at each other when he came home from school. Nothing unusual in that. His father had been stationed in Vietnam and returned a changed man - it seemed fighting was all he remembered how to do. Dan's mother, on the other hand, had got used to independence and now treated her husband as an occupying force.

Dan ignored the shouting, went upstairs to his bedroom and shut the door. The walls reverberated with the muffled sound of this particular conflict. The boy lay on his bed and tried to read a book but he couldn't concentrate. The yelling intensified.

Then there was silence.

Dan waited, holding his breath. He knew the battling would begin again and no amount of hoping or wishing would change that.

Only, this time, the house stayed ominously quiet.

He got up and opened the bedroom door. The unaccustomed silence was more frightening than the argument. Yet he knew his parents were both in the house, or he would have heard the front door slam.

Nothing. No sounds of his father trying to explain away his outburst. No muted crying from his mother as she put ice on her bruised face.

Dan crept quietly down the stairs and into the kitchen.

Wilma Salty lay on the floor in a pool of blood, one leg at a strange angle. Her mouth was open and so were her eyes.

A knife stuck out of her chest.

Dan knelt beside his mother. There was no point in feeling for a pulse. Even at this young age, Dan knew his mother was dead.

"Aw, no, mom." He rocked back on his heels. "Aw, no."

He pulled the blade from her lifeless body and put it on the kitchen table. Opened the living room door.

Alex Salty was hunched on the couch, head in hands, his face ashen.

"Oh God, I'm so sorry," he said weakly. "I'm so very sorry."

Dan had heard it all before.

He walked through the kitchen and into the backyard. At the end of the garden was a shed where his father kept tools. Dan found the key under a flower pot where he knew his father hid it. He unlocked the door, took Alex Salty's shotgun from a rack and went back to the house.

"Have you called the police?" His father looked up as Dan entered the room. "I didn't mean...."

The words died in his mouth as he saw the gun in his son's hands.

In Vietnam, Alex Salty had been trained to act first and think later. He leapt from the couch and bolted out the front door. But, as a soldier, he had taught his son how to handle a weapon. Dan followed him.

His father sprinted down the garden path and onto the street, zig-zagging as he ran. The boy calmly raised the shotgun to his shoulder, took aim and fired.

Salty was catapulted into the air and landed, face down, in the street.

Dan dropped the shotgun. Across the road, he could hear a neighbour screaming.

He ran back into the house and sprinted upstairs to his bedroom. Opening the top drawer of his bureau, he grabbed his savings, fourteen dollars in all. There was also a small business card. He took that as well.

He could hear police sirens as he darted down the stairs. The teenager fled through the back door and across the gardens, vaulting fences.

By the time the police had surrounded the house, he was on the bus to Denver.

29

D.B. Salty sat back and lit another cigarette.

"My fingerprints were on the knife that killed my mother. Naturally, I got the blame for that murder as well."

"I didn't know," Apathy said in a small voice.

"Neither did Emily. It wasn't something I wanted to talk about."

They listened in silence to the fire crackling in the grate.

"My turn now." Colin cleared his throat loudly. "In nineteen tickety-boo, U.S. Army Intelligence had a very clever idea. They set up a facility in Arizona to see if troops could kill goats by concentrating their mental powers on them."

"Excuse me?"

"Actually, it's true. Didn't work – though one soldier claimed to have offed his pet hamster just by looking at it."

171

"Colin knows a lot of stuff," Dan grumbled. "Most of it useless."

"In 1974, they had a better idea. A test was circulated through U.S. schools, devised by a scientist named Markus Kelty."

Apathy's eyes narrowed at the mention of Kelty's name, but Colin was warming to his story.

"It was supposed to highlight children's strengths and weaknesses, in order to make them easier to teach – but was withdrawn after a national outcry by child psychologists, who protested it had no value in that area whatsoever."

"Which was perfectly true," Dan added.

"Absolutely. It was actually a cleverly disguised psychological test of another type. A con, if you like." Colin raised his glass in admiration. "I appreciate a good con."

"It was designed to show which children had sociopathic personalities," Dan said sourly. "The results were given to U.S. Army Intelligence and they made a list of all the children who had these... symptoms."

"When those kids left school, the army intended to approach and recruit them," Colin continued. "People with sociopathic tendencies lack normal empathy. They don't really understand how other people feel and don't fit into society well. Ideal raw material for being moulded into army killers."

"And you took that test?" Apathy asked her father.

"Showed up as a true blue, certifiable nut job." Dan shook his head angrily. "But it didn't make me bad. Lots of people with sociopathic personalities live perfectly normal lives."

"Well… you *did* shoot your father," Colin said disarmingly. Dan ignored him.

"A few months after the test, I was approached outside my school by a Major Whittaker from Army Intelligence. The Major said the military was interested in recruiting me when I graduated. Gave me a business card and told me to keep quiet about it."

"The card in the drawer." Fascinated by the story, Apathy lifted her glass of wine from the table and took a sip. "The one you took with you when you ran from the police."

"I was in deep trouble. I didn't know who else to call."

"Major Whittaker came and rescued your father." Colin picked up the thread. "Offered him a deal with the devil."

"He said that the police also had psychologists. That, if they caught me, they'd find out about my personality and lock me away for life. So he offered me a way out. The army were doing research in a place called Sheridan Base in the Mohave Desert. If I agreed to take part, they'd set me up with a false identity afterwards and I could go free."

"Your father foolishly accepted."

"I was fourteen years old!"

"What happened?" Apathy took another taste of wine. She was starting to get used to it.

"Something went wrong with the experiment." Dan picked up a burning coal from the hearth, tossed it back into the fire and blew on his fingers. "The whole base went mad and your grandmother got me out."

"I know. My mum told me the rest of the story."

"Your mom didn't know the entire story." Dan glanced at the clock on the mantelpiece. "It's getting late."

"I slept plenty in the van." Apathy looked daggers at Colin. After a moment, Dan shrugged and carried on.

"Louise brought me up in Diamondback trailer park and, eventually, your mom and I left and settled in Austin." He took the corkscrew off the mantelpiece and opened another bottle. "One day, I got a message from Louise asking me to come back. Just me." He looked tentatively at Colin.

"She really should know," the younger man said uneasily.

"Then you better tell her."

Colin looked suddenly lost, his knee jiggling nervously.

"My whole mess began on a winter's day, December 1994." He set down his glass on the mantelpiece and clasped his hands together.

"That was the day *I* killed my mom."

30

1 9 9 5

Louise Martin opened the door and enveloped Dan in a fleshy hug. She had dark circles under her eyes and her hair was now more grey than brown.

"Welcome home, honey," she beamed. "You're a sight for sore eyes."

"You too, Louise. How's tricks?"

"There's a racoon living in the garbage can and the kitchen needs painting." Louise ushered Dan inside. "What about Emily?"

"In blissful ignorance." Dan was equally brief. "Where's Colin?"

"He's in the shed."

"You locked him *up*?"

"He's collecting firewood." Louise gave Dan a scornful swipe.

"Yeah? I don't like the thought of him anywhere near an axe right now. How much does he know?"

"Enough to make him pretty nervous."

Dan plonked his bag in the middle of the floor.

"Then we better have a little talk with him."

Colin sat on the couch, hands on his lap. He hadn't grown much since Dan saw him last and it looked like he was always going to be a head shorter than his adopted brother. Still, he was good looking, with a bowl of straight black hair, bright blue eyes and a gap in his teeth that mirrored his mother's.

He and Dan exchanged pleasantries, then quickly ran out of things to say. Dan and Emily had left when he was eight and they hadn't been back too many times because of the distance. The prolonged absence and the age difference had stopped them ever being close.

Colin knew something was up. His knee bounced up and down, one foot drumming the floor as it always did when he was nervous. Louise and Dan sat opposite, drinking Coors. Neither said anything, unsure of how to start the conversation.

"I know something's happening to me." Colin started the ball rolling. "And I know it's got something to do with why we live out here in the middle of nowhere."

"Can't argue with that." Dan looked at Louise for assistance.

"Give it your best shot, honey. I don't know *what* to say."

"In some Indian tribes," Dan began falteringly. "There was a ritual the braves used to go through before they became a man."

"The Vision Quest," Colin broke in. "The young warrior would travel to somewhere totally isolated. There, he would seek a vision usually in the form of an animal, a bird, or a natural force like thunder and lightning."

He closed his eyes as if reciting from memory.

"This would be his guardian, a reflection of the Great Spirit in each seeker, and it would remain all his life to help and protect him, especially if he kept his heart purified."

Dan looked suitably impressed.

"Colin knows a lot of things." Louise smiled at her son approvingly.

"I read a lot." The boy admitted. "Not a lot else to do around here."

"We need you to go on a sort of Vision Quest for a while." Dan nodded to a weighty bag lying beside the window. "You'll have a tent and provisions and… eh… books if you like."

"But you have to stay isolated until we come and fetch you," Louise added.

"That doesn't sound like a quest. More like a quarantine."

"Jeez, you have smart kids," Dan whistled.

"It all came from me, hon." Louise almost smiled.

"You know about the experiment at Sheridan base fourteen years ago?"

"Mom told me. It all went wrong."

"Well, *that's* an understatement." Dan leaned forward in his chair. "We never worked out exactly what the scientists were trying to do. We *do* know that they produced something that killed everyone on the base except Louise and me."

"You really don't know why?"

"We've had years to come up with theories." Louise sat down next to her son. "I was pregnant with you at the time. That's the only explanation I can think of why I wasn't affected. And this thing... we think.... it..." Her voice choked with emotion.

"We think it bypassed Louise and went straight into you," Dan finished.

"What is this *thing* you're talking about?" Colin looked down at himself with barely disguised repulsion.

"I honestly don't know. We just know it makes people go crazy."

"What's going to happen?" Colin's leg drummed harder. Louise put her arm around him and gave a reassuring squeeze.

"It's going to come out of you, baby," she said softly. "Soon, we think."

"Will it kill me?"

"No, it won't," Dan broke in quickly. "It won't do you any harm at all. But we think it will hurt other people, just like at Sheridan. That's why you have to be completely isolated when it happens."

"You won't be totally on your own." Louise ruffled her son's thick hair. "Dan will come and check on you every day."

"And why won't it affect him?"

"It's hard to explain." Dan rubbed his temple awkwardly. "But you see, I have this personality trait…"

"No need to go into the gory details," Louise interrupted. "Let's just say we're pretty sure he's immune."

"That's how we know that you'll survive." Dan took a long swallow of his beer. "Because I was the subject of the last experiment they did at Sheridan base and I'm still alive."

He wiped froth from his mouth.

"But whatever it was killed all these people, originally came out of *me*."

The Curse of Apathy Walton

The larvae of the Cicada bug live underground for most of their lives before emerging in their thousands and becoming fully formed insects. The largest of these, Brood X, only surfaces every 17 years

In some parts of Northern America, however, the larvae have begun emerging much earlier in their cycle. As yet, scientists, have no explanation for this anomaly

31

1995

Dan helped Colin erect his tent in a clearing on the slopes of Mount Peters. There was a breathtaking view across miles of silver birch and they could see Lake Champlain twinkling like a strip of Aluminium in the distance. Dan sucked in lungfuls of mountain air.

"God, it's beautiful up here," he enthused. "And if there's a living soul within miles of this place, I'll eat my own underwear."

"Please don't."

"You can't build a fire in case a ranger sees it and investigates, but I packed you a gas stove." Dan sidled up to the boy, who was staring, transfixed, at the view. "You gonna be OK?"

"I've lived in the woods all my life." Colin stuck his hands stoically in his pockets. "But how do you know this... thing is

183

going to happen *now*? I don't want to be up here until I turn into some beardy mountain man."

"Ants." Dan shielded his eyes and gazed across the vista. "They started popping up all over Sheridan base just before the massacre. Louise said the same thing's been happening here."

"That's all you got to go on?"

"Plus your age. I was almost sixteen when it happened to me. I'm sure age has something to do with it, but don't ask me what."

"That's pretty vague."

"If we're wrong, the worst thing that's gonna happen is you get to spend a few days surrounded by the tranquillity of nature."

"True."

"There was one other thing. The personnel at Sheridan started acting funny in the days before the disaster. You notice that with the people in the trailer park?"

Colin's eyes opened wide. "Yeah, I did!"

"Arguments? Fighting? That kind of thing?"

"No." Colin bent and began unpacking the rucksack. "They seemed much more open and friendly than usual. Kept wanting to come to the cabin and party."

"Really?" Dan was taken aback. "Well, I'm no scientist, but I know it doesn't do any harm to take precautions."

"You know, I'm not scared at all." Colin reached out his hand, surprising Dan with the adult gesture.

"See you in a couple of days. I'm off to do a quick rain dance and hunt some buffalo."

Colin knew woodsmanship. He hung his provisions in a tree to stop black bears investigating the new food supply, cleared the film of snow away from his bivouac and dug a latrine. For the rest of the day, he explored his surroundings until the muscles in his calves ached. That night, he read his books by a small kerosene lamp and slept with the tent flap open so that he could see the stars. This far from the city, the night sky was awash with pinpoint lights. He fell asleep listening to the whirr of crickets.

The next day was just as uneventful. Dan arrived at noon with a huge pastrami sandwich and a bottle of Gatorade.

"You got the good end of this deal," he wheezed, collapsing onto the grass. "Louise's truck can only manage halfway before the track gets too snarled. I'm gonna have to run myself ragged just to bring you a lunchtime treat."

"Watch where you sit." Colin took a bite out of his sandwich. "There are a few ants around. The cold kills them straight away, but they're determined little buggers."

"Listen. I've been waiting for the right time to tell you," Dan had regained his breath sufficiently to hold a conversation. "I got news. Me and Emily are gonna have a kid. You'll be an uncle."

"Congratulations!" Colin spat out crumbs through a wide grin. "What did mom say?"

"She doesn't know yet. I didn't want to tell her until this was all out of the way. I wanted her just to be happy, not to have to worry...."

"About me?"

"Yeah, about you."

"You're a decent guy, Dan. You always looked out for her."

"I'll look out for you too." He passed Colin the Gatorade.

"I promise."

The next night passed as uneventfully as the last. Colin rose with the sun, made breakfast and sat with his back against a tree, reading a book.

Then he began to feel strange.

It was a little like heartburn with an accompanying sensation of light-headedness. Within half an hour, he was drenched in sweat and shaking badly. But the boy had spent the last two days mentally preparing. He wasn't afraid.

He put down the book, drew his knees up to his chest and held them, taking deep, even breaths.

"Just stay calm," he repeated over and over. "After this, life will go back to normal."

He closed his eyes and rocked backwards and forwards.

"Just stay calm. Just stay calm. Just stay calm."

He felt the ground begin to vibrate.

His eyes shot open. His throat constricted and he tried not to gag.

All around him, the forest floor was moving. Frosty leaves, twigs and moss undulated as if the very ground had turned to liquid. Colin sprang to his feet, back to the tree.

Then they emerged.

Hundreds of wriggling grubs, pushing their way through the frozen soil. Not ants but sticky white blobs of flesh. Only there weren't hundreds. There were thousands. The boy looked around in terror, trying to comprehend what he was witnessing.

The fat squirming slugs surged from the ground, bloated and half-formed, with stumpy mucus coated legs and waving antennae. They squirmed, carpeting the forest floor in an unspeakable writhing mass.

There weren't thousands. There were *millions* of them.

Colin looked down and screamed.

His boots had vanished in a thick, squirming pool of translucent goo.

He ran. Branches whipped at his face, lacerating his cheeks. He tripped over a root and sprawled, hands sinking into the wriggling white sea. He leapt up with a cry of horror, waving his arms in the air.

More by luck than judgement, he found the trail leading downhill. He put his head down and sprinted, breath coming in terrified gasps. All around him, the squirming monstrosities cracked open the earth and pushed their way through the snow to the surface. They began to swarm up the trees until the boy was running through an oozing, pearly forest.

Dan was about to climb into the truck for his trip to Mount Peters when Colin burst into the clearing. The boy was screaming and slapping at his body. White blobs clung to his jeans and jacket, even to his face.

He collided with the vehicle and fell to the ground, sobbing uncontrollably.

"Oh, Christ!" Dan knelt beside the hysterical boy, brushing off the remaining bugs. "Colin. Colin! I'm here! It's OK!"

"Not ants!" the boy screeched. "THEY'RE NOT ANTS!"

"I know. I know!" Dan hauled Colin to his feet and tried to push him into the vehicle. "We have to get you out of here!"

There was a sharp retort and the glass of the jeep's side window exploded.

Louise stood on the porch of her cabin, rifle in hand. A wisp of smoke rose from the barrel. She raised the gun, sighted and fired again.

Dan leapt to the side as a dent appeared in the vehicle's door where he had been standing.

"Stay down, Colin!" He scurried on hands and knees behind the back of the Jeep. "She doesn't know what she's doing! She'll kill you!"

Louise clicked another round into the breech, her face twisted into a manic sneer. Dan leapt to his feet and headed for the shed, zig-zagging across the open ground. Louise fired again. The bullet nicked the shoulder of Dan's leather jacket and he overbalanced and sprawled across the ground. He scrambled up again and glanced at the shed. It was too far to reach. Louise was a crack shot.

"Louise! It's me. Dan." He held his hands above his head. "You have to listen! Your daughter is pregnant, do you hear me? Emily and I are going to have a baby!"

Louise faltered.

"Your daughter. She's going to have a child." Dan slowly put his hands down. "We're going to have your grandchild. Please don't kill me."

For a few seconds, fear, rage and compassion struggled for dominance on the woman's face. Then Louise raised the gun to her shoulder. Dan opened his mouth for one last plea.

There was a sharp crack to his right.

Louise jerked backwards and collided with the wall of the cabin. Her legs buckled and she tumbled over the porch rail, landing face down in an undignified heap. Below her twisted body, a crimson stain spread across the snow.

Colin slumped against the truck. The pistol he had taken from the glove compartment dropped from his fingers as he sank unconscious to the ground.

Dan scooped up the gun and ran to Louise. He rolled the woman onto her back and felt for a pulse, but one look at her shattered chest told him she was dead.

"Aw, mom." He rocked back on his heels. "I'm so sorry."

He felt a stinging sensation on the back of his hand. Half a dozen ants were clinging to the hairs. Dan's head snapped up.

"Fuck! The trailer park!"

He prised the rifle loose from the dead woman's hand and staggered to his feet. There were more ants swarming over the stock of the weapon.

He turned and sprinted in the direction of Diamondback.

32

1995

Yolanda Butters was painting her nails when the doorbell rang. Tutting to herself, she went to answer, wafting the purple talons in front of her face and blowing on them.

Dan Walton stood in the doorway, his brother draped over one shoulder.

"Well, hey! *You* boys been partying hard, by the look..." She stopped as she saw Louise's vehicle parked in her driveway. One window was missing and the side of the truck was pockmarked with bullet holes.

"What's going on, Dan?" She stepped back as the young man knelt down and laid Colin flat in her hallway. "Is he OK?"

"He's fine. Just out cold." Dan shut the door behind him. "You're Louise's best friend, Yolanda. I didn't know where else to go."

"What you boys *done*, Danny Walton?" Yolanda let Dan carry Colin into the living room.

"You knew Louise better than anyone. I'm guessing she told you *something* about her past."

"Like what?"

Dan arched an eyebrow.

"She spun me some crazy story once. She was drunk and I didn't believe her." The woman leaned forward and fingered the hole in Dan's jacket. "This what I *think* it is?"

"Was the story about a place called Sheridan base? In the Mohave Desert?"

"That was the one. But none of what she said made sense."

"Did Louise tell you about her past and what she thought might happen someday?"

"Once. When she was drunk. I thought it was nonsense and I told her to sober up. She never mentioned it again."

"Everything she said was true, Yolanda." Dan hauled Colin onto the couch and laid him flat. "And it's happened."

"Dan." The woman pulled at his sleeve. "Where's Louise?"

"Louise is dead, Yolanda." Dan checked the boy's pulse. "Everyone at Diamondback is dead."

The woman sat down heavily on her coffee table.

"How did she die?"

Dan hesitated.

"I shot her. I didn't have any choice."

"This is crazy, mad, you hear me?" Yolanda sounded more angry than afraid. "I'm gonna call the cops."

"That's your prerogative, but Colin didn't do anything and he's no threat anymore. I swear to you, the army will be right behind the police and they'll take him away. Nobody will ever see him again."

Yolanda looked at the boy, unconscious on the couch. She had known him since he was a baby.

"You promise what Louise told me was the truth?" Everyone knew Dan never broke his word.

"I promise."

Yolanda took a deep breath. "What do you want me to do?"

Dan pulled a roll of banknotes from his pocket.

"I'm going back to Diamondback and dump the truck before the police show up. That's cutting it fine, but the trailer park is pretty isolated, so I might just make it. Then I'll try and escape over the mountains."

He dropped the money on the table.

"This kid's innocent. Wrong place, wrong time."

"What do you expect me to do with him?" Yolanda squirmed on the coffee table and knocked over her nail varnish. A purple puddle spread across the table and dripped onto the carpet. "Goddammit to hell! You killed *Louise*!"

"She was my mother, Yolanda. Nothing you can say will make me feel any worse."

"She *told* me this might happen." The woman's lip trembled. "I didn't *believe* her."

"There's a young runaway turned up at Diamondback a few days ago." Dan patted his pockets for a cigarette. "I'm gonna put his body in Louise's cabin."

His shoulder's sagged as he realised he didn't have any smokes.

"You'll most likely be called to identify the bodies, being her best friend."

"And you want me to say the poor kid is Colin? That it?" Yolanda fetched a pack of Marlboro Lights from the mantelpiece and handed one to Dan.

"I can't tell you what to do." He lit the cigarette, hands shaking. "But this boy just saw his mother die. I reckon he deserves a chance to live his life rather than rot in some military facility."

"I guess I could drive him to Westport when he wakes up. Put him on a bus."

"I know I'm asking a lot."

"I ain't doing it for you. I'll do it for Louise." Yolanda lit a cigarette of her own, her hands shaking as much as Dan's. "I should have trusted her. She was a fine, fine woman."

"She was," Dan agreed. He raised a sceptical eyebrow. "You're taking this very calmly."

"I grew up in the Denver projects," Yolanda replied evenly. "I seen my share of violence. And I know you ain't some punk with a chip on your shoulder. If you were, you wouldn't admit to shootin Louise and you wouldn't have saved your brother."

"Thank you, Yolanda."

"Now, I gotta ask you to leave before anyone sees the truck. I don't intend to go to jail for aiding and abetting a murderer."

"I understand." Dan pulled a scrap of paper from his pocket. "You got a pen?"

Yolanda fetched a biro from the mantelpiece and gave it to him.

"Louise and I took a lot of precautions in case we had to go on the run again. I have a Post Office Box in New York under a fake name." He scribbled on the paper. "If Colin ever needs to reach me, all he has to do is write and tell me where he is."

He handed back the pen.

"Make him memorise it. Don't leave any evidence, just in case he's caught."

"I guess I can do that."

"I appreciate your help, Yolanda."

Dan turned to go but the woman laid a hand on his shoulder.

"How you gonna live with what you done, Danny Walton?"

"Dan Walton didn't do this." Dan removed the woman's hand.

"The notorious D.B. Salty did."

Apathy finished her wine. She silently held out the glass and Dan refilled it. Colin leaned back in his chair, looking at the ceiling. His knee had begun bouncing up and down again.

"I'm sorry, Uncle Colin."

Colin didn't reply.

Apathy grabbed Dan's arm as he withdrew the bottle.

"I'm sorry for you too, dad."

Dan tensed. Then he gave a brief smile and returned to his chair.

"Cicada bugs," Colin said. "That's what the insects were. They live underground as larvae and enormous swarms come out to breed every seventeen years. Brood X, they call them."

His knee rattled faster.

"They weren't supposed to come out. They weren't *due* to come out."

"The thing Colin and I had inside, it attracts ants." Dan rubbed tired eyes. "We didn't realise it could affect other bugs as well."

"Plus it drives humans crazy."

"Homicidal is the term I'd use." Dan opened his cigarette packet and offered one to Colin. The man took it without looking at his companion.

"The rest of the trailer park?"

"Went nuts, of course. It was them or me. I couldn't let them get anywhere near a populated area and spread what had gotten into them."

Apathy stared into the fire. Colin and Dan drank silently. Outside, an owl hooted.

"You think Louise survived Sheridan cause she was pregnant with Colin," Apathy said. "That right?"

"Whatever came out of me went straight through her and into him," Dan said. "Only explanation we ever came up with."

"And my mum turned up at Diamondback when she was pregnant with me. In the middle of the outbreak."

Dan nodded. Colin clasped his hands together as if he were praying. Apathy picked up her wine glass and twirled it in her fingers.

"So... now I'm the age you and Colin were when both disasters happened."

"That's right."

"And you've kidnapped me and taken me to the middle of nowhere." Apathy stared at the fire. "A place where there are no other people."

"I have."

The girl cupped the glass with both hands, still not looking at the men.

"I think I understand."

33

Apathy excused herself and went to the toilet. Closing the door, she leaned on the sink, taking deep breaths and staring at herself in the mirror.

"Well... you're your father's daughter, for sure," she muttered to her reflection. "A danger to the bloody public."

Dan fidgeted in his chair, waiting for Apathy to return. He puffed up his cheeks and exhaled noisily. He looked around and slapped his hands on his knees.

"Seen my newspaper around, Col?"

"Eh?" Colin arched an eyebrow. "You haven't had the pleasure of your daughter's company for fourteen years. And you want to read the sports section?"

"I thought we could do the crossword together."

"Just talk to her, D.B."

"I don't know what to *say*."

"Then try listening."

"I guess." The glow from the fire flickered across Dan's face. "Are you ready?"

"Good to go." Colin reached out a foot and gave his partner a kick. "It'll be fine, D.B. You'll manage. I'll only have to stay away for a few days."

He reached up and swept his hand across the mantelpiece. When he opened his fist, there were three ants crushed in his hand.

"Maybe even less."

"You sober enough to drive? What if the police stop you?"

"Don't try to con a con man." Colin held up his glass. "My wine bottle's filled with grape juice."

"Get going then. See you soon."

"Keep it together, D.B. You and your daughter will be fine."

He winked at Dan and let himself out the front door. A few minutes later, the van started up and moved off down the rutted track, away from the cottage.

Apathy returned to the room and smiled shyly at her father.

"So, how long do we have to stay here?"

"Not long, I hope." Dan returned her smile. "It'll be ok. Don't worry."

"I'm not worried. Well... not *too* worried. But why can't my mum know where I am?"

"Because she'd come right here. Like Louise, she'd probably succumb to what you have inside, but she'd turn up anyhow."

"Did Uncle Colin leave?"

"Had to. He may not be immune either. As far as we can tell, only I am. Something to do with my… eh… unique personality." Dan scratched his temple uncomfortably. "You really don't want a short, fat maniac running around waving the kitchen cleaver."

Apathy laughed at the image, despite herself. Then she stopped suddenly.

"What will you do when it's all over?"

"What do you mean?"

"I… eh…" Apathy struggled with the words. "I mean…"

"Will I come and live with you? Is that what you're asking?"

"I suppose that would be up to mum."

"I bet she's pretty mad at me, honey."

"We can explain to her."

"I think I'll let *you* do the explaining. She might shoot me on sight."

"But you promise you'll try."

"I'll try."

"Dad." Apathy said quietly. "You didn't promise."

Her father poured himself another glass of wine.

"Once you release what's inside, I'm betting the army won't be interested in you anymore." He put the bottle down on the hearth and sipped from his glass, looking at his daughter over the rim of his glass. "But I'll still be a wanted man."

"You can explain! Tell them what you've told me."

"Baby. The U.S. military isn't going to admit to any of this. If I'm ever caught, I'll be deported and face the death penalty – not that the army will let me live long enough for that to happen."

"It's not fair!" Tears stung Apathy's eyes.

"Don't you worry." Dan patted his daughter's arm. "Colin's the best con man in the world. He'll find a way out of this for us, no matter how unsavoury."

Colin parked the van a mile from Amblin Cottage and climbed into the back of the van.

The rear was filled with equipment that the pair used in their 'psychic' investigations. He took a phone off its hook, attached it to a shiny metal box and switched on a homemade scrambler. Then he dialled.

"I want to get in touch with Catherine Naish, U.S. Military intelligence." He said. "No... I know she's not listed. But I'm sure you can find her... I understand, yes. Yes. Yes."

His tone switched to a coldness that cut through the static like a razor.

"Listen to me, lady. You relay this message to U.S. military intelligence. Say that Colin Walton called with information about Kirkfallen Island. Tell

Naish I want her personal cell phone number. I'll call back in one hour. And this line isn't traceable, by the way."

Colin hung up before the switchboard operator could say anything else. His face was slicked with sweat and the black fringe stuck to his head.

He took a deep breath and dialled another number.

"Apathy?" The voice on the other end was one Colin hadn't heard for many years and it sounded close to panic. "Is that you? Please say it is."

"I'm afraid not, Emily." The man took a deep breath.

"It's your brother, Colin."

34

2000

Lieutenant Colonel Catherine Naish sat at her desk, hands flat on the highly polished surface, staring at her mobile. In the corner of the room, two men were crouched over a tracking device - one wearing headphones and the other holding a digital recorder.

The mobile rang, the vibrations inching the device towards Naish's left hand. The man in the headphones gave her a thumbs-up signal.

The woman snatched up the phone.

"Naish here."

"This is Colin Walton." The voice on the other end sounded calm and composed. "I intend to make this brief."

"Good," Naish snapped. "I don't like time wasters."

"That will be your last interruption."

"How do I know you're who you say you are?"

The person at the other end hung up. Naish looked at her companions in astonishment. Headphones grimaced.

"No chance of finding *that*."

The mobile rang again. Naish pressed receive and held it tentatively to her ear.

"I can do this crap all day." It was the same voice. "You'll have a much better chance of locating where this call is coming from if you shut up and listen."

"My lips are sealed."

"You're missing a kid from Kirkfallen Island."

"All the children on the island are accounted for, thank you."

"Not my daughter. She vanished with me fourteen years ago."

Naish stayed silent but a sick feeling bubbled up in her stomach.

"We escaped to the mainland. The debris the other islanders reported was a ruse."

"Can you prove this?"

"I'm talking to you, aren't I? It's been a long time but I'm sure you recognise my voice."

"Where are you? Where is the girl now?"

"We're in Disneyland, Naish. I have a job as Mickey Mouse."

"What are you after, Colin?"

"I want *you* on Kirkfallen, fast as you can get there." The voice was quietly forceful. "No excuses. The girl and I will arrive by boat in the morning and I need clearance to moor. And I'd like a copter to airlift a couple of other people to Kirkfallen too."

Naish forced herself to stay calm. She had to try and stall the person on the other end of the phone.

"Nobody gets clearance to land on the island."

"Oh, I think you can make an exception."

"What if we sink the boat? Just to be on the safe side."

"You've only got my word that she'd actually be on it. Might be a decoy." Colin's voice turned glacial. "Guess wrong and the little lady will be on a plane under a false name and heading for the USA."

"You wouldn't!"

"She's just turned sixteen now. Do you want to test your experiment in the middle of America's largest city?"

"I can't just turn up there without alerting my superiors!" Naish blustered. "They'll come out with a Goddamned army."

"Do what you have to do. This girl is due to release what's inside her pretty soon. You don't want her to be wandering around Manhattan when she does."

The sick sensation crept across Naish's chest.

"I'll be there." She almost choked on the words.

"Good." Colin sounded almost cheerful. "I'll call back once more with a couple more details. You won't have time to trace this call, by the way."

"What are you after, Colin?" Naish repeated.

"My daughter and I have been in hiding for fifteen years." The voice laughed bitterly.

"We want to come home."

The line went dead. Naish glanced at the men in the corner.

"Where's he calling from?"

"No idea, Ma'am. This guy knows what he's doing."

"I want a jet prepared ASAP." Naish got up and paced the room. "Patch me through to Brigadier Potter at HQ and have him place Radcliff Naval Base in the Scottish Hebrides on full alert. Prepare an emergency satellite transmission to Kirkfallen Island."

Naish ran a hand through her greying hair.

"I have to talk to Edward Stapleton."

35

Apathy and her father sat in silence, staring into the roaring fire. Now and then Dan sneaked a glance at his daughter, averting his eyes every time she stared back. His hands shook slightly whenever he lifted the glass to his mouth.

"What do we do now?" She took a sip of her own wine.

"There's a game of Twister in the cupboard." Her father tried a tentative smile. Apathy understood that he spent his nights with Colin, not some stranger he'd met that day. Even if that stranger happened to be his daughter.

"Eh... dad?" she asked finally. "What are you actually like?"

Dan Salty thought for a while.

"There was a Russian scientist in the 1930s called Professor Luria," he replied. "He went to the furthest reaches of Siberia and conducted a survey of the natives. Asked them to describe themselves. This was an area almost untouched by civilisation or industry, you understand."

He took another slurp of wine.

"They would say things like 'I have four cows' or 'I grow potatoes'. Luria persisted, asking what they were like as people. Were they good or bad? Were they happy or sad? But they didn't really understand the question. They'd simply repeat, 'I have four cows'. See. This was what was really important to them."

"Did Colin tell you that?"

"Yeah. More useless information courtesy of the walking encyclopaedia." Dan leaned back in his chair and looked openly at Apathy for the first time. His expression was one of complete surprise.

"I have a *daughter*."

"Is that better than having four cows?"

"Colin was right. You *are* a firecracker." Dan gave a sharp laugh. Then his face became blank. "I've no idea how to act around you."

"Do you… love me?"

"I'm not sure." Dan lowered his eyes. "Do you love me?"

"No," Apathy replied evenly. "I don't know you."

"We should probably have played Twister."

The teenager shifted awkwardly in her chair.

"You… eh… work as a con man."

"It was Colin's idea," her father replied half-heartedly. "We started off doing fake séances.

Seemed harmless enough and we didn't need social security numbers or permits. Colin is a whiz with technology. He put together all this equipment for us to use. Tiny transistor radios and transmitters to make it seem like the dead were in the room. Our clients would hear voices coming from nowhere. See strange images out of the corner of their eyes..."

Dan stopped mid-sentence.

"It's not very nice, is it?" He sounded as if the notion had crossed his mind for the first time.

"Dad." Apathy said quietly. "What exactly is inside me?"

Dan poured himself more wine. His bottle was almost empty and his hands trembled. Apathy wondered if it was from nervousness or just the fact that he had consumed so much alcohol. She was vaguely alarmed at how much he was drinking.

"I need to show you something." He pushed the chair roughly back, strode to the kitchen drawer and pulled out an old Instamatic camera.

"I'm going to take your picture." His hands were still shaking and Apathy realised, with a shock, what was causing the tremors.

Her father was afraid.

He looked through the viewfinder and clicked the shutter. The camera whirred and a small square of plastic slid out of the bottom of the machine.

"This is what's inside you."

He thrust the photograph at his daughter.

In the picture, Apathy was seated by the fire, washed by its orange glow. Behind her was a shadowy female figure. She was almost transparent, long dark hair spilling over her face. Her hands were raised, as if in fury, above her head. The nails were long and black, like the talons of a bird of prey. One gleaming eye shone through the lank hair, glistening with unrepressed hatred.

Apathy felt herself go numb.

The girl in the picture was a grotesque caricature of a human being but there was no mistaking its identity.

It was her.

Apathy slowly put the photograph on the table.

"And I'm the only person in the world like this?"

Dan crumpled up the picture into a tight ball and pulled a lighter from his pocket. He lit the plastic square and dropped it into the ashtray.

"Am I?" the teenager insisted.

"Actually, no. There's an island in the Atlantic called Kirkfallen with a whole bunch of these horrors trapped on it."

"Like Jurassic Park?"

"I'm not kidding." Dan watched the sooty flames consume the picture, spiralling into a miniature helix of black smoke. "It's part of the military project I was mixed up in all those years ago."

"Can't you do anything about it? Shouldn't you tell someone?"

"Yeah. That'll look plausible." Dan extinguished the dying flame with a nicotine-stained thumb. "Mass murderer D.B. Salty contacts the authorities and tells them he really didn't have a choice when he killed all those people. He was just part of a top secret experiment that went wrong thirty years ago. They'd lock me up and throw away the key."

He gave a bark of laughter.

"They really *would* lock me up and throw away the key."

"But Colin could back up your story."

"It would be worse if anyone actually believed us. The first whiff of real suspicion? Your uncle and I would be assassinated. And, poof, everything on that island would be gone."

"So, you aren't going to do *anything*?"

"I didn't say that." Dan winked at her. "There's a little secret about Kirkfallen that Colin told me."

He got up and dropped the camera back into the drawer.

"All the same, I'm not going to risk my family." He pulled a manila envelope out and showed it to his daughter. "I've met some shady characters in my line of work. These are fake passports for you, Col and your mother. You're going to Canada."

"But I'm at school here! I can't just go on holiday."

"It's not a holiday." Dan dropped the envelope on the table. "You're going there for good. It's the safest place in the world for you both."

"I don't want to go to Canada!"

"It's a complicated situation," her father retorted coldly. "I promised to keep my family safe and I intend to do so."

"But you're not coming?"

"You stand a much better chance of settling over there if you don't have a wanted murderer tagging along."

"This can't be happening!"

"Baby. I've spent most of my life thinking that very thought."

"My God, you *are* a sociopath!" Apathy blurted. "All this talk of staying away to protect my mum and me? It's all crap."

"Apathy!"

"No. You just didn't care enough about our feelings to look after us properly! You used your stupid promise to get you out of any real responsibility. You didn't want the hassle of a wife and child!"

The teenager pushed back her chair and ran into the bedroom, slamming the door. Dan got awkwardly to his feet and followed her. He rested his head against the wood and listened to his daughter weeping.

"Goddammit!" he breathed, marching back into the kitchen, hands balled into fists.

Hearing the creak of a floorboard, he turned.

"What are *you* doing back?"

Colin stepped forward and punched his friend hard in the stomach.

Dan doubled over, air whooshing from his lungs. Colin stepped around him, demonstrating an agility that belied his size and build. With his other hand, he clamped a chloroform filled rag over Dan's mouth. The larger man slumped unconscious to the floor.

"I'm sorry, D.B."

Colin pulled Dan from the cottage and into the shed next door. He laid his friend out on the floor, trying to make his position as comfortable as possible.

"There's been a change of plan."

Kirkfallen Island

We tend to think of sociopaths as murderers or serial killers. But though most sociopaths have very little empathy and will cheat and lie without qualm, they do not turn out to be murderers. If they have no good reason to kill, they won't

In fact, according to psychologist Martha Stout, about one in twenty-five individuals living among us can be classed as sociopathic

36

Gene, Millar and Poppy were up at dawn. Since it was Saturday, there was no school or chores, but the teenagers had their own task.

The night before, Millar had removed several long pieces of wood from the communal scrap pile, telling the adults it was for repairs to the gang hut. They already had plenty of spare rope and tools left over from building their hideaway.

They hauled the timber out to Pittenhall Ridge in a tractor and trailer. Poppy kept lookout on a nearby hillock while Millar and Gene constructed two ladders by lashing the wood together and nailing on wooden steps. They roped the ends of the ladders to each other to form a loose hinge and, as a finishing touch, stuffed heather and gorse into the rope to camouflage what they'd made. Lying flat on the ground, the ladders were almost invisible.

Poppy gave them the all-clear and they carried the contraption to the fence at a point where the barbed wire top had rusted away. Leaning one side against the mesh, they flipped the other over the top so that they could climb down on the Jackson Head side. When they were safely over, they pulled the ladders behind them and laid them on the grass.

The trio made their way over the promontory, keeping a sharp eye open for the holes they had been warned about. After a few minutes, they reached the abandoned facility.

It looked like a giant World War II pillbox, the concrete blackened by age or, more likely, by fire. Island foliage had already begun to reclaim the structure - grass grew on the top and moss and scrub poked from the walls. The entrance was on the north side, surrounded by scorched concrete pillars. Above was a faded sign.

MacLellan Research Facility.

But the thick metal door was free of rust or foliage. And it was open.

"Do we really want to go in there?" Poppy tried one last attempt at reason.

"Nope. But it sure looks like we are." Millar switched on his flashlight and got as far as the entrance. He stopped and took a deep breath. Then he backed away quickly, almost falling over his own feet.

"What are you doing? Dancing?"

"Oh God. I think I have claustrophobia."

"I've known you for fifteen years, you slacker." Poppy shook her head. "You never mentioned *that* before."

"There aren't any enclosed spaces on Fallen." Millar's forehead had broken out in a sweat. "But I've never been *here*."

"And I thought I was the girl in this trio." Poppy brushed past him and marched through the doorway.

"I guess you're right." Millar ran a nervous tongue over his lips. "If *you* can fit in there, it can't be *too* enclosed."

Even so, it took the teenager several hesitant tries before he could bear to walk into the darkness.

The upper corridors were dark and grimy, foliage pushing its way through cracks in the ceiling. The trio crept silently along the passageways, shining their torches into doorways. Millar was breathing in short, ragged bursts.

"Calm down, will you?" Poppy spread her arms wide. "It's a corridor, not a rabbit warren. I can't even touch the walls."

"It's still the narrowest thing I've ever been in," Millar whispered. "And it's dark!"

They reached a stairwell and descended, Millar whimpering softly. Another corridor stretched into the darkness and a flight of stairs headed into the depths.

"Maybe we should split up to cover more ground," Gene suggested.

"Maybe you should have your head examined," Millar squeaked.

"You should take a peek in this room." Poppy shone her flashlight through the nearest doorway.

The teenagers gathered round to see what she was looking at.

The room was larger than the others. A blackened plaque on the door read **Ready Room 4** and a large table sat in the centre with chairs around it. Scorched metal cabinets lined one side and a cheap clock hung on one wall.

"Notice something unusual? Everything in this base is supposed to be burned up, right?"

"Yeah. My dad said the place was destroyed by an explosion. You can still see black marks on the walls."

"But the table and chairs are fine," Millar said. "And look at the time."

The children concentrated their flashlights on the clock. They could see the second hand moving.

"That's battery-operated," Poppy volunteered. "My parents have one just like it."

"No battery lasts for sixteen years." Millar turned to his companions, his eyes wide.

"Jesus, guys. This place is still being used!"

37

"We have to go deeper." Gene swung his flashlight towards the stairs. "There are more levels."

"Have you lost your senses?" Millar's face was hidden by shadow but his tone of voice admirably conveyed his distress. "We don't know *what's* down there."

"That's kind of the point. If we knew what was below us, we wouldn't have to go look."

"If I go any deeper, I'm gonna have a hairy fit!"

"I'm with Millar on this one." Poppy was still shining his flashlight around Ready Room 4. "If someone's using this place, they might catch us here."

"Don't you want to know what's going on?"

"I'm curious as hell now, but I am *not* going further underground!" Millar patted his chest in distress. "Makes me ill just thinking of it."

"Then I'll go myself." Gene stuck out his chest and made for the stairs.

"Don't be stupid," Poppy blocked his way. "We can't leave without you. We'd have to remove the ladder and you'd be stuck."

"Then wait if you like, but I need to see what's down there."

"What's gotten into you, buddy?" Millar joined Poppy's human barricade. "I really think it's time we asked our parents?"

"Then they'll know we've been here, genius." Gene tried to push past his friends. "You have to believe me. The clue to what's wrong with Fallen is tied up with this base."

Poppy looked quizzically at her agitated friend.

"What exactly do you know that we don't, Gene?"

The teenager gave a groan. He had to tell his friends *something*.

"I overheard my parents having a completely weird conversation last night," he said. "It didn't make much sense, but they were talking about sacrificing kids."

"Yeah, right!" Millar almost choked. "I'm tired of eating turnips as well but we're not living in the middle ages."

"Give it ten minutes. That's all I ask. There's a nice clock on the wall there, so you can time me."

Poppy and Millar hesitated.

"What can happen in ten minutes, guys?"

"Get going then." Poppy stepped back. "But if you meet some hulking monster, try and handle it on your own."

"I thought you weren't going downstairs, Poppy," Millar said pleasantly, earning himself a quick slap on the head.

"I won't be long." Gene pushed past his friends before they could protest again and made his way down the inky stairwell.

"Can we go into the big room?" Millar pleaded once his friend was gone. "I think I'm having palpitations. I really *hate* it here."

Poppy nodded. They returned to the Ready Room and sat on the chairs.

"So, who do you think is using this place?"

"The adults in the village, I guess." Poppy played her flashlight around the empty room. "That might be the real reason we're not allowed on Pittenhall Ridge. To stop us seeing them going in and out."

"What do you think they do here? Have orgies?"

"Don't be disgusting."

"Then I don't get all the secrecy."

Millar tilted the chair back and put his feet on the table. Now that he was in a large room, his confidence was slowly returning.

"What do we care whether our parents come here or not?"

"My thoughts exactly." Poppy's black brows knitted together. "Gene should leave this alone."

"Wait a minute." Millar slammed the chair down. "What if it's *not* our families who are using the base?"

"Why didn't I think of that? It's really a retirement home for goblins."

"No, listen. You can't get on or off Jackson Head by sea because of the cliffs." Millar stroked his chin, leaving black smudges down each cheek. "And the fence cuts off the promontory from the rest of the island."

"Your point?"

"We've always thought the barrier was there to keep people *out* of Jackson Head."

"What else would it be for?" Poppy licked her fingers and wiped her friend's dirty face.

"Stop that!" Millar grabbed the girl's wrist. "What if it was built to keep something *in*? You've seen *King Kong* a million times, right?"

"Is this another comment about my size?"

"It's about an island that's always shrouded in clouds, just like this one. And it's terrorised by a monster." Millar's voice held no trace of mockery. "So the islanders build a barrier to keep it away from them. Only that isn't enough."

The boy took off his hat and rubbed his flattened hair.

"They also give it human sacrifices to stop it breaking out."

"I see what you're getting at. But nobody on this island has been sacrificed."

"What about the Orbisons?" Millar scrambled to his feet.

"I think we better get Gene."

38

Poppy and Millar inched along the corridor, flash-lights held in front of them. They had gone down two flights with no sign of their friend. Most of the doors were open and they shone their lights into each room as they passed.

"Can you take my hand?" Millar begged. "Please? I'm finding it really hard to breathe."

"Jeez, you really are claustrophobic."

Poppy reached out. It was the first time she had ever held a boy's hand and it made her feel odd. But in a good way, she had to admit. She had a slight crush on Millar, though she would never dream of telling him.

"Notice something funny about this place?"

"*Funny* and *this place* are not compatible words in my head." Millar leapt back as a rat scurried up the corridor. "Try terrifying."

"I think I'll shout for Gene."

"Then stand at the end of the corridor. I want a chance to escape when some hairy beast attracted by the noise starts snacking on you."

"That ought to give you at least half an hour." Poppy flexed a beefy arm.

"You find humour in the weirdest situations, know that?"

"Boo!"

The voice came from right behind Millar. He spun around with a guttural cry, flattening himself against the wall.

Gene stood in the shadows, shining a torch under his chin.

"What the hell…!" Millar pushed the teenager violently against the wall. "I got a weak heart, you know!"

"I think a faint heart is the term you're looking for." Poppy let go of Millar's hand, suddenly embarrassed. "You find anything, Gene?"

"Come with me." Gene led his companions down the corridor, Millar still muttering curses under his breath. They came to a door marked **Communications** and stepped inside.

"Look at that."

The Communications Room was bare except for one table and chair. On the table was a metal box with a small screen, the back a mass of wires leading to two car batteries. Poppy leaned over and peered into the workings.

"What is it?"

"Looks like a homemade sonar or radar device of some sort." Gene tentatively nudged a couple of the wires. "But it's not rusty. It's getting used."

"Fascinating." Millar was still sulking. "Can we go now?"

"There's a couple more rooms you need to see." Gene reversed back into the corridor and the others followed. He led them a few more yards and opened a door marked **Experimental Chamber 1.** It had a narrow observation slit at head height.

The whole room was painted sky blue. In the corner was a bed. Next to that were sets of shelves lined with children's books, while posters of superheroes decorated the walls.

"*This* is unexpected. Is it some sort of crèche?"

"With a lock on the outside of the door?" Millar asked. "That's just creepy."

"There's an identical room next door. **Experimental Chamber 2**." Gene tugged Poppy back into the corridor. "And then it gets stranger."

The next door was labelled **Armoury**. He pushed it open and the trio entered.

The original gun racks were there, bent and twisted. But hanging on the misshapen metal were weapons of every sort. Gene moved his flashlight across them.

There were at least a dozen rifles, a couple of shotguns and an array of handguns. On the next wall were catapults, bows and arrows and spears made from lashing spikes of metal to carved poles. The flashlights played across Zip guns and Molotov cocktails – bottles filled with tractor fuel and topped with wads of cotton. Axes. Saws. Scythes. There was even some kind of flame thrower that appeared to be constructed from a propane tank and a weed sprayer. The last wall was lined with metal drums – a hazard label on the front.

"Like I said." Gene pointed to the racks. "Everyone on this island knows how to build."

Millar walked past the rows of deadly implements and gave a shudder.

"This is genuinely scary."

"I'll tell you what's scarier." Gene swung his torch around.

There was a table in the middle of the room. On it lay a huge Bible.

"We've got a room full of homemade weapons here," Poppy snorted. "You're worried about a *Bible?*"

"Check out the page it's open at."

"The Book of Revelations." Millar leaned closer. "And there's a passage underlined."

And I looked, and beheld a pale horse: and his name that sat on him was Death, and Hell followed with him. And power was given unto them over the fourth part of the earth, to kill with sword, and with hunger, and with death.

39

The teenagers left the ruined installation, talking in urgent whispers.

"What did we just see back there?"

A seagull on top of MacLellan base gave a guttural screech and all three recoiled, bumping into each other.

"I got no idea," Gene admitted. "But I'm really quite alarmed now."

"So, what are we going to do?" Poppy blinked in the open sunlight.

"Well, I'd advise getting out of here, pronto."

"First smart thing you've said all day," Millar turned to head for the fence and fell flat on his face. He reached out for what had tripped him up.

"What the?"

Poppy gave a cry of fear.

The ladder was lying on the ground next to Millar.

"It's certainly a nice bit of camouflage. Then again, you were taught well."

Gene whirled round, recognising the voice immediately.

His father was sitting on a grass verge a few feet away.

"Dad?"

"Don't worry, I'm not mad at you." Edward Stapleton held a bulky object. He also had a walkie talkie clipped to his belt.

"Satellite phone." He glanced down at the piece of equipment in his hand - a device none of the teenagers had dreamt existed on Kirkfallen.

"I keep it hidden in your mom's underwear drawer." He winked at Gene. "Figured you'd never go looking in there."

"Dad? What is going *on*?"

"You three are certainly due an explanation." Edward Stapleton walked over to his son and laid a hand on his shoulder. "I guess I've been putting it off."

He gave an awkward smile.

"For about fifteen years, in fact."

"Are you going to sacrifice us, Mr Stapleton?" Millar's voice was a terrified whisper.

"Interesting question." Edward motioned for the trio to sit down. "I have something to tell you. When you hear it, I hope you'll understand why I kept it secret for so long."

Gene's father wore only a shirt and jeans, sleeves rolled up over his brawny arms, but his forehead was beaded with sweat.

"But first, you need to read this."

He opened a leather bag and pulled a manila folder from inside. Emblazoned on the cover in red were the words **TOP SECRET**.

"It's time you learned about the Stopwatch Project."

The Stopwatch Project

The first insect pheromones were discovered by German researchers in the 1960s. Then, a 1971 study by University of Chicago Professor of Psychology, Martha McClintock Stern, provided evidence for the existence of pheromones in humans

Since humans are vastly more complex than insects, these have been much harder to detect and categorise

40

TOP SECRET
The Stopwatch Project
Head of Project: Colonel Markus Kelty, MD, PhD.
Project Assistant: Dr Catherine Naish, PhD.

The Stopwatch Project was suggested by Dr Markus Kelty and stemmed from classified research he conducted for the U.S. Army during the Vietnam conflict. His work was based on the study of insect pheromones carried out by civilian laboratories throughout the 1960s. The first human tests were carried out by Dr Kelty on Vietcong prisoners.

Pheromone Research
Pheromones are hormones - chemicals released by insects that allow them to communicate with others of their species. Pheromones differ from sight or sound communication in that they are virtually impossible to detect and are effective over a long range. Most of the pheromones dis-

covered so far have been found in social insects like ants and honeybees. These included...

The Alarm Pheromone: This allows ants to trigger alarm in other ants, who will then attack any perceived danger. The pheromones drive the insects into a frenzy and they will even attack each other in such an uncontrolled state.

The Mandibular Pheromone: This is a pheromone passed among worker insects, causing them to coordinate nearly all their activities.

However, there is evidence that humans also produce pheromones. Dr Kelty began to research this at Sheridan Military Base in the Mohave Desert. The Stopwatch Project (Mark I) was an attempt to see if the alarm pheromones in ants could be isolated and combined with human pheromones to trigger aggressive behaviour in people.

The experiments yielded partial success. When injected with a concentrated insect pheromone, volunteer test subjects became uncontrollably violent and had to be restrained, to stop them from harming themselves and others. It was noted, however, that one soldier – Asher Wylie - seemed unaffected by the experiment.

After a battery of tests, it was discovered that Wylie suffered from a form of sociopathy. Another pheromone experiment was then done on a sociopathic inmate from

Dobson State Correctional Facility. He, too, was unaffected. It appeared that a lack of certain human characteristics, such as empathy or conscience, in sociopathic individuals rendered them immune to the alarm pheromone.

Dr Kelty then proposed a two-pronged approach to his research. He devised a test for schools that, on the surface, would appear to be a teaching aid. In fact, it would allow the U.S. Military to ascertain which children in the state school system had sociopathic personalities. It was hoped that these children could be recruited by the armed forces when they graduated. Their lack of societal checks would make them excellent covert operatives, who would be banded together to form an elite squad called the Stopwatch Unit. As well as a ruthless fighting force, they could be used as monitors, or even test subjects, for further clinical trials into the alarm pheromone's effect on humans.

In the meantime, research continued at Sheridan base, using long-term prisoners from the state penitentiary.

In 1980, tests were conducted on a 15-year-old sociopathic volunteer named Daniel Boone Salty. The effects were catastrophic. Unlike previous test subjects, the boy somehow spread alarm pheromones to the rest of the base. Protective suits had no effect, for the pheromones were amplified to astonishing proportions by swarms of ants, attracted by Salty's hormone release. In the ensuing frenzy, the entire complex wiped itself out.

Dr Kelty hypothesised this incident was the result of a one in a million chance. Daniel Salty was injected just as puberty was bringing on enormous changes to his own hormones. Somehow, the alarm pheromones reacted with these changes to produce a massive and deadly emission, attracting and amplified by thousands of ants. One so over-powering it spread through the base like a virus.

After a change of government administration, it was decided that these experiments posed a threat to national security - a repeat of the Sheridan disaster might result in pheromone emissions reaching a population centre. Since these were amplified by both humans and ants and, given that ants are indigenous to 95% of the earth's surface, the result could mean a nationwide epidemic. However, it was recognised that Dr Kelty had discovered a devastating biological weapon.

It was at this point that Dr Kelty proposed a safer alternative to the project. He would set up another base on the isolated island of Kirkfallen in the Atlantic. Key personnel, including the Head of Security and the Communications Officer, would be from the newly formed Stopwatch Unit. Their sociopathic personalities would leave them unaffected by an outbreak of alarm pheromone and enable them to contain any potentially hazardous situation.

The base became operational in 1996.

While the teenagers finished reading, Edward Stapleton plucked tufts of seagrass and let them fall through his fingers.

"I was one of the Stopwatch Unit," he said softly, glancing at the concrete structure behind them. "In fact, I was the Communications Officer for this base, when it was still in use."

"You used to be in the army?" Gene spluttered. He didn't even want to think about the reason his father had been recruited. "You used to be stationed *here*?"

"I'm still in the army." Edward held up the Sat Nav phone. "And I just been talking to my boss. She's on her way."

"What happened to the base, dad?" Gene whispered. "Why was it abandoned?"

"There's no point in hiding the truth anymore, so I'll tell you."

Edward tossed the satellite phone contemptuously onto the grass.

"Because life, as we know it on Fallen, is about to end."

41

1996

Edward Stapleton sat on a hillock gazing out to sea. The wind came in gusts, surprising him with sudden changes of direction. Waves careered up the beach and then retreated, watery children playing a game, leaving frothy ridges in the sand.

He heard a polite cough behind his back.

"You found my favourite spot." Dr Markus Kelty was standing a few feet away, a half-eaten sandwich in one hand. "Mind if I sit?"

"You're the boss, Sir." Stapleton began to get up but Kelty motioned for him to stay where he was.

"How come you're not in the mess with the rest of the men?"

"I like it here and I'm not exactly a team player."

Kelty stood a while longer, eating the rest of his lunch. Edward didn't know how to make conversation with a superior officer, so he stayed quiet, wishing the doctor would go away.

"Mind if I ask you something?" Kelty said eventually.

"I guess not."

"How come you joined the army?" The question came out of the blue.

"Is this some kind of check?"

"No, soldier. It's one human being curious about another."

"Before I left school, I was approached by a Major Whittaker, who suggested I might like to sign up." Stapleton stretched his legs. "When I told him I planned to be a fireman, he gave me the old importance of defending my country speech."

Stapleton gave a resigned shrug.

"Whittaker then told me how much money a person with my... special talents could make."

"That convinced you?"

"He also hinted broadly that a fireman who had tested positive for a sociopathic personality wouldn't have much of a career arc."

"I'm sorry."

"No, you're not, Sir. You designed the test."

Kelty ran a hand down his face.

"Do you know what we're doing here? You're the Communications Officer, so don't pretend you don't."

"I hear the scuttlebutt."

"And what do you think?"

"I have no opinions. I'm in the army."

"Nicely put." Kelty finally sat down and unfastened the top button of his shirt.

"I've finally made a breakthrough, you know," he said unexpectedly.

"I'm happy for you." Edward clamped his jaw shut. He was dangerously close to insubordination.

"Are you?" Kelty tossed the crust of his sandwich to the screaming gulls. "Really? I mean… off the record."

"Is it worth it?" Edward flinched as soon as the words were out of his mouth but Kelty didn't seem fazed.

"I'm hoping so, in the long run."

They sat staring at the ocean for a while. Then Kelty began to talk, long chin resting on the arm draped over his knee.

"The Stopwatch Project exists because the army wants a weapon. One that will put an end to the struggle for supremacy on this planet once and for all."

He swatted at an overconfident gull that had come too close, diving for crumbs.

"But it's a struggle that can only be won at a terrible price."

"You must agree with their aims if you've spent twenty years working on it. Sir."

"Drop the Sir, malarkey. I need to talk to someone."

Kelty rubbed tired eyes. There were tight lines around his mouth and his hair seemed to have more white in it every day.

"It's not a trick. Honestly."

"I don't see how this... weapon can work," Edward said cautiously, still wondering if the exchange was some sort of trap. "You take a human, fill him full of insect alarm pheromone and let him release it in some hostile country. That correct?"

"Broadly speaking, yes."

"What if it spreads right around the globe? How is that a victory for anyone?"

"Imagine a pheromone outbreak started in Asia." Kelty seemed perfectly calm, as if he were discussing the weather. "In that dense population, it would multiply like wildfire. Spread across Africa, Europe, China, India – everyone would go nuts. Too crazy to fire nuclear weapons or instigate any conventional response. Too mad to fly planes or sail boats. They'd just start killing each other with whatever came to hand. Rifles, farm implements, household appliances. You name it."

"What would stop that outbreak reaching the USA?"

"The Atlantic and Pacific Oceans." Kelty pointed to the rolling waves. "The pheromone weapon is a human/ant hybrid. Human pheromones are strong – but they need to be amplified and carried by millions of ants to have a long range effect. No people or ants to carry the outbreak? It grinds to a halt."

He crumpled up the sandwich wrapper and put it in his pocket.

"There are no people or ants in the ocean - and the only landmass that is near both Asia and the American continents is Alaska – with a small human population."

"And it's too cold for ants." Edward suddenly understood.

"The plague would never reach America."

"What about the survivors of your infection? The people who aren't affected?" Edward jerked a thumb at himself. "People like me?"

"You'd be burying the dead for years. Most of the world would revert back to the Stone Age. We'd have won hands down."

"And you call *me* a sociopath."

"Let me give you a hypothetical situation." Kelty looked at the sky, conjuring up a scenario. "You encounter a child you know is carrying an infectious disease. He is approaching a heavily populated area and you have no way of isolating him. What do you do?"

"A child?"

"A child."

Edward Stapleton swallowed hard.

"I kill it."

"And how would you feel about that?"

"I'd feel I just saved a lot of people."

"And the child?"

"I did what I had to do. Took one life to save many."

"My point exactly." Kelty patted the man on the shoulder. "Having a sociopathic personality doesn't make anyone a monster. Just makes it easier for them to kill."

Edward Stapleton's face reddened.

"Anyway," Kelty continued. "The military swear they'd never actually use the Stopwatch Project. It's just meant to be a... deterrent."

"And you believe them?"

"Not at all, but I guess it never stopped me." Kelty gave a short bark of laughter. "I thought of myself as a visionary."

"That's not a vision I'd like to have in my head when I try to sleep at night." Edward didn't try to conceal his distaste. If Kelty wanted honesty, he would damned well get it.

"This planet is dying, Edward." His superior lay wearily back on the grass. "Becoming buried under the weight of its human population. Unable to cope with the pollution we cause, the environmental changes we generate. We don't think about it now, but in twenty years, we'll begin to realise that we're going to wipe ourselves out. By the time we do, if I'm any judge of human nature, it will be too late to reverse the process."

"You *want* an outbreak to happen?" Edward felt his head spinning. "You could *live* with that?"

"Wouldn't have to. Despite what I've done, I haven't got a sociopathic personality. I'd be dead as well."

The gulls screamed and weaved in the grey sky. Edward Stapleton looked around the deserted promontory. Tried to comprehend the enormity of what he was hearing.

"What's it like?" Kelty pulled a bottle of water from his pocket.

"What do you mean?"

"To be like you. Not to be able to feel how others feel." He twisted off the top and took a swig. "Not to be stopped by your emotions."

Edward thought for a while.

"It's lonely."

"You know what turns certain sociopathic individuals into serial killers? I did a study of this, by the way." Kelty offered over the bottle of water. "They don't fit in. They don't feel a part of society. In some people, that's enough motivation to take revenge on their own race."

"You're being a bit simplistic."

"Why look for a complicated answer when an easy one will do?"

Edward took the bottle. His lips were dry and cracked by the salty air. The fresh water washed away the saline taste. He drank greedily.

"Now, imagine a place where everyone was just like you. You wouldn't feel alone anymore."

Kelty took the water back, splashed some into his hands and applied it to his face.

"You wouldn't be swayed by prejudice, by religious ideas, by patriotism, by any of the things that make the masses kill. You'd actually deserve to inherit the earth."

Edward thought about that for a long time.

"The problem is," he offered eventually. "I can still tell right from wrong."

He unclipped the holster on his belt and pulled out his pistol.

Kelty frowned.

"What are you doing?"

"Considering ending the project." Edward calmly swung the gun and pointed it at his superior's head. "Feel like appealing to my better nature? How far do you think that will get you?"

"This wasn't on my study."

"Don't make me out to be a fiend, Colonel." The soldier flipped off the safety catch. "I don't have to give in to my demons."

"Like I said." To Edward's astonishment, Kelty went back to staring at the rolling swells. "Sometimes you have to kill to make things better."

"If you have any last words, now's your chance. Not that someone like *me* will care."

Kelty took a deep breath.

"I never told anyone this, but my real name is Markus Kirkemeyer. And when I was a child, my own father handed me over to the Nazis because my mother was Jewish."

Kelty unfolded his arms and put his hands behind his head as if he were discussing a family outing.

"She and I were sent to a concentration camp. She died. I didn't." The doctor gave a thin smile. "My father and I had just attended one of Hitler's Nuremberg Rallies."

"What has that got to do with anything?"

"My father had always been a decent man. Patriotic, yes, but a decent man all the same. So why did he do something so horrific?"

Kelty took one hand from behind his head and removed a set of dentures from his mouth.

"In the camp, I wash sho malnourished that, by the time the Americansh came, all my teesh had fallen out."

"Please put those back." Edward felt queasy at the sight. Without his dentures, Kelty looked like an animated cadaver.

"At firsht I thought it musht have been my fault." He returned the teeth to his mouth. "That I was some kind of monster. Then I thought it must be because my *father* was a monster. Neither of these, as you can imagine, were acceptable explanations. So, I've spent my life trying to find another reason."

The doctor closed his eyes and shivered.

"Then it came to me. You put a mass of people together and whip up their emotions? They lose all sense of who they are. Become immersed in the feeling of the crowd. It's called mass hysteria."

"Stop stalling." Edward's gun never wavered. "If you have a point, get to it."

"Mass hysteria. The kind of total conditioning that overcomes reason. You find it at football matches. Lynch mobs. Political rallies. Fraternity parties. Wars. Religious gatherings. And it's caused by *human* pheromones."

"I've never heard that theory before."

"Cause it's mine." Kelty thumped his heart. "Though I don't see a Nobel prize heading my way any time soon."

"I don't think they give them out to *mad* scientists."

"Very droll." Kelty gave a chuckle. "Y'know, I was so grateful to the American soldiers who rescued me from the camp, I joined the U.S. army myself. Served in Vietnam."

The doctor seemed to have forgotten all about the gun.

"But when I came back to the States, I found another kind of movement." He grinned at the thought. "The Hippies. Peace and love. Change the world for the better. Fuelled by concerts and love-ins and hang-outs where everyone was together and hoping for a better world. People releasing pheromones that weren't harmful but positive."

Kelty treated the soldier to a knowing leer.

"I got quite into the free love thing, in fact."

"That's more information than I needed to know."

Kelty stopped smiling and tucked his hands into the pockets of his army regulation shirt.

"It was a doomed movement, of course. Soon swamped by a world that was filled with hate. But it existed for a while."

"And this means something?"

"Whether we're talking about ants or humans, there's more than *one* type of pheromone."

Kelty's eyes positively twinkled and, for a second, he looked much younger.

"The alarm pheromone makes insects attack anything that moves. Humans too, as we found out. But there's also a type that makes insects *coordinate* their actions – the Mandibular Pheromone. If you could create a worldwide outburst of *that* type, people would be compelled to *work* together. *All* people Edward. Irrespective of race or religion."

"Shame your research went in the opposite direction."

"I still remember the Nuremberg Rallies." Kelty sat up and stared out across the horizon, a lost look on his face. "And even though I was Jewish, and the tirade was directed against *me*? It still felt *wonderful.*"

He rubbed his temple as if trying to alter the memory.

"For many years, I *wanted* to create a deadly phero-mone plague. I wanted everyone under the influence of pheromones gone, leaving only those who could think clear-ly. Logically."

Kelty gave a shuddering sigh.

"Oh yeah. Just what the Nazis preached. I was trying to create a master race. That's how influenced I was."

"And now?" The soldier suddenly had an inkling of where the conversation might be going. "Are you saying you've changed?"

"I fell in love with a lady, Edward." Kelty seemed awed by this simple statement. "A bit late in life, I know, but it made me see things in a different light. Therefore, I've been misleading the powers that be about what I'm actually up to."

He sighed.

"But I can't do it for much longer without getting rum-bled."

Edward Stapleton slowly holstered his gun.

"Why are you telling me this?"

"Because I like you and I'm going to need you." Kelty felt safe enough to stand up. "So I'll ignore the fact that you were a hair's breadth from executing a senior officer."

"Sure wouldn't look good on my record."

"Tomorrow afternoon, You are to come out here and stay put. Don't go anywhere near the base. That's an order."

"Why? What's going to happen, Dr Kelty?"

"I have a plan." Kelty buttoned his shirt back up to the collar again.

"I'm going to try and undo the harm I've done."

Edward rubbed his bare arms, where goosebumps had formed. The teenagers looked at each other. Millar nudged Gene.

"What happened next, dad?"

"I did what Kelty told me. I was at the other end of the island when I heard explosions. He'd corrupted all the records and destroyed the base. I knew Kelty was responsible because I ran to Jackson Head in time to see him taking off in a boat with a woman. The one he loved, I guess."

The wind gusted and Edward looked up, as if surprised to find himself back on the island.

"He even waved to me, can you believe it? Next day, I was picked up by the U.S. Navy."

He pulled a stone from the grass and flung it at the base. It bounced off the ruined concrete, sparking a white puff of powder that was carried away in the breeze.

"I didn't tell them about our... conversation. After all, Kelty spared my life." A doubtful look slid over his face. "I suppose I trusted him in the end."

"Dad." Gene bit his lip. "What you were saying about your... eh... personality. Does this mean you don't love me?"

"You're the best thing that ever happened to me." Edward Stapleton reached out an arm. Gene shuffled over and his father pulled him close. "I'd give my life for you."

"Eh... if the base was destroyed?" Millar asked shyly. "Why are you still on Fallen?"

"I'm part of Kelty's great con." Edward jerked his thumb at the blackened ruin of the MacLellan facility. "Obviously, I haven't got time to go into it right now."

He shook his head.

"But even I couldn't have guessed just how far Kelty was willing to go."

42

Calton Hill. Edinburgh

1996

Naish sat on a chipped green bench, coat fastened up to the neck. An icy wind blew across the top of Calton Hill, strong and cold enough to keep all but the most hardened joggers away. Even so, she counted a handful of people dotted across the scrubby green expanse. A well-wrapped couple stood, hand in hand, gazing at the spires of the dozen gothic buildings pricking the grey Edinburgh sky. An old woman in a huge green jacket and fur hat read a book a couple of benches back and a lone dog walker pulled at the lead of his unwilling canine, a hundred yards away.

Despite the years, Naish recognised Kelty's confident walk immediately as he made his way over the brow of the hill. Hands in greatcoat pockets, briefcase under his arm, he looked neither right nor left. She rose when he reached her and gave him a quick kiss on the cheek. Kelty's thinning hair was pure white now and deep lines puckered his eyes and mouth. They sat down, huddled together against the elements.

"The wind is cold in October," the doctor said conspiratorially. "But the birds will return in spring."

"Quit pretending you're in some spy movie. There's nobody watching. I didn't spend years in Army Intelligence without knowing how to lose a tail."

"That's my girl. Now unfasten your coat so I can have a feel."

"You really *have* missed me."

"I want to be sure you're not dumb enough to wear a wire."

Naish unzipped her coat and Kelty quickly patted her sides.

"Thank you." He glanced warily around. "Won't you get into trouble for this?"

"Nothing I can't handle," Naish snorted. "I knew you wouldn't talk to me if I had... eh... company."

"Then I'll make this brief."

"What exactly are you *doing* here?" The woman angrily fastened her coat back up. "You've been missing for months and the authorities sorely want to question you. Why were you stupid enough to surface again?"

"Is the Stopwatch Project still active?"

"Why would it be?" Naish flicked a golden leaf that had blown against her coat. "Sheridan base was destroyed. The Kirkfallen base is destroyed. There's not a shred of data left."

"Maybe the army should take a hint."

"So what happened? Was Kirkfallen a repeat of Sheridan?"

"I'd have thought that was obvious." Kelty blew into his hands.

"Then, what makes you think the Stopwatch Project will ever be reinstated?"

Kelty opened his briefcase and took out two newspaper clippings. One was regarding the Diamondback Massacre and the other about the identification of D.B. Salty.

"Dan Salty may have ended the outbreak at Diamondback, but he sure as hell didn't start it. He's a spent force."

Kelty pulled another sheet of paper from the briefcase.

"This was faxed to me by Army Intelligence right after Diamondback. Salty's adopted mother, Louise Walton, died in the slaughter. It doesn't take a genius to figure out she must be Louise Martin – the only other survivor of the Sheridan disaster."

"What of it?" Naish tried to sound nonchalant.

"Louise Walton had a sixteen-year-old son called Colin." Kelty tapped his nose. "Sixteen? Is it possible Louise was pregnant when she was at Sheridan base?"

"I suppose so."

"Then her son caused this, not Dan Salty."

"I see what you're getting at. You think Louise's unborn kid absorbed the pheromone outburst that killed everyone else at Sheridan, leaving her unharmed?"

"I can't think of a better explanation."

"And then he unleashed hell at Diamondback trailer park, at the same age as Dan Salty was when he destroyed

Sheridan." Naish pulled the collar of her coat tighter as the wind whipped her long dark hair around her face. "You're thinking it lay dormant in Colin all that time."

"Sounds about right." Kelty began putting the clippings back into his briefcase. "According to the military report I got, the army certainly believes so. They picked him up right after the massacre."

"Then, you already know the answer. The Stopwatch Project is still operational, despite recent.... setbacks."

"I was afraid of that. But it won't work, Naish." Kelty gave a disapproving glare. "Dan Salty and Colin were flukes and both have used up their pheromones. All my data was destroyed and no scientist knows how to re-create the serum I used to set Dan off."

"I'm sure they'll try."

"Even after two bases being wiped out?"

"Let's hope they'll be very careful."

"You know they won't. They're too arrogant."

"Talk about the pot calling the kettle black." Naish pushed tangled hair back from her face. "Anyway, it's nothing that I can change. I'm not part of the project anymore."

"You're going to be, I guarantee it." Kelty winked at her.

"Why did you come back, Markus?" Naish looked apprehensively around. "Soon as you called, wanting to meet, the army flew me over to Scotland. I'm sure you considered this might be a trap."

"Of course. Top Brass would love to prise whatever knowledge they can out of me. In all sorts of unpleasant ways, I imagine."

"So, why put yourself in such danger?"

"To be alone with you for a few minutes."

Kelty looked around. The dog walker was closer now, the wind whipping at his scarf. The woman with the green coat was still reading her book.

"The military will hunt me down eventually, so I figured I better give them what they want."

"I don't understand," Naish frowned.

"There's a key to a safe deposit box in your coat pocket. I put it there when I was patting you down."

"Now, I *really* don't understand."

"In that box is the last batch of active Stopwatch serum. I saved it from Kirkfallen."

Kelty sat back and stared at the sky.

"It's invaluable, as the military won't be able to replicate it."

"Any substance can be broken down and copied. You know that."

"Don't be foolish, Naish. They can't even do it with Coca Cola." Kelty wiped his nose with his sleeve. "They'd need to know the exact process of making it and I've stopped that ever happening again."

"You sabotaged the Kirkfallen base, didn't you?" Naish said quietly. "I always suspected it."

"That I did. Wiped the data and killed everyone working on the project."

"Then why are you giving me a serum you went to such lengths to destroy?"

"When they get nowhere, the military will put you back on the project. You were my assistant and the only qualified person left. Hell, they might even promote you and stick you in charge."

"I don't want the job."

"Yes. You never approved of what I was doing, thank God." Kelty put a hand on her shoulder. "But here's why you're going to take it and what you're going to do."

He leaned forward and whispered in her ear.

"You have *got* to be shitting me." Naish's eyes widened. "I can't! It's treason!"

Kelty's lip curled.

"For once in your fucking life, Catherine Naish, have the guts to act on your convictions. People who blindly follow orders are as bad as those who give them."

"What do you mean? I've always..."

"Why would anyone take their pet to a big green space and then keep it on a leash?" Kelty interrupted.

He nodded towards the dog walker, now only twenty yards away.

"I knew you'd betray me, Catherine. In fact, I counted on it."

He gave her a kiss on the cheek.

"If you won't do the right thing out of decency, perhaps you'll do it from guilt."

"Oh, Markus. I didn't..."

"It's *Doctor* Kelty, Naish."

He reached inside his pocket and brought out a gun.

"Markus, no!" Naish leapt to her feet. "There are soldiers…"

"There always are." Kelty smiled sadly. "But they'll get nothing more out of me."

He turned and fired. The dog walker looked surprised, then toppled over. The dog bounded away, free at last.

Kelty turned and ran towards the brow of the hill, greatcoat flapping behind him. There was a sharp crack and the doctor spun sideways, clutching his leg.

"Don't kill him!" Naish sprinted towards Kelty, waving her arms. "He's the only one who knows the…"

She skidded to a halt as the doctor raised his gun and pointed it at her.

"No. He's bluffing!" she yelled. "Don't sho…"

There was another sharp retort and Kelty fell backwards. A plume of red spouted from his chest and was whipped away by the wind.

"Markus, no!"

A man in a black leather jacket emerged from the bushes a hundred yards away, sniper's rifle in hand. He ran over to her.

"You OK, Major Naish?"

The woman knelt over, trying not to retch.

"What did he say to you, Major?" the man asked urgently.

After a few seconds, Naish straightened up and patted her cheeks. She picked up Kelty's briefcase from the bench.

"What did he say to you?" The sniper repeated.

"That's above your pay grade." Naish tucked the briefcase under her arm.

"But, if you must know, he was saying goodbye."

43

The trawler *Lillian Gish II* gouged a furrow through scudding whitecaps, scrappy clouds and sea-gulls duelling in the sky above. Colin stood at the prow with the skipper, both wearing woolly hats and overcoats.

"This isn't what I signed up for." Captain Hall wiped salt spray from his handlebar moustache. "You didn't say anything about a girl coming along."

"For what I'm paying you, I could bring the London Symphony Orchestra." Colin pushed his hair more securely into his hat.

"Don't you think it's about time you told me where we're going?" Hall indicated the expanse of heaving grey and green in front of the ship. "I doubt this is a seal spotting trip."

"Set course for Kirkfallen Island."

"Are you crazy?" The Skipper turned on his companion. "*Nobody* gets permission to land there. No

267

ship ever has – rumour is, it's owned by the U.S. military or something. I'm not getting boarded or blown out of the water, no matter how much you're offering!"

"Get on the ship's radio and contact Kirkfallen." Colin pulled a scrap of paper from his pocket. "This is the frequency. Ask for an Edward Stapleton. He'll give you permission."

The skipper snatched the paper and glared at it. Without another word, he stomped towards the wheelhouse.

Colin waited, hands in his pockets.

After a few minutes, Captain Hall returned, sliding on the spray soaked deck. His face registered deep suspicion.

"We have authorisation to land," he grumbled. "You must know some pretty high up people."

"When we moor, set us ashore, then head back to the Hebrides." Colin took back the scrap of paper. He opened his fingers and it was whipped over the side by the wind. "The second half of your payment will go into your bank account on one condition. You tell *nobody* about this."

"You don't have to worry about that. I'm pretty sure we're doing *something* dodgy."

"I'm going below. Let me know when we reach our destination."

Colin entered the cabin, shrugging off his overcoat. Apathy was sitting on a bunk, glaring at him.

"Well?" she said, stretching her thin arms. "When are we meeting my dad?"

"I told you. He'll be following us shortly."

Colin flopped onto the bunk opposite and pulled the red hat from his head. His static-filled hair gently floated down to a more normal shape.

"I don't know how your mom figured out where we were but the area was suddenly crawling with police. He's covering our tracks while I get you to safety. Can't risk the authorities returning you to Edinburgh in your condition."

"Yeah. And where exactly are you going to hide me that's safe?"

Colin patted the wall of the boat.

"This old crate is taking us to Kirkfallen Island in the Atlantic Ocean. It's completely isolated. Perfect, in fact."

"Where the monsters are?"

Colin raised a thick eyebrow. "Hmmm…. I figured Dan might mention that."

"He did. But I still don't understand how you both know about this place?"

"The next part of the story, I guess." Colin rubbed his red hands to restore circulation. "You ready to hear it?"

"I think my days of blissful ignorance are well and truly over."

"After the Diamondback Massacre, Dan got away by walking over the hills. I, unfortunately, was put on a bus." The *Lillian Gish II* listed slightly as the ship changed course. "Did you know that 75% of all wanted criminals in the U.S. are caught on interstate Greyhound buses?"

"I'm underwhelmed with indifference."

"I managed to get about twenty miles before we were stopped at a military roadblock. I had no ID and no explanation for where I had been or where I was going. It didn't take a rocket scientist to work out who I really was."

Colin sighed ruefully.

"And some of these guys *were* rocket scientists."

"They caught you?"

"Yup. The military tested and probed and poked me for months. They took blood samples, tissue samples, DNA samples. Samples of *everything*."

Colin's mouth set in a tight line.

"I didn't realise, at the time, what some of these samples were for."

"What did they find?"

"Nothing. I'd already released what was inside me. Even so, they kept me in custody for almost a year. Then they hit me with a bombshell. A Colonel Naish informed me I was to be relocated to a place called Kirkfallen Island. It wouldn't be so bad, she said. It wasn't a prison. More like a community. More like a... family."

Colin slapped his hands on his knees to stop them bouncing up and down.

"They liked to play God, these people. They did it with D.B. and they did it with me. Then Naish told me what some of those samples they took were really for. Artificial insemination."

The engines changed rhythm as the trawler picked up speed.

"I was sixteen years old. And she informed me I now had a daughter."

44

The walkie talkie on Edward Stapleton's belt crackled and a gruff voice cut through the static.

"Edward, it's Wentworth. Are the kids gone yet? I've been hiding in this damned bunker for an hour, trying to stay out of their way. Over."

"That's my dad!" Millar gasped.

"Eh... They're sitting right next to me, Geoff. They can hear everything you're saying."

"Damn!"

"We're a little out of practice as a smooth-running military unit," Edward apologised. "It's been almost fifteen years since we did anything but farm and fish."

"My dad's gonna kill me." Millar moaned.

"No, I'm not." The voice came over the air again. "I'm more likely going to beg your forgiveness, but that will have to wait."

"What's our status, Wentworth?"

"We just got a radio message from a trawler called the *Lillian Gish II*. They have Colin Walton and his daughter on board, asking permission to land."

"*Colin Walton*?"

"The very same. I gave them the all-clear like Colonel Naish ordered."

There was more crackling and Wentworth Watt came through again, loud and clear. "But that's not his daughter with him. It can't be."

"We know that. But Naish obviously doesn't." The confusion was plain on Edward's face. "I don't know what the hell Colin's playing at."

"It's not him that worries me," Wentworth said. "It's the fact that Naish is on her way – and she won't be coming alone."

"Now that the Orbisons are dead, the army was going to arrive anyhow."

The children glanced at each other but kept quiet.

"But they weren't due for another week. This could really put a spanner in the works."

"Alert the appropriate people, Wentworth. Then wait for my instructions."

"Will do. Over and out."

Edward clipped the walkie talkie back on his belt and nodded towards the entrance of MacLellan base. A few minutes later, Wentworth Watt emerged from the doorway. Millar stood up, clutching and unclutching his hands. His father strode over and pulled the teenager into a bear hug.

"Are you OK?"

"No time, Wentworth." Edward nodded in the direction of the village. "I'll finish up here."

Wentworth gave a throaty growl. He hugged Millar one more time, then stepped away.

"Just remember I love you."

He kissed his son on the forehead, then headed for the fence. He produced a key from his pocket, opened the padlock on the chain-link gate and ran off in the direction of the village.

"You were talking about a guy called Colin Walton." Gene looked up at his father. "Is he related to the Waltons who used to live here?"

"Who are the *Waltons*?" Millar butted in, dismayed that Gene might actually know something he didn't.

"We've always claimed nobody ever left this island, Millar. A man called Colin Walton did."

Edward cast his eyes across the Atlantic swells.

"What I don't understand is why he's on his way back."

He clapped his hands together and pulled Gene to his feet.

"No matter. U.S. troops will be here soon and, when they arrive, you are going to play a pivotal role in our survival."

"I'll do my best, Sir."

"Don't ever *Sir* me again. You're not a soldier."
Edward patted his son on the cheek. "Here's the last
part of the Fallen story. The *good* part."

His eyes glinted with sinister charm.

"The part the military would kill us if they knew."

45

1996

Naish stood so close to the scudding surf that it occasionally rolled over her boots. She wore a U.S. army uniform with insignia on the shoulders indicating the rank of Colonel. Behind her, where the beach surrendered to firmer, higher ground, a group of squaddies were building cottages. Further inland, a tractor combed rich, dark furrows into soil that had never felt the tear of a plough. Gulls circled angrily in white fluttering crowds as their habitat was torn apart.

She spotted Edward Stapleton and Colin Walton walking along the shoreline and waved them over.

Colin wore the same sullen expression that permanently darkened his face. Naish couldn't blame him. The poor lad was only sixteen and she had sentenced him to imprisonment on this island, for God knows how many years. If that wasn't bad enough, she had lumbered him with a family. A

277

daughter he didn't want and a partner the army had chosen for him.

Edward Stapleton saluted when he reached her, but it was slack and cursory - a gesture that went well beyond insolence. Naish let it pass.

"Well. Here we stand at the limit of our universe," Edward said disdainfully, drawing a line in the sand with his boot. The water rushed up and immediately eradicated the mark.

"This may be the last time you'll see me, so I need to talk to you alone." Naish adopted her sternest tone.

"What I'm about to impart stays between us."

"Yeah. And who are we gonna tell?" Colin shot her a look of undisguised hatred.

"Please listen. I'm about to put my life on the line."

Colin and Edward looked at each other. Naish pointed up at the wheeling cacophony overhead.

"What with the birds and the surf and the cloud cover, nobody can monitor us – not even if the army had a spy satellite pointed right at this spot."

"Get to the point." Colin, having gone through the stages of anger, unfulfilled hope and then despair in the last few months, had now perfected a rebellious insolence that befitted his teenage years.

"Let's go over why you are here one more time, so it's straight in your minds." Naish kept her expression neutral. "What's your cover story?"

"The Kirkfallen community is a social and scientific experiment." Edward recited what he had learned by rote. "An attempt to see if an isolated island environment can sustain a community. We will be testing scientifically modified fertilisers, crops, pesticides and polymer fishing nets to see which combinations produce the best food yields. In order to do that, we have to live in near isolation."

"And why is that?" Naish prompted.

"We can't have boats from the mainland anchor here in case they introduce rats or insects or even stray pollen into our environment, negating the research we are doing."

"Very good, Mr Stapleton."

"Except it's all bull." Edward didn't bother to say Ma'am. His displeasure was more contained than Colin's and all the more biting for it.

"Yes. The wheels behind the wheels." Naish spun a circle in the air. "Only Army Intelligence knows the secondary role of Kirkfallen. For years, the Stopwatch Unit has acted as a covert force sent to other countries to… eh… fix problems."

"You mean an assassination squad." Colin picked up a shell and threw it with all his might into the waves. It vanished without a ripple.

"If you want to put it that way." Naish put her hands behind her and cracked her back, a gesture that reminded her of Doctor Kelty. "But now the powers that be feel the Stopwatch Unit would be more useful if they became part of an experiment on Kirkfallen."

"Forced retirement," Edward added acerbically.

"Every two years, eight members of the Stopwatch Unit, four men and four women, will be moved here. They'll have been partnered up and the women will all have had a child."

"Whether they wanted to or not."

"It's called following orders, Edward," Naish said pointedly. "It has been impressed upon the unit that this deep cover operation is of the highest national importance."

"The consequences of disobeying these orders were also impressed upon us," the man sneered.

"The idea is that you will train your children from birth to hunt, farm and be totally self-sufficient. A new generation, trained in survival techniques."

"A new assassination squad in the making." Colin turned his back on Naish and watched the soldiers hauling planks of wood that was to be his home. His *prison.*

"It gave me the leeway to issue the islanders with weapons so they could teach the kids to shoot." Naish retorted. "You may need that advantage someday."

"Do we have to go over this again?" Colin was unrepentant. "Haven't you tortured us enough?"

"Be quiet for one minute, will you?"

The teenager lapsed into churlish silence.

"There's only a very small, very high up band of people who know the *real* purpose of Kirkfallen." Naish continued. "The Stopwatch Project Mark III. Each pregnant woman has been injected with an ant/human pheromone concentrate, designed by doctor Markus Kelty, which is then absorbed by the foetus."

"A fact none of them are too happy about, I imagine." Edward thought about his own child, back in one of the huts, and fought to suppress his anger. "I'm certainly less than pleased."

"They were willing to kill and to die for their country," Naish cautioned. "Now they don't have to do either. Think of it as a blessing in disguise."

"It's a pretty damned convincing disguise," Edward snapped. "And I never killed anyone. I was a radio opera-tor."

"Each child is completely normal – the pheromone over-load doesn't even show up in the bloodstream." Naish refused to be drawn into an argument. "But when the chil-dren reach a certain state of puberty – just as they turn sixteen – they'll release a storm of alarm pheromones which will drive anyone around into a homicidal frenzy."

"The Stopwatch Unit won't be affected, of course." Ed-ward gave a bitter laugh. "We all have sociopathic personalities, which make us immune. Handy, since the pheromone emissions are amplified by both humans and ants, causing a plague of total rage."

"That's right," Naish continued. "If everything is hunky-dory out in the world, any child about to release phero-mones will be quarantined in the old MacLellan base until its emissions are over. The land around Jackson Head will be regularly saturated with insecticide, so there's no chance of the infection spreading. That child will then be deemed safe to return to the USA. Its parents will be released from all obligations to the army and given a *very* handsome pension."

"And if everything isn't *hunky-dory*?"

"If world events reach a point where the existence of the United States is threatened, the children on this island closest to sixteen years old will be taken and infiltrated into the danger zone. Soon after that, they will release their alarm pheromones and Europe, Africa, China, India and Asia will turn into a bloodbath. All threats to the USA will be wiped out."

"God, that's cold." Edward bowed his head.

"That's why their ages are two years apart," Naish pressed on. "Those twenty-four Kirkfallen children can combat any future threat for years to come, whenever that menace may arise."

"And millions of people will die." Colin spread his hands in a last futile attempt at reason. "Nothing justifies that. *Nothing.*"

"What if the whole race is on the brink of the abyss?" Naish felt the need to argue despite her own distaste at the situation. "What if this is the *only* way to stop mass pollution or a nuclear strike by terrorists?"

"Don't even try to defend this or give me some greater good crap."

"I won't." Naish warily scanned the sky. "In fact, I've been lying to the people behind the scheme."

She made the statement so plainly that it didn't register on her companions for a few seconds. Colin and Edward stared vacantly at her.

"Could you repeat that?"

"Kelty said nobody else would be able to duplicate his research and, as usual, he was right. Annoying man that he was."

She gave a regretful sigh.

"He left me a batch of serum – enough for two dozen injections. Then he told me what it *actually* does."

"What am I missing here?" Colin looked suspiciously at his companions.

Edward shuffled uncomfortably, stirring the sand with his boot.

"Kelty told you what he was up to." Naish cottoned on immediately. "Didn't he?"

"He hinted. I bet I can guess."

"Then tell Colin." The woman made a snap decision. "I figure he deserves to know."

"I think Kelty managed to synthesise a different type of pheromone," Edward said. "Not the Attack Pheromone but something called a Mandibular Pheromone. One that makes people *co-operate* their actions rather than kill each other."

"Correct. And *that's* what the children coming to this island carry inside." Naish drew closer to the men. "If one of these kids is seeded into a population, it won't destroy anyone. It will *influence* them. They'll be pacified. United. Loving, hopefully."

"Oh, well that's fine!" Colin exploded. "Playing at being Gods wasn't enough for you people. Now you've moved on to *creating* them."

"I haven't got a lot of options here!" Naish wiped salt spray from her eyes. "I'm just a figurehead. But I'm older and wiser than I was when I began working for Kelty. I won't be responsible for mass carnage, no matter what the reason."

"But we don't *really* know what an outburst of Mandibular Pheromones will do either," Edward argued. "What if it turns everyone into some kind of zombie?"

"Better than killing each other." Naish spread her hands in exasperation. "Pheromones exist, Edward. Someday, some other country will figure out how to use that as a weapon. And they *will* use the attack pheromone. There won't be people like Kelty and me around to double-cross them."

"Who else knows about this?"

"Only the two of you." Naish took Edward by the arm. "Right before he died, Kelty asked you be put in charge of Kirkfallen. The Stopwatch Unit are trained to obey orders without question, but they won't take kindly to being posted on this barren dump. Kelty thought you'd be a stabilising influence."

A tinge of jealously crept into her voice.

"I think he admired you."

"If I'd known being stable was going to land me here, I'd have gone on a rampage long ago."

"You would have ended up on Kirkfallen anyway, just not in command." Naish gripped Edward's arm tighter. "You have to make sure these kids are brought up in the most decent and open-minded way you can, because they may have the power to make the world *work* together. They have to be educated, able, self-sufficient and environmentally conscious. Traits the world can *use*."

"So you entrust their upbringing to a bunch of socio-paths!" Colin raised his hands to Edward in a conciliatory gesture. "No offence, buddy."

"None taken. I'm a bit perturbed by the idea myself. What if the Stopwatch Unit kill the children or try to use them as bargaining chips?"

"Out here you're hardly holding a strong hand," Naish replied. "Anyone who pulls a stunt like that will cease to exist for real."

"I agree, that's a fairly powerful incentive to behave."

"Listen, Edward." Naish lowered her voice, even though the three of them were utterly alone. "I believe there are silent people, high up in the military, who *want* a war. They will use these children, whether there is a real threat to or security or not."

She folded her arms defiantly.

"Only they won't get the result they expected. The kids will produce the Mandibular Pheromone rather than the Alarm one."

"This makes us traitors to our country."

"Of course it does. But I now consider myself a human being first and a soldier second."

"What if we reported you?"

"I'd be dead within the hour. And heaven knows what will happen to you and the children."

"And we'll just take your word for this?" Colin arched an eyebrow. "How do we know it isn't a ruse to stop us causing trouble?"

"She's telling the truth." Edward looked shell-shocked. "Kelty *said* he had a plan to make everything right."

"If I could go back and change the last twenty years, I would."

Naish ran fingers through her short, bobbed hair. It was a gesture that made her look uncertain and vulnerable.

"The inhabitants of Kirkfallen are stuck here and I can't do anything about that. But you're also the Stopwatch Unit, which means nobody will check on you. You're an elite military squad and Top Brass can't conceive of you not doing your duty. You'll be visited twice a year by a submarine from Radcliff Naval Base. Medical check. Provision drop. That's it. Anything more obvious and other nations might start getting curious about this little operation."

She turned to Colin.

"As for you? Wrong place, wrong time."

"Story of my life, isn't it?"

"Since you were a carrier yourself, we knew for sure your offspring would have the genetic makeup to absorb pheromone injections." A surge of surf enveloped the woman's legs but she made no attempt to back away. "So, I recommended you be part of this, rather than having you die in a convenient… accident."

"Thanks for nothing." Colin stared at the ground, his emotions in turmoil.

"I don't want to sound melodramatic, but the fate of the world rests on your shoulders." Naish turned to Edward. "You up for the challenge?"

Edward thought for a moment. Then he saluted. A proper salute, this time.

"The Stopwatch Unit is at your disposal."

Apathy swung her legs off the bed.

"But you're not *on* the island," she said to Colin. The boat gave a lurch and she put a hand on the wall to brace herself. "What happened? Where's your daughter?"

"I imagine Kirkfallen has excellent medical resources now," her uncle replied quietly. "And some of the Stopwatch Unit are trained medics. But when the colony started, there were only a handful of us and Radcliff Naval Base was seven hours away."

His foot began to drum on the floor again, his fleshy chin quivering.

"I didn't want to have a child. But she was such a tiny, pretty thing." Tears trickled down his cheeks. "I thought she had a cold. Nothing to worry about. Then she just... died."

"Oh." Apathy came and sat on the bunk beside him, uncertain of what to say. "Uncle Colin..."

"It's all in the past." But the tears still came. Apathy took his hand and squeezed it.

"Did they let you go after that?"

"Not with what *I* knew." Colin wiped his eyes with the back of his hand and sniffed loudly.

"I escaped."

46

The funeral was a brief, almost insignificant affair. All the island's inhabitants were there - the Stapletons, the Ainsworths, the Watts and the Waltons. Three of the families carried their own children – a painful reminder to the Waltons of what they had lost. But there was nobody else on the island to look after the babies.

Afterwards, they made their way back to Edward Stapleton's cottage and silently drank whisky, emptying one of the few precious bottles on the island. The infants were asleep in the bedroom, oblivious to the tragedy.

Libby Walton was hunched listlessly in one corner, ignoring everyone else. It occurred to Edward that he'd never asked her real name. Though she was older than Colin, the poor kid couldn't be more than nineteen. She must have been one of the final recruits to the Stopwatch Unit and now she was stuck here with nothing but regrets and a partner

289

barely knew. A girl with no happiness in her future and probably not much in her past.

"We need to inform Radcliff Naval Base about this," Wentworth Watt poured himself another shot of whisky.

"What for?" Libby Walton snarled. "So they can dig my kid up and do an autopsy on it?"

Colin stared at the floor, unable to give her any comfort.

"I need to talk to you all outside." Edward picked up the bottle. "Let's give these two a few moments alone."

Neither Colin nor Libby acknowledged him, lost and lonely in their misery. The rest followed Edward out of the cottage.

"We need to decide, right now, what this community is supposed to be." Their Commander shut the door behind him. "We've been royally shafted and I don't think anyone here would disagree."

"I have to say, this isn't what I signed up for." Geoff Ainsworth scratched his thick neck. "Ain't gonna do much defending my country sitting on this rock."

"It's a bum deal." Alison Ainsworth agreed. She was a short dumpy woman whose green eyes shimmered with dissatisfaction. "I'm never gonna get my figure back."

"We're the Stopwatch Unit." Sonja Watt took a sip of her whisky. "We carry out the jobs nobody else will do."

"No. We're the Stopwatch Unit because we don't have any qualms about killing." Edward lowered his voice to be certain that Colin and Libby couldn't hear. "I don't think our superiors even see us as real people."

"What are you getting at?"

"On this island, I'm your Commanding Officer. I'm also just like you." Edward placed his hands on his hips. "From now on, if you're going to obey orders without question, you'll obey mine."

"If you think I'm gonna kowtow to you every day for the next fifteen years, you're gonna be sorely disappointed." Geoff Ainsworth snapped. "Far as I'm concerned? We're as good as prisoners."

"That's the spirit." To the other's surprise, Edward gave a broad smile. "The beauty of sociopathic personalities, eh? They don't respond well to unfair treatment."

"Not much we can do about it." Sonja voiced what they were all thinking.

"Maybe not." Edward mentally crossed his fingers. This was the moment. If he could bind them all in complicity, right now, there was a chance he could make this whole scenario work to his advantage. Part of him felt bad about using a dead baby to further his aims, but he shrugged it off. He guessed he had that kind of character.

"We're not gonna tell our superiors about the kid dying. She was a Goddamned American citizen and they were going to use her as a weapon from the day she was born."

He folded his arms defiantly.

"I'm done blindly obeying. From now on, *this* is our country, to defend if need be." He stamped his foot on the springy turf. "So the first thing we're going to do is help the Waltons escape."

The others stared at him in disbelief.

"What?" Edward spread his hands. "They're no use to anyone. They're certainly not part of the experiment anymore. They're no more than kids themselves."

There was silence from the rest of the group.

"Or you could just sit back and take what's been done to you like good little soldiers."

"They couldn't make it, anyhow." Geoff Ainsworth took the whisky bottle from his 'wife' and swigged, not bothering with a glass. "The three boats we've got aren't much more than glorified canoes. It's 250 miles to the mainland and none of us are sailors."

"Colin's been boating on Lake Champlain since he was a little boy," Edward countered. "That boy's better trained in survival techniques than *we* are. And he doesn't have a child to slow him up," he added unnecessarily.

"Even if they reached land, the army would hunt them down."

"Not if they thought the Waltons were dead." Edward took the bottle and swallowed heartily. "Come on," he gasped, the alcohol burning in his throat. "We were *trained* in subterfuge."

"What's in it for us?"

"A sense that we're at least partly in charge of our own lives?"

It was the moment of truth and they all knew it.

"Well?" Edward prompted. "Are we going to stand together on this?"

The group bunched together, whispering to each other. Finally, Alison Ainsworth raised her glass.

"If I put my ass on the line for you, I expect to be treated as an equal."

"We all do." Sonja Watt added.

"You got it."

"You still haven't explained how you'll pull this off."

"Right before dawn, we take a bag of planting seed and scatter it over one of the boats. Come daylight, there will be a flock of seagulls obscuring the craft. With the clouds that are always draped over this place, it'll make those vessels invisible. Under that cover, you start stripping the boat and throwing the debris into the water. I've been watching the currents and I'm pretty sure the flotsam will end up on the rocks at Pittenhall Ridge. Leave nothing but the bare hull and motor."

"That's pretty clever," Geoff admitted, seeing immediately where the plan was going.

"Colin and Libby will set off under cover of dark tomorrow night." Edward swigged from the bottle again. "Next day, we report that we've found debris from a missing boat at Pittenhall. That the Waltons must have died trying to get away with their daughter. Agreed?"

"What if there are homing devices hidden on the boats?"

"We're too far out for a signal to reach. In this case, Kirkfallen's isolation gives us the advantage."

They heard the soft cry of a child from inside the cottage.

"Are we agreed? Or do you want to stay faithful to your jailers?"

The others thought for a while. One by one, they nodded their approval. Geoff and Alison, recognising the sound of their own offspring, turned to go inside.

"Before you leave." Edward scratched his cheek. "Could you all give me just one salute? I'd kinda like that."

"Yeah, right." The others trooped back inside.

Edward Stapleton leaned against the wall of his cottage and let out the breath he seemed to have been holding the entire conversation.

He had them. Now they could all know the truth.

The next night, the unhappy couple were ready to go. Libby sat in the boat, which had been stripped to its timbers and loaded with supplies and fuel.

"There's no compass on the island, or you could have it." Edward was almost invisible in the darkness.

"I know how to steer using the stars and the sun."

"Of course you do." Edward held out his hand and Colin shook it. "Good luck."

"Thank you for what you've done, Eddie."

"There's something I have to tell you before you leave." Edward kept hold of Colin's hand. "Something I've never told anyone."

"If you're going to say you love me, I'll be extremely uncomfortable."

Edward smiled.

"When I was stationed here years ago, I saw Markus Kelty leaving in a boat. After the place had been destroyed."

"And?"

"He had a woman with him." Edward finally let go of Colin's hand. "He said he had fallen in love. It was an open secret on the base that he'd been seeing a young researcher named Aiki Conroy. She's listed as having burned up along with everyone else, but he took her with him."

"You never told anyone this? Not even Naish?"

"I thought Kelty deserved a chance at happiness. But Naish says he's dead."

"So?" Colin couldn't muster much sympathy for the doctor. "What about it?"

"Naish said there would be 24 children injected with the Stopwatch serum and put on this island. But I was at MacClellan base long enough to know the serum was produced in batches of 25."

"Maybe Naish dropped one."

"Maybe Kelty kept one." Edward stuck meaty hands into his pockets. "And injected his partner."

"Why would he do that? Unless she was…"

"Pregnant?"

"Shit!" Colin caught on immediately. "That means, someday, her kid will release pheromones!"

"Kelty believed it was inevitable anyhow." Edward glanced back towards the tiny lights of the fledgling Kirkfallen community. "He was a conceited man and I wouldn't put anything past him."

"Then why give Naish any serum at all? If he'd already set the ball rolling."

"Another of his smokescreens, I guess. If the army had what they wanted, they'd concentrate on that and not go snooping into where Kelty had been in the last few months of his life. He was protecting his family."

Edward picked at his lip.

"Besides. If his child released Mandibular Pheromones, it might well find itself controlling everyone. An egoist like Kelty would have surely enjoyed that idea."

"Are you saying he sacrificed himself to hide some theoretical kid?"

"Why not? He was willing to kill for what he thought was the greater good." Edward took his hands from his pocket and folded his arms. "I got the feeling he was willing to die for it as well."

"Well, *that's* just dumb."

"Yeah? Then, pray you never find yourself in the same situation."

"Isn't it more likely that Naish just dropped a vial and Kelty wasn't as smart or as altruistic as you seem to think?"

"Probably." Edward didn't sound convinced. "Still…. if you make it, you might want to try and find this Aiki Conroy and see if she had a child. Just to check."

"*If* I make it?"

"Sorry. *When* you make it."

"I'll do my best." Colin agreed. "I certainly owe you one."

"People like me have to prepare for any eventuality." Edward took a deep breath. "That's why we've begun stockpiling homemade weapons in the old MacClellan base."

He smiled thinly.

"If the army ever find out the true results of the project and try to get rid of us, they'll be in for the fight of their lives."

Colin and Libby reached the west coast of Scotland two days later, soaked, frozen and utterly exhausted. With nobody but each other for company, they had talked properly for the first time. The fact that they might die on the journey or miss land altogether had helped with the dubious bonding process.

They lay on a deserted beach and watched the tide pull the boat back out to sea. Colin had broken a hole in the bottom so that it would sink and leave no trace. Eventually, Libby sat up.

"Well, I did join the army to travel," she said, a little too cheerfully.

"Where are you going to go?"

"I don't know." Libby hugged her knees, a gesture Colin was now familiar with. "Thank you for getting me to safety, though."

They sat for a while, watching their boat drifting in circles and slowly sinking. Libby was shivering and Colin put his arm around her.

"So, I joined the army. I had a kid without even the fun of sex. It died. Now I'm on a beach in a foreign country without any money or identity. And I'm only nineteen."

She hugged her legs tighter.

"This life is turning out to be some ride."

She turned to Colin.

"What about you?"

"Let's see." Colin scratched his stomach. "I lived under a false name for years. I've faked my death twice. I'm now part of the biggest double-cross in world history. I reckon I'm cut out to be a con man."

"You win," Libby giggled. "Where you gonna start?"

"I have a PO box number in New York memorised. If I write, an old friend called Dan Salty will come for me. He wasn't bad at conning people himself. I can probably persuade him to go into partnership."

"Sounds like a plan."

"You could always come along," Colin ventured.

Libby tried a grateful smile, but her mouth refused to turn up at the corners.

"I could. But I'm a loner, Col. I don't mix well with people." She rested her head briefly on her partner's shoulder. "I got a glimpse, though. A glimpse of what others cherish. A home. A family. A great guy. It's a shame that life isn't for me."

She tilted her companion's face towards her and kissed him on the lips.

It was the first kiss Colin had ever had.

"Good luck, mister." She thumped her chest. "What little is in here? You actually managed to touch it."

Then she was on her feet and running.

47

"What happened to Libby?" Apathy reached up and wiped a tear from her uncle's cheek.

"God knows. She was trained to blend in and I never tried to find her." Colin's voice was laden with regret. "I'm a part of a life I'm sure she wants to forget."

"Did you ever track down Kelty's partner and her kid?"

"Yup," Colin replied dismissively. "When Kelty kicked the bucket, she remarried a man called Andrew Flintheart," "I kept an eye on them but the whole family died in an accident."

Apathy gave her uncle a few moments of silence. But she had too many questions to hold back.

"So, how did you find her? How did you find *me,* for that matter?"

"Dan had a theory that your mother fled to Scotland. It was where our ancestors came from. Apparently, she'd always wanted to go there."

"Yeah. Shame we ended up in a shitty tower block."

"I searched for years." Colin continued. "All I had to go on was that someone filled with pheromones influenced others in a small but significant way."

Apathy remembered all the fights that revolved around her at school. The fact that her mother always seemed to have a pent up dissatisfaction with life. Now she understood why. She had caused it. The realisation squatted like an ugly toad in her gut.

"I also knew that those pheromone emissions showed up on photographic paper," Colin continued.

"And *that's* how you found me?"

"Hell, no!" Her uncle looked shocked. "I wasn't going to get arrested taking Polaroids of kids left, right and centre. No. One day, Dan was talking about you. He was drunk."

"He talked about me?"

"He talks about you all the time."

Apathy sat back on the bunk, surprised and pleased.

"Anyhow, he told me a story I'd never heard before. How he and Emily had joked about calling you Apathy Amazon or Norman D. Landing."

"You didn't?"

"Yup. I pretended to be a truancy officer and called every school in the country, asking if they had a pupil by either of those names. And there you were."

"How long ago *was* this, Colin?"

The short man looked pained.

"Over a year."

"And my dad never tried to contact me?" Apathy's lip trembled.

"He's a wanted murderer. Can't really afford to have his picture in the local paper, winning the three-legged race with you at sports day."

Colin shrugged.

"He looked out for you, though. Remember the bullies that picked on you at your last school? How they suddenly stopped for no reason?"

"What about it?"

"They stopped because D.B. paid a little visit to their parents." Colin raised his eyebrows. "I seriously doubt they'll ever bother anyone again."

He fished in his pocket for cigarettes, signalling this particular conversation was over.

"I've told Colonel Naish that you're my daughter." He stood up and paced the room. "She'll find out pretty quickly that's not true, but it will be too late. By that time, we'll be on the island. Your father wanted you someplace safe."

"Why do you think Kirkfallen is safe? I wasn't injected with Mandibular Serum. I got the original nasty one. And there are people there."

Apathy's eyes widened.

"If I release those pheromones, won't it affect the other children and drive them crazy? Won't it affect you? You're not a psychopath."

"Naish is bound to quarantine you while she checks out my story. The island was designed for it."

"You better hope so."

"And I used to live on Kirkfallen," Colin reminded her. "I know how to keep out of harm's way. As for the kids? Sociopathy is fifty per cent hereditary."

He lit his cigarette and tossed the match out of the open porthole.

"You seem OK, probably because your mother was normal, but the kids on Kirkfallen *all* have sociopathic parents – which means they'll be sociopathic themselves. Even if you aren't quarantined, you won't affect them at all."

"Christ. They won't exactly be a lot of fun to hang out with, will they?"

"Not necessarily. Me and Edward Stapleton always got on fine."

"Does that mean I can tell him the truth?"

"Oh, he knows you're not my daughter but he'll keep that to himself. Naish is bound to come with an army escort and he'll have to pretend that everything is going according to their plan. Otherwise, the whole population might all be… disappeared."

"Thanks for putting my mind at ease."

Apathy closed her eyes and let out a heartfelt sigh. Colin sank into the seat opposite.

"I want you to promise me something." The teenager opened one eye. "Promise me you wouldn't con your own niece."

Colin returned Apathy's stare.

"I promise."

He pulled his coat on and let himself out of the cabin.

Then he staggered to the rail and threw up over the side.

48

Dan sat on a wooden crate in the shed and cursed. He had checked the door, but it was locked from the outside. He could see a big key blocking the keyhole – only a few inches away but impossible to reach. He had shouted and pounded on the door but nobody came to his assistance.

Dan had no idea how long he'd been trapped, though it seemed like hours. He didn't know where his half-brother had gone, but he must have taken Apathy, or else she would have set him loose.

He was going to kill Colin for this.

It was bitterly cold in the shed. Dan considered lighting a fire but he didn't want to risk burning the place down, especially since he was inside. He wondered if he could set the door alight and break the weakened timbers before the whole shed went up. It was worth a try.

He searched around the empty shed, looking for something to burn and found a newspaper stuffed between a pair of cinder blocks and the wall. Pulling it loose, he fished a lighter from his pocket, still unsure if this was a suicidal course of action.

The paper was dated the day before and folded open at page seven. Dan glanced at the lead article.

Freak 'Accident' May Be Murder

A police investigation into the death of an Aberdeen family has ruled out an accident as the cause of death and are now pursuing a murder inquiry.

Andrew Flintheart, 36, his wife Aiki 30, and their daughter Elspeth, 15, of 32 Westmoreland Drive were found dead on Wednesday 18th December.

Police originally believed the family's death was due to an accidental gas leak. However, subsequent evidence found at the scene now points to deliberate interference with the external gas supply.

"As a result of this new evidence, we are now treating the deaths as murder." said a spokesman for Aberdeenshire police.

*Neighbours of the Flintheart family reported that they were visited by a short, black-haired man the day before the family's death. He was last seen driving off in a white van with **G.B. Paranormal** on the side. Police are appealing for more witnesses.*

Dan let the paper fall from his fingers.

"Oh God, Colin," he croaked. "What did you do?"

He heard the throb of a car engine approaching and dropped the newspaper. The noise grew louder, finally pulling up outside. A door slammed. Footsteps approached and the key turned in the lock. Dan got up off the crate, trembling both with cold and rage.

"What the fuck are you playing at?" he shouted. "What have you done with my daughter?"

The door swung open and Dan recoiled.

"Emily?"

Emily Walton slapped him hard across the face. Dan blinked. This was the second time today a member of his family had hit him.

Emily cuffed her husband again.

"You irresponsible, horrendous bastard!" she yelled, raising her hand a third time. Dan caught her wrist and held on tight, staring in astonishment at his wife. Her eyes were bloodshot from crying, her face twisted in fury.

But she still looked beautiful.

"How did you find me?" he gasped.

"Colin called me," Emily snarled. "You kidnapped your own daughter! You didn't tell me my brother was alive! You didn't even try to *find* me!"

"We've been looking for years! We only came across you a few months ago."

"Liar!"

"It's the truth." Dan let go of her hand and waited for the next blow. "You've been in hiding and I had no idea where. Someone like me can hardly take out an ad in the *Times*."

Emily began to sob. Dan started to put his arms around her and then stopped, unsure of just how to act. Damn! He didn't know how to comfort either his wife or his own daughter. It struck him again just how incomplete he was as a man.

"Colin's taken Apathy," he said, trying to divert Emily's attention. "I don't know why and I don't know where he's gone."

Emily pulled a wad of paper from her pocket.

"Colin also left me a *long* letter. I found it in my flat. Do you know how disturbing *that* is?"

She thrust the papers into his hand.

"He's taken Apathy to a place called Kirkfallen Island."

"Why?" Panic gripped Dan. "What for?"

"Read it!"

Dan sat back down on the crate and began to scan the sheets. Once or twice he risked a glance at Emily. She stood in front of him, breathing heavily.

God, she looked good.

Then he came to a line in the letter that froze the breath in his throat. He read the rest without a pause. When he had finished, he held the paper out.

"Shit."

Emily took the letter and fished a lighter from her pocket. She flicked the flame to life, set the paper alight and dropped it. They both watched the pages curl and turn black until nothing was left on the floor of the shed but a pile of black ash. It reminded Dan of his relationship with his wife. With everyone, in fact.

"According to Colin, there will be a military helicopter here soon. Get ready to be on it."

"I know. I can read."

"You're going to rescue my daughter, Dan Salty."

"I will. I promise."

"Your word no longer means anything to me." Emily turned her back so he couldn't see her tears. Dan helplessly watched her shoulders rise and fall.

"Have you got makeup in your car?" he asked tentatively.

"What?" Emily whirled round. "You vanish for fifteen years! You abduct my daughter. You put her in the hands of a maniac. Now you're telling me I'm not *pretty* enough!"

"You sure look fine to me," Dan replied softly. He glanced down at the discarded newspaper. "But I have an inkling of what Colin might be up to. And for it to work, you're going to have to look stunning."

"Yeah?" Emily stepped forward and tugged at his unkempt, greying locks. "Well, you need a haircut."

"Then cut it. And I've got dye in the cottage."

"You've got what?"

"I'm a con man and a wanted killer. I've lost count of the number of colours my hair's gone through."

Emily looked at the pile of ash on the floor.

"All these years I thought you killed Louise. And your own mom too." She sat on the packing case beside him. "Not that I'll ever forgive you for the sins you *have* committed. But I should have known you wouldn't do something like that."

"Emily, you don't have to come with me."

"Yes, I do. You know I do."

"Then let's get ready." Dan stood up and held out his hand. Emily waited a few seconds then let her husband pull her to her feet.

"You look pretty good yourself," she said, looking him in the eye.

"Then make me better. Dan Walton has made too many mistakes in his life to keep living."

He set his jaw in a determined line.

"But a lot of people are gonna be sorry they crossed swords with D.B. Salty."

Operation Louise

The first pheromone ever identified (in 1956) was a powerful sex attractant for silkworm moths named Bombykol. A team of German researchers worked 20 years to isolate it, removing glands at the tip of the abdomen of 500,000 female moths

It has been calculated that if a single female moth were to release all the Bombykol in her sac all at once, she could theoretically attract a trillion males in that instant

49

By the time Colin and Apathy paddled to the shore, the *Lillian Gish II* had turned and was heading back to Scotland. Their dinghy was met by a line of dour-faced men and women who silently pulled it out of the surf. Edward Stapleton reached out and helped Colin and Apathy from the tiny craft, skipping back from the jerky, seaweed laden froth. Behind him stood three teenagers – two boys and a girl.

Apathy smiled shyly at them and they stared back with unconcealed fascination. The teenager realised they'd never seen a girl who wasn't raised on the island.

"Good to see you again, Colin," Edward said curtly, sounding anything but pleased. "We need to talk."

He turned to Gene, Poppy and Millar.

"You going to stand there like a bunch of hillbillies or would you like to introduce yourselves to our guest?"

313

"Hi. I'm Poppy." The girl stepped forward, elbowing Gene and Millar out of her way. "What's your name?"

"Apathy Walton."

"Cool," Millar chimed in. "You wanna see our gang hut?"

"Eh… OK." Apathy smiled at him. She rarely met anyone who didn't laugh at her name the first time they heard it. "I'd like that."

"I'm Gene Stapleton." A handsome boy with a fringe of straight black hair stepped forward, formal and well mannered, hand outstretched. "Welcome to Fallen."

Apathy smiled again and shook the boy's hand. For some reason, she was reluctant to let go.

"I'm delighted to meet you."

"The gang hut will have to wait." Edward cut short the introductions. "Apathy, you'll be billeted at a place called MacLellan base. A Colonel Naish will be here soon and she'll want to give you some tests. Poppy, you escort her. Take a tractor."

"A tractor?" Poppy patted her bobbed hair daintily. "That's not very ladylike."

"I'm asking you to drive it, not push it. Wentworth? You go with them in the second tractor. Put a trailer on the back and take eight men. I want the base… eh… spick and span for our visitors."

"You got it."

Poppy beckoned to Apathy and she followed the girl, turning to wave to Colin as she left.

"What's the status with the land buggies?" Edward turned to Geoff Ainsworth, lurking behind his shoulder.

"Two hidden. One spare."

"Get on up to MacLellan base with Wentworth and load the weapons onto the spare. Bring them back and hide them in the crofts."

"You really are expecting trouble."

"I've been expecting trouble for over a decade."

Edward steered his old friend away from the welcoming party.

"What the *hell* are you doing here?" He glanced at Apathy, being led to the tractors by Poppy. "You and I know that girl isn't your daughter. So who is she?"

"She's my niece." Colin watched Poppy and Apathy climb into a nearby tractor. It jolted twice, then chugged forward, catapulting gobs of earth into the air. "I told Naish I wanted two other people flown here as well, and she agreed."

"Why would she do that?"

"It's my brother, Dan Salty, and his wife, Emily. The army has been after Dan for years, though he's kept his mouth shut the whole time. At my insistence, by the way."

"So why bring them here? Why now?"

"Because here they're no threat to the army." Colin watched the rumbling vehicles vanish into a dip. "Dan and Emily have been on the run for most of their lives and it has to stop."

He took in the simple crofts dotting the green hill beyond the shore. Smoke curled from some of the chimneys.

"I'd like them to have a proper home where they're not looking over their shoulder every day."

"The girl is his daughter, am I right?"

"Yes. And she's hot - with the wrong kind of pheromone. Once she reaches the Maclellan base, make sure you have her quarantined right away."

"What the hell have you brought down on us?" Edward snapped. "Christ, you couldn't have picked a worse time to turn up."

"I'd no choice," Colin replied sadly. "See, I had to warn you about…"

Sonja Watt came pounding across the field.

"Sonar's picked up incoming helicopters," she panted. "God, I'm out of shape."

She didn't seem out of shape to Colin. Years of farm labour had toned her body to the point where she resembled an Olympian athlete.

"You have sonar?"

"Well… duh." Sonja sneered. "We used to be the Stopwatch Unit. The old radio mast on top of MacLellan base was easy to repair and we can build an early warning system out of tin foil and bubble gum."

She turned to Edward.

"And it picked up a lot of helicopters."

"How many?"

"Seven."

"Are you sure?"

"No," Sonja snorted. "The operator stopped counting after five and made a guess."

"Seven helicopters are bad?" Colin asked uncertainly.

"Only one type of helicopter flies in formation. The kind that carries troops." Edward pulled the walkie talkie from his belt and waved a finger at Colin. "I'm afraid your little trick has really put the wind up the powers that be."

He held the device to his ear.

"Mr Ainsworth. We have seven troop-carrying birds approaching Fallen. I repeat, seven. Over."

"Then you were right." Even over the air, Geoff Ainsworth sounded suitably alarmed. "Sounds more like an invasion than a visit."

"We knew they were coming, now that the Orbisons are dead. Colin's arrival just speeded them up."

Colin shifted his feet uncomfortably. Who were the Orbisons? He silently cursed the army for getting here so fast. He had expected at least a day on Kirkfallen to get the lie of the land.

"Listen, Eddie," he said. "I got to tell you something…"

"It'll have to wait." Edward motioned for Sonja to go back to the village. "Gather up all the children and put them in the barn."

"I'm on it, Sir. And welcome home Colin. I think."

Then she was off and running.

"She called me Sir." Edward looked unaccountably pleased. "Been a while since I heard *that*."

"You're putting the children in a barn?" Behind Colin, Sonja Watt had already reached the village.

"Yeah, well, the Hilton was all out of rooms." Edward pointed to a large wooden building on the eastern perimeter of Kirkfallen, visible over the thatched roofs. "The storage barn is the biggest building on the island and it's out of sight from the place we call Reardon Flats. That's the obvious place for helicopters that size to land."

The walkie talkie crackled to life again.

"We're rounding up the kids now." It was an islander named Doug McCombie. "Have them in the shed in a few minutes. How close are the choppers?"

"About the same." Edward put a hand on his hips and his whole bearing changed. "Mr Ainsworth? You still listening?"

The walkie talkie fizzled into life again.

"Here, Sir."

"Go to Code Red. Hopefully, our ruse will work. If not, I'll give the order to begin Operation Louise."

"Understood. Over and out."

Edward put the device away.

"Louise was my daughter's name," Colin was taken aback. "I called her after my mother."

"I know. It's sort of a reminder."

"Of what?"

"We watched those kids grow up, Col. They're our only kin and they're better people than us."

Edward swept a hand round, indicating his village.

"Now think about this. What if they take one, put it into a foreign country and don't get the result they expected?"

"They'll be pretty furious."

"Damned right. And the rest of them will be considered useless. Worse, they'll be a liability."

"And I stuck Apathy right in the middle of it," Colin said listlessly.

"The odds are well and truly stacked against us, but we're the Stopwatch Unit and not to be underestimated."

Edward tapped the weapon at his side.

"Operation Louise means we fight to keep them alive."

Apathy let the breeze blow through her hair. The seagrass waved and the air had a fresh, biting tang. The tractor throbbed beneath her and seagulls screamed and whirled around the vehicle until she felt she was in the centre of some great natural engine.

"This place is wonderful!"

"Of course it is." Poppy was hunched over the wheel. She glanced bashfully at her companion. "You're very pretty."

"Me?" Apathy ran a hand through her dishevelled hair. "Thank you."

"So? What's it like out in the world?

"It's frightening." The answer came out before the teenager had time to think.

"Really?"

"There's lots of good stuff too." Apathy considered what she'd just said, before deciding her companion deserved the truth. "But mostly, it's frightening."

"I'm not worried." Poppy threaded thick fingers through her own short locks in an unconscious imitation of her companion's gesture. "I'm going to get to the real world soon. Then on to Hollywood."

"I've always wanted to visit there myself."

"No. I'm going to be famous." There was no trace of irony in Poppy's voice. "I'm a very fine actress and I'll do all my own stunts."

"Good for you."

"I know I'm not thin." Poppy thought about the films she had seen. "But neither was Mae West and she was a big star."

"Mae, who?"

"I guess you're not a movie buff like me."

"I don't go to the pictures all that often."

"You've been in a cinema!"

"Eh… A few times."

"Well, I'm going to Hollywood. The boys just don't understand." Poppy changed gear and the tractor lurched forwards. "But now I have a girl to talk to. A girlfriend!"

She gave a huge grin.

"You can show me how to do makeup and stuff. Make me look pretty as well."

"I will if you teach me how to drive a tractor."

"You got it. Should I grow my hair?"

Apathy regarded Poppy's manly bob.

"No… em… short hair is in right now."

"Great. See. I knew you'd help me!"

She pounded the steering wheel with a beefy hand.

"Now I have a new friend and a makeup artist! When this is all over, I'm going to be in the movies."

"When what's all over?"

"I can't say too much." Poppy gave Apathy a sly wink. "But soon, it won't matter what I look like. Everyone will love me anyhow. They might even build a monument right here to show where I lived. It'll say **Poppy Ainsworth: Star**. Nothing too fancy."

She spun the wheel to avoid a large rock.

"But, yeah. A monument with my name on it."

50

The helicopters settled, like giant bluebottles, onto Reardon Flats, north of the village - disgorging a mass of camouflaged troops. Now, the copters were guarded by a ring of soldiers carrying assault rifles. The rest of the force had bivouacked outside the village, though a detachment had alighted early and was stationed at Jackson Head near the fence.

Colonel Naish had made the information hut her HQ. She looked at her watch nervously.

"Commander Stapleton will be here in a few minutes," Poppy's mother said.

Alison Ainsworth had been assigned as Naish's escort and now stood to attention beside the window - ramrod straight - every inch a soldier.

"He's worried about the impact of so many strangers on the children, so he's taking... precautions."

"Yes. I didn't actually see any kids." A short, balding man in a Brigadier's uniform was browsing through the books on the shelves.

"That's one of the precautions, Sir."

"I'm rather keen to meet this Commander Stapleton." The Colonel shut a volume of Shakespeare's Sonnets and a puff of dust wafted into his face. Naish looked at her watch again, perspiration shining on her forehead.

A tense group stood outside the information hut.

"You ready?" Edward gave Colin a nudge. Stapleton was wearing full battle dress. Beside him was Sonja Watt, also in uniform. Her boots were polished and her hair was tied back in a ponytail.

"I think so."

Edward leaned forward so his lips were inches from Colin's ear.

"I'm about to lie through my teeth. And whatever I say, you go along with it. Do not contradict me under any circumstances."

"No problem. You're the one with the gun."

"Good man." Edward wiped sweating palms down the back of his trousers and adjusted his tunic. He hadn't worn this outfit for fourteen years and it didn't seem to sit right on his body anymore.

"Gene!" He called out. "We're ready."

Gene Stapleton appeared from around the side of the hut. He looked terrified.

"It's fine, boy. It'll be OK." Edward licked his fingers and parted his son's hair. "Just tell them the truth. The people in there are mean and ruthless and they'll know if you're lying. Remember that."

"I will, dad. But I don't understand why they want to talk to me."

"You don't have to. It's called following orders. Welcome to army life."

Edward straightened his shoulders.

"Let's do this."

They entered the information hut with their Commander in the lead. The soldier in Edward took in his surroundings immediately. Alison Ainsworth at the window. A man with the rank of Brigadier by the bookshelf. Three armed soldiers against the far wall. Another by the door. Colonel Naish in the centre of the room.

The Brigadier saluted. Edward and Sonja returned the gesture with perfect fluidity. Colin and Gene bunched behind them, awed by the situation.

"Stand easy, Commander Stapleton. My name is Brigadier Potter and I have a few questions."

"Sir. Yes, Sir." Edward relaxed slightly. But only slightly.

"Where are the children, Commander?"

"The youngsters have no experience of outsiders, Sir, especially armed ones. Nor do they have any idea they are part of a military operation. I thought it best that they be kept out of the way until you and I had talked."

"Understandable, if a little *too* cautious." The Colonel turned to Naish. "This is the boy?"

"Gene Stapleton, yes."

"Come and sit." Colonel Potter indicated a seat next to him.

Glancing at his father, Gene moved over and sat down. Edward didn't look back.

"Tell me what happened last week. The day the Orbisons died."

"I was out at Pittenhall Ridge, drawing birds." Despite his obvious trepidation, Gene's voice was calm and clear. "I was near the fence. I know I'm not allowed there but it's the only place that I can draw…"

"Just the bare bones of the story will do." The Brigadier smiled at him but there was no kindness in his eyes.

"I saw the Orbisons walking hand in hand away from the place." Gene shot another look at his father but Edward was still staring impassively ahead.

"And then?" Potter put his hands on the desk in front of Gene and stared into the teenager's eyes.

"I don't know. I came over all sick and dizzy and think I must have fallen asleep."

Gene was obviously desperate to please, but there wasn't much else he could say.

"When I woke up, the Orbisons were gone."

"Thank you, son. You can leave."

Gene scooted out of the door in obvious relief.

"We found the Orbisons on the rocks at the bottom of Pittenhall Ridge," Edward said once the teenager had left. "Looked like they threw each other off."

"So they went mad." The Colonel concluded. "Due to the boy's pheromone release, we assume."

"As far as I can ascertain."

"Why didn't the infection spread?"

"Pittenhall Ridge is next to Jackson Head," Edward replied. "It's bound to have absorbed the insecticide we use there. There wasn't enough of a concentration of ants or people for the outburst to reach the rest of the island's children."

"Very good." The Colonel seemed satisfied with the answer. "Now. What's your story, Mr Walton?"

"I'm familiar with the set up here." Colin didn't bother with military protocol. "I know that, in the future, this island will be one of the few safe places on earth. I wanted my family to survive, so I arranged to have them brought to Kirkfallen."

He shrugged non-commitally.

"That meant telling a bit of a white lie. Apathy is actually my niece."

"Your definition of a white lie beggars belief - and let's not forget you deserted the island in the first place." Potter's voice was soft but the menace in it was unmistakable.

"I didn't desert. I'm not a soldier." Colin refused to be intimidated. "In my situation, I imagine you'd have done the same."

Naish drew in a sharp breath. The Brigadier took his hands off the desk and stepped back.

"Yes. I probably would have," he chuckled. "It was a canny move, Mr Walton, and it worked. Dan and Emily are in Private Ainsworth's cottage and they're mad as hell at you."

He tapped the side of his nose.

"But it's better to have them here than on the loose, knowing what they know."

"Thank you, Sir."

The Colonel fixed Colin with an owlish stare. "So, where's your real daughter? And her mother, Libby Walton."

"They didn't make it." Colin's demeanour was as rigid as the soldiers around him. "I barely managed to reach the mainland myself."

"It was quite a feat of seamanship, I'll admit." Colonel Potter nodded sagely. "So why the cock and bull story about Apathy being yours?"

"Wanted to make sure I had your attention."

"You certainly got that. I must say, I admire your chutzpah."

"Does this mean we can stay?"

"I suppose so. Although, I did consider putting your whole family in a helicopter and dropping them in the ocean."

"You're a humane man, Brigadier Potter."

"Here's how it's going to play out." Potter put his hands behind his back in an official manner. With the blackboard behind him, he resembled a stern school-master.

"Mister Stapleton, you are relieved of command. Since your son has obviously released his phero-mones, your family will accompany us back to your home, the United States of America. You will be giv-en some tests, sign a secrecy agreement - and then be free to go on with your lives. Is that acceptable?"

"Sir. Yes, Sir."

"Emily and Dan Walton – or should I say D.B. *Salty* - will also accompany us for testing. Then they will be returned to Kirkfallen."

"That wasn't part of the deal," Colin interrupted.

"I wasn't aware we had a deal. They'll be brought back unharmed, I promise."

"And the rest of the children?"

"Your appearance has brought home just how... precarious our position here really is." Potter rolled his eyes theatrically. "It's time to act. Poppy Ains-worth and Millar Watt will be relocated to the Far East. It's time the Stopwatch Project proved its worth."

There was a hushed silence throughout the room. Sonja Watt and Alison Ainsworth exchanged imper-ceptible glances but remained rigidly to attention.

Everyone considered the enormity of what was being decided.

"I'll make sure the unit is informed," Edward said evenly. "Begging your pardon, Sir, but we know our duty. Was a whole battalion as your escort really necessary?"

"Probably not." The Brigadier took off horn-rimmed glasses and wiped them on the tail of his uniform. Without them, his eyes were just as big and bulbous. "But I'm also a cautious man and I don't appreciate all these loose ends suddenly appearing. Plus, I didn't want you going native on me."

"Understood."

"That will be all. I'd like to see the children before I leave, but I'll make sure the majority of my men are back on the choppers first. Before we do, I'd like a chance to speak to the Stopwatch Unit."

"They expected as much, so most of them are digging out their old uniforms. We keep them hidden from the kids," Edward added self-consciously. "Let's hope they still fit."

"That's not really necessary, Mr Stapleton."

"I know, but the unit hasn't had a proper inspection for years. It would be a big boost for their morale. I can have them assembled on the beach in half an hour."

"Very well." Colonel Potter gave in. "In the meantime, I'll have a look round the village."

"Sergeant Ainsworth will be happy to escort you."

Alison Ainsworth looked far from happy but kept silent.

"Mr Walton." Potter turned to Colin. "Once we're gone, the remainder of the Stopwatch Unit will help you build a home and give you a plot of land."

"Sounds good to me."

"And I suggest your family learn to farm real quick." He dismissed Edward's group with a wave of his hand. "We've no use for slackers here."

Gene was waiting for his father outside.

"Well done, son." Edward put an arm around the teenager, still trembling from his ordeal. "Go to the croft and tell your mom I'll be there as soon as the Brigadier has finished his snoop around."

"Dad? What *happened* to the Orbisons? Did I do something to them?"

"Later, son." Edward pushed the teenager brusquely in the direction of their home. "Now's *really* not the time."

Gene bit back a reply and left just as the Potter and his entourage stepped out of the Information Hut and set off on their tour of the village. As soon as they were out of earshot, Colin rounded on Edward Stapleton.

"What's going on? I'm a con man by trade and something back there sure smelled fishy to me."

"You're a *what*?"

"Long story."

"*That* was a bit of subterfuge," Edward said.

"Who the hell are the Orbisons?"

"Orbison was their cover name. They were both army doctors."

Edward loosened his top button. He was far more muscular than he had been fifteen years ago and his uniform was uncomfortably tight.

"They didn't know it, but the army sent them here as human guinea pigs. When the first of the kids were quarantined, they were supposed to be there to monitor what happened. If the Orbisons went crazy, then Top Brass would know their experiment worked."

"What if they harmed the kid?"

"Our people would be present too. And remember, sociopaths like us aren't affected by pheromone release."

"Sounds like they *did* go nuts."

"They didn't." Edward hesitated, then plunged ahead. "Gene hasn't released his pheromones yet."

"What?"

Sonja put her head down and began inspecting her rifle.

"Gene hasn't released his pheromones yet," Edward repeated. "I knew he sneaked off to Pittenhall Ridge to sketch birds every Sunday and the Orbisons liked to walk there too, so I slipped a tranquilliser into the boy's food at breakfast. He slept through the whole thing."

"What thing? What killed the Orbisons?"

"Sonja and I did." Edward's expression was unreadable. "The survival of this community depended on the army believing the Stopwatch Project worked exactly as they'd hoped. We had no choice."

"You bumped the doctors off without a thought?"

"No. We thought about it." Sonja jutted out her chin defiantly. "Then we bumped them off."

"That's pretty damned nasty."

"We weren't picked to be in the Stopwatch Unit because we were Boy Scouts," Edward replied contemptuously. "We used the old bag-of-seed-scattered-over-the-ground trick, so the air was thick with birds. Prevented any spy satellites spotting the murder. Worked for getting you off the island, too, as I recall."

"Oh," Colin's said awkwardly. "Well, I do appreciate a good con."

"It worked. Everything has worked the way we wanted." Sonja's voice was tinged with pride.

"Gene will go to the USA and Poppy and Millar to the Far East," Edward continued. "But when they release their pheromones, it will make people *co-operate*, not kill each other. We might even achieve world peace."

He gave a snigger.

"Think of it. World peace achieved by a group of sociopaths, trained to do nothing but kill."

Colin licked his lips nervously.

"It's not going to happen, Eddie."

"What do you mean?" Edward's hand went instinctively to the revolver strapped to his side. "Is this something to do with the warning you were talking about earlier?"

"You were right about Markus Kelty all those years ago," Colin said. "I found his daughter. Her name was Elspeth Flintheart."

Colin warily eyed the sidearm.

"When Dr Kelty died, Aiki Conroy married a car salesman. I been keeping an eye on her the last few months and I don't think she had any idea what Kelty had done to her."

He fished a cigarette from his breast pocket with trembling hands.

"Problem is, Aiki Conroy was injected with Mandibular Pheromones, just like all of your kids… but as her daughter approached sixteenth, she began slowly releasing alarm pheromones."

Edward went white.

"Oh, my God. That can't be right."

"Humans are far more complex than ants." Colin picked his words carefully. "I guess that was Kelty's real problem. He could never really see the difference between the two species."

"I think the clue is in the number of legs," Sonja said witheringly.

"Let him speak," Edward commanded.

"Pheromones do different jobs for insects," Colin continued. "But they don't operate that simply in humans. Kimberly Flintheart became a teenager with all the fears and worries that entailed. And her parents weren't getting along. When that happened, she stopped producing Mandibular Pheromones and started emitting alarm pheromones instead."

Colin bit his lip.

"That got me thinking about when I was at Diamondback. I was happy then. And the others at the trailer park became much more friendly and sociable. But I was supposed to be filled with the *alarm* pheromone."

"You were. Your release made everyone at the trailer park go kill-crazy."

"Because I was scared out of my mind." Colin lit his cigarette, cupping shaking hands around the flame. "I've had plenty of time to think about it and Kelty was wrong. It doesn't *matter* what kind of pheromone we have inside. The stress of release will always produce the stronger pheromone, the alarm pheromone."

"So, what happened to Elspeth Flintheart?" Edward asked. "Is she still a danger?"

Colin held his breath for a long, long time. When he exhaled, the words came out wrapped around a thread of poisonous smoke.

"She and her family are dead."

"Excuse me?"

"Gas explosion. Don't ask me any more about it."

"And you have the temerity to call *me* cold." Edward curled his lip. "Was D.B. Salty part of this?"

"He had no idea." Colin took another vicious drag. "My brother's seen too much killing."

He held out his hands in a pleading gesture.

"Point is, you put Poppy and Millar in China or the Middle East? They'll be terrified. They'll produce alarm pheromones. And they won't survive the carnage they've created."

Edward stared into the man's eyes, trying to find a glimmer of a lie in what he said. He recognised nothing but pained honesty.

"And you came back to alert us about it?"

"I did." Colin held Edward's stare. "Figured I owed you that much."

The Commander let out a long sigh.

"Thank you."

51

"What the hell do we do now?" Sonja Watt groaned. "How are you gonna stop Potter taking Gene, Millar and Poppy with him?"

"We fight," Edward said. "Our hand has been forced."

"We were only expecting a small military contingent." Sonja jerked a thumb at Colin. "Because of this bastard, there are seven giant helicopters filled with crack troops."

"And just one of those choppers has enough space to hold all the kids on the island."

"Are you nuts?" Sonja shook her head. "Even if we got our hands on a copter, where would we take them?"

"The British mainland," Colin interrupted. "These things are bound to be pretty fast. You'd be there before you could be intercepted."

"We're in the US military. We'd be whisked off before the story ever came out."

337

"It's a helicopter full of bloody kids!" Colin insisted. "Land them in Glasgow City Square, if you want. The UK authorities won't just hand them over, no matter what cover story the US military concocts."

"And then what?"

"I imagine the British Army will put you back here with round-the-clock NATO surveillance. I'm sure the children will be allowed to leave once they pass puberty."

"That'll sure sour US relationships with the rest of the planet."

"My heart bleeds."

"What you're suggesting is impossible." Sonja calmed down, deciding that a logical argument was her best course of action. "*If* we could steal a chopper. *If* we could disable the other six. Then what? The kids are in the barn and the terrain is too hilly to land anything there."

Edward thought for a few seconds.

"What if we could get the kids up to the Maclellan base? We could easily hold it until they all boarded."

"We could move them if we were only up against the squad we expected. But not a whole *battalion*. We wouldn't stand a chance."

Her Commander ran a hand across his forehead.

"We're the Stopwatch Unit," he said. "We do the jobs no one else can."

"I didn't spend fifteen years on this rock to die because of some fat scam artist!"

"And just how did you expect to die?" Edward moved Colin gently out of the way and faced down his second in command.

"In my bed. In Kansas." Sonja replied dispiritedly. "That's where I come from."

"Sonja," Edward said softly. "The game is up. It's now or never."

Sonja covered her face with her hands, breathing heavily. Then her head snapped up and she saluted her Commanding Officer.

"What are your orders, Sir?"

"Are the moles in place?"

"They are."

"Then switch the walkie talkies to our secure channel and give the signal." Edward returned the salute.

"Tell them to begin Operation Louise."

The Battle of Kirkfallen

Studies have shown that 98% of soldiers who engage in active combat are later found to have been traumatised by their actions

The other 2% are usually diagnosed as being 'aggressive sociopathic personalities' who basically have no qualms about killing

The Battle of Kirkfallen

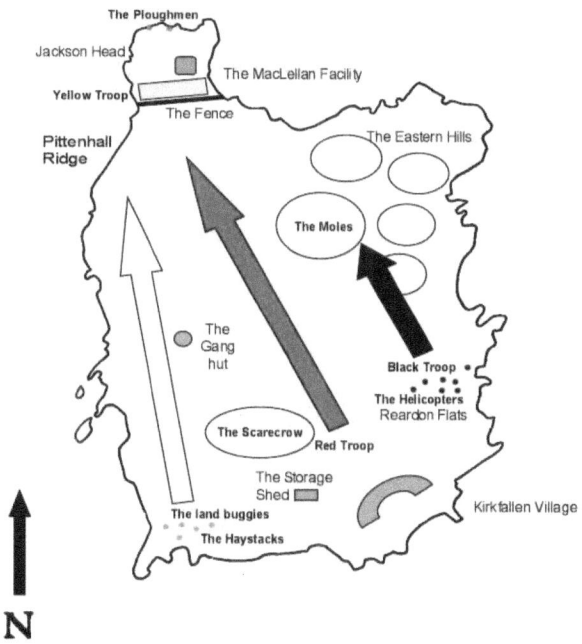

52

Edward posted two of the Stopwatch unit outside his cottage. The Brigadier had been and gone but the sentries would warn the occupants if any of his men approached the dwelling.

Inside, the highest-ranking members of the Stopwatch Unit gathered in the cramped living room. They lined the walls, some smoking furiously. The air was thick with a grey fug, a the sense of nervous anticipation almost palpable. Gene sat on a stool in one corner, pale and frightened.

"There are a lot of troops at the fence but only a handful in MacLellan base itself, along with a couple of army doctors." Edward looked around. "Wentworth Watt and his contingent will take care of them. Then, at least, we'll have one stronghold."

"Tell them not to kill the doctors," Annie Stapleton said. "We're bound to have casualties by the time we get there."

"Will do."

Colin watched in horrified fascination. He was seeing a side to these people that had lain dormant for years and it scared the hell out of him.

"What about the kids?"

"Doug McCombie and Deep Singh will be in charge of the children."

The men breathed out cigarette smoke in unison. They knew they had the biggest responsibility of all the Stopwatches.

"And my compliments to you, Doug, for being so far-sighted in your planning, in case it came to a fight."

"Now get out of here," Annie tisked. "You're stinking the place up."

"Is Walter De Guglielmo in place?"

"He's been there for an hour."

"Good. Now, we need to get one chopper in the air and disable the others." Edward spread a hand-drawn map of Kirkfallen across his kitchen table and sketched seven circles just northeast of the village at Reardon Flats. "Any ideas?"

Annie Stapleton joined him at the table. She was wearing a plain green dress and had a sidearm strapped to a belt around her waist.

"The other helicopters will have to be destroyed." She smoothed down the map as if it were her best tablecloth. "How many soldiers are guarding them?"

"About forty," Sonja Watt grunted. "The same as our *entire* fighting force."

"Perhaps we could take them in one surprise rush."

"They're much better armed than we are. We might manage, but there wouldn't be many of us left."

Sonja bent over the map, as if looking hard enough would produce some miraculous answer.

"Certainly not enough to get the kids to Jackson Head and then defend it against the 400 men left."

"I've got an idea." Edward thought for a second. "Fred Wolper used to fly choppers, didn't he?"

"Yup. So did Doug McCombie."

"He's already got the kids to contend with. Let's use Wolper." Edward rubbed his chin. "Sonja? We're going to need your son, Millar, to help."

"Yeah. That'll be right."

"That's a direct order, sergeant Watt."

"And this is a direct refusal."

"I'll do it." Gene stood up and stepped out of the shadows. "Whatever you're planning, I'll do it."

"You stay exactly where you are, young man." Annie grabbed Gene by the scruff of his neck.

"You can't ask Mrs Watt to risk Millar if you're not prepared to risk me." Gene retorted, slapping his mother's hand away. "Anyhow, what do you care?"

"Don't you say that!"

"I'm a military experiment!" the boy shouted. "And you knew! You've been lying to me for years! Don't you understand how I feel about that?"

Annie and Edward looked at each other and Gene realised, to his horror, that they probably didn't.

"Baby, we were trying to protect you!" His mother finally blurted out.

"How? By killing the Orbisons and putting the blame on me? You think I wouldn't figure it out?"

Gene waited in the forlorn hope that his mom and dad would deny it. But they simply hung their heads.

"If that's protecting me, I'd really prefer you didn't anymore." The boy's voice became hard and flat. "If you want me to accept what you've done, you better make me part of it."

"No, Edward." Annie's eyes sparkled with fury. "I won't let this happen!"

The others looked guiltily around, not wanting to be bystanders in this particular argument.

"Millar is in the storage shed with the other kids." Sonja pushed home her point. "Gene is right here."

"I've put my sister, my niece and my brother right in the firing line." Colin moved behind Gene and put his hands on the boy's shoulders. "I don't care who goes, but someone better do it and do it fast."

Annie Stapleton gave a quiet moan.

"Dad," Gene said. "Good or bad, this is my home. *I* want to help save my friends."

Edward knelt in front of Gene. His face twitched and he put a hand to his cheek to hide it.

"Ok. Go get Fred Wolper."

53

Fred Wolper roared up to the soldiers guarding the helicopters and did a spectacular wheelie in the land buggy. Gene was crouched on the passenger seat, holding onto the roll bars above his head.

"Wow!" he enthused, jumping from the vehicle onto the springy seagrass. "These are incredible!"

He started towards the choppers, a look of near rapture on his face.

"Oi! Oi!" Wolper leapt from the buggy and made after him. "I said you could look, that's all. These men aren't here to give these things a wash and polish – they're guarding em."

He gave the approaching soldiers an apologetic shrug.

"He's Commander Stapleton's son. He's never seen helicopters close up before, so the boss said he could have a quick peek."

Gene was trying to inch past the guards. Wolper gave him a slap on the back of the head.

"Settle down, will you?"

"Is that a pilot?" Gene waved his arms at a man in a jumpsuit standing in front of the nearest chopper. "Do you really fly this thing? It's totally incredible!"

The pilot strolled over, helmet under one arm.

"You've never been in a helicopter?"

"No, Sir." Gene pushed past the soldiers. "But I'm gonna fly one of these someday." He gave the airman a perfect salute and one or two of the guards laughed out loud.

"You wanna see it properly?" The pilot asked laconically, secretly pleased by the attention.

"Are you kidding me?" Gene's jaw dropped open. "I'd die to look inside."

"C'mon then." He turned and sauntered back towards the chopper. Fred Wolper went after them.

"Don't you touch *anything*. You hear me?" He took a few cautious steps and stopped. "Christ, these birds are impressive."

"Big, ain't they?" One of the guards offered him a cigarette.

"Been a while since I seen hardware like that." Fred waved the offering away. "No thanks, I gave up."

The pilot climbed into the chopper cockpit and pulled Gene up after him.

"Don't go inside!" Wolper beckoned Gene back, but the boy wasn't watching.

"I'm like an old woman," he explained to the guards. "But he's the Commander's son."

Inside the cockpit, Gene plonked himself in the co-pilot's seat.

"This is the most exciting moment of my life!" He scanned the array of buttons and dials. "What does everything do? Where's the ejector seat?"

"Doesn't need one," the pilot said proudly. "This baby can fly rings round anything else in the sky."

"Mr Wolper." Gene leaned out of the open cockpit door. "You *have* to come and see this!"

"I don't think that's allowed," Fred called back. "You be careful."

"Go on. Knock yourself out." The guard with the cigarettes stepped back to let Fred Wolper through.

"You sure?"

"Fred! Come on!"

"Yeah. Otherwise, the kid's gonna have a fit."

Fred moved slowly towards the chopper, two soldiers on either side. He reached the cockpit and ran his hand along the sliding door.

"Man, this machinery is epic!"

He stepped back in appreciation and slammed his elbow into the chest of the guard to his right. As the man crumpled, Fred gave a quick chop with his left. The other guard staggered away, clutching a broken nose.

"What the...?" The pilot rose in his seat to see what was going on.

Gene's arm shot out, rigid fingers burying themselves in the man's throat. The pilot fell back, choking, into his seat.

With one fluid movement, Wolper hauled himself into the cockpit and grabbed the pilot by the collar. He pulled hard and the man flew out of the door and landed on the grass outside. Fred slammed the door behind him and vaulted into the empty seat.

The soldiers guarding the choppers were well trained. As Fred engaged the engines, they ran towards the helicopter, unslinging their weapons and opening fire.

Gene threw his arms over his face. Bullets thudded across the windscreen, sending up showers of sparks.

"Relax, kid." Fred grabbed the joystick. "This thing's packing more armour than an Armadillo at a jousting match."

Above him, the rotors began to spin. Gene lowered his arms. Other pilots were racing for their machines, one or two already climbing in.

"Now, where the hell are the guns?" Fred pulled back on the stick and the chopper rose slowly into the air.

"You mean you don't *know*?"

"Kidding!" The man flicked a cover on the joystick and pressed down. Twin gouts of flame burst from either side of the cockpit. The soldiers dived for the ground as the earth was torn up around them.

Fred pulled back on the stick and the chopper rose jerkily into the air. He pulled to one side, finger still on the button. The helicopter turned, almost leisurely, in a circle and huge chunks of metal flew from the nearest choppers. He thumbed a few more switches on the console in front of him and pulled the joystick back. The chopper vaulted up, then hung in mid-air. Rockets whooshed from the bottom of the craft and four helicopters exploded on the ground.

The last two choppers began to rise slowly. Gene thumped Fred's shoulder, but the man seemed to have eyes in the back of his head.

The craft swivelled in the air and headed straight for the other birds. One helicopter tried to evade the suicidal charge, nose-diving into the ground and bursting into flames. The other spun to return fire but it was too late. Fred released another rocket at point-blank range and the chopper disintegrated.

"And that's *all* she wrote!" Wolper whooped.

He pointed the copter at the ground and fired. The soldiers scattered in every direction, but not before twenty or so of the slowest were cut down.

Gene clapped a hand over his mouth, trying not to retch.

"Sorry, lad. But this is what we do." Fred pulled a walkie talkie from his belt and held it to his head.

"Commander Stapleton, all the birds are clipped and Gene is safe." His voice was exultant. "You now have air support."

"Thank you, Mr Wolper. Put my son on."

Gene grabbed the device and held it to his ear.

"Dad?" He was close to tears. "This is horrible!"

"Keep it together, boy." Edward Stapleton's voice was cold and calm. "It's them or us. Unfortunately, that's what it's come down to. Put me back on to Fred."

Wolper reached out and snatched back the walkie talkie.

"Boy's fine, Commander." He opened the throttle. "Now get the rest of the children to Jackson Head. We'll cover you. Look after my girl, Gemma."

"Will do. You take care of Gene."

"You mean my co-pilot?" Fred grinned. "Don't you worry. We'll tear em up, boss."

And they rose further into the air, Gene gripping the sides of his seat.

Inside the storage shed, Deep Singh and Doug McCombie put their fingers to their lips. The children were huddled in one corner - the youngest clutched in the arms of their mothers.

"We are about to play a little game." Deep Sing winked at the children. "We are going to try and get right across the island without anybody stopping us. So you have to stay very, very quiet for as long as you can."

The children nodded. His wife, carrying their four-year-old son, smiled encouragingly.

Doug McCombie slid aside a bale of hay, revealing a trapdoor underneath.

"Been digging this tunnel for five years," he said with obvious satisfaction. "I just *knew* we'd need it someday."

He pulled up the wooden flap, flakes of dirt and straw dancing in the air as it rose.

"Mr Singh will go first."

"Lucky we eat a lot of carrots on Fallen," his companion mumbled, vanishing into the dark hole like a magician's rabbit in reverse.

"The rest of you follow him. It's a tight fit but it's perfectly safe. Comes out behind one of the hay bales. You wait till Mr Singh gives the all-clear, then follow him. We'll make for Jackson Head."

He clapped his hands like an enthusiastic scout leader.

"This will be so exciting! None of you have ever been there before."

Bob McCombie raised a hand.

"Yes, Bobby?"

"What about all the new soldiers?"

"Well, I'm not supposed to tell you this, but what the hey?" Doug beamed at his son. "They're not soldiers. They're actors, shooting a movie on Kirkfallen. Can you believe it?"

Judging by the look on Bob McCombie's face, he certainly *didn't* believe it. But his father's enthusiasm had convinced most of the kids.

"The plot is that the baddies are trying to stop a group of very special kids from escaping – that's you lot. So they'll come after us, but all your parents will fight them. It's like we're all extras."

"Are we getting paid for this?" Bob didn't raise his hand this time.

"Not unless you're in the actor's union. But you do get a trip in a giant helicopter to go see the mainland."

That was exciting. The older children began frantically whispering to each other.

"There will be lots of guns going off and people getting knocked for six, but you just ignore all that." Doug waved them towards the trapdoor. "All you have to do is run as fast as you can and don't stop for anything."

His smile faltered.

"Some of your parents might fall down like they've been shot, but that's all part of the scene, so no need to worry. You just have to keep going. It all has to be done in one take."

"I can't believe Poppy's missing this," Marcie Gold remarked dryly. "She'd probably run in slow motion just to get noticed."

The children began to file into the hole, some tremulous with anticipation, one or two shaking with fear.

Bob McCombie was in the middle. He stopped halfway down and tapped his father on the leg.

"Can you get on your radio and tell mom I love her?"

"I will, son." Doug fought an overwhelming impulse to hug the boy. "And if Deep and I go down, you have to keep the others moving. Understand?"

"If this was just a movie," Bob said quietly. "You'd know already whether you make it or not."

"I need you to keep them moving, kiddo," Doug repeated. "Do you *understand*?"

"I understand," his son replied tearfully.

"Good boy." Doug reached out to touch him but Bobby had vanished from sight.

"I love you."

He hoped Bob had heard. The others filed silently past and lowered themselves into the hole.

Doug shut the trapdoor and leaned heavily on his rifle. He heard a shuffle and his head shot round.

Millar was standing with his back to a hay bale. His knuckles were white where they held onto the binding twine.

"What are you doing? Get after the rest of them!"

"I won't go in there," Millar whispered fearfully. "I have claustrophobia."

"What? It's only thirty yards!"

"I can't go into a hole." The teenager began to sob. "I just can't!"

"There are troops all the way around this shed, boy. I have to hold this place as long as possible. Make them think the children are still inside."

"I'll stay with you," Millar pleaded. "I can shoot. I'm a good shot."

"Don't you get it? The tunnel is the only way out."

"I can't go into a hole! Please! You can hold this place twice as long if I help you."

Doug slammed his hand against a wooden crate and Millar gave a squeak of fear. Then, the man unholstered his pistol and handed it over.

"I used to play football when I was a kid." His voice softened. "You know what they say in football?"

"No," the teenager replied tearfully. "There aren't enough older kids on the island to make a team."

"They say the best defence is a good offence. That's what they say." Doug sighed.

"So... New plan. We're going out the front door. When I give the signal, you run up the hill towards the scarecrow at the top. Don't stop for anything."

"I won't, Mr McCombie."

"It's Doug. You're a man now. Let's go."

Millar sniffed and crept away.

Doug looked longingly at the trapdoor. His only means of escape.

"My God. Who knew being one of the good guys could be so *hard*?"

He slammed a magazine into the breech and headed towards the door.

54

In the quarantine room, Apathy was beginning to feel queasy. She lowered herself gingerly onto the bed, her legs trembling.

The door flew open and Poppy Ainsworth burst in, radio in hand.

"I need you to stay…" the girl stopped in mid-sentence. "You all right?"

"I don't feel very well. Maybe it was the injection the doctors gave me."

"They only took blood." Poppy came over and placed a calloused hand on her companion's forehead. "Jeez… you're burning up."

There was a shout from the level below them, then a cry of pain.

"What's going on?"

Poppy ran to the door and looked into the corridor. Apathy was startled to see a long knife tucked into the back of her belt.

"Our parents are taking over the base!" she said with bated breath. "We're all going to escape in one of the big helicopters!"

She came back and knelt in front of Apathy.

"Try to hold on. I'll come for you when we're ready to go. You can sit next to me on the chopper." She slapped a large thigh. "We're going to the mainland! I'll be able to eat hot dogs, whatever they are, and go and see a Broadway show."

"That's nice." Apathy tried to concentrate on what the girl was saying.

"It's wonderful! I'm going to get a job as an actress, soon as I get there."

"I can't go." Apathy let her head drop, exhausted. "I've got the same pheromone thing you do. Only, with me, they're bad ones and they're about to break loose. I can't go near the mainland."

"But you can't release bad pheromones!" Poppy recoiled. "All the other kids are on their way. The quarantine won't work if they're here."

"It's fine." Apathy waved her hand weakly. "None of you will be harmed. You're all..." She struggled for the words. "You're just like your parents."

"What do you mean?"

"You all have sociopathic personalities." Apathy was too dizzy to be tactful. "I'm sorry if you didn't know."

"Of *course* I know." Poppy took a deep breath. "My parents told me about themselves a long time ago. I knew the history of this place long before Millar and Gene did."

She stood up and adopted a theatrical pose.

"But my mom and dad said never to tell, and I'm an actress, so I know how to play dumb. The boys never suspected."

Apathy made a supreme effort. She pulled herself up on the bed and raised her head.

"And doesn't it bother you?"

"Our parents have always been good to us." Poppy checked the corridor again. "I don't know if they act the way real people are supposed to, but none of the children have ever known anything else."

She closed the door quietly.

"Sure, they're only *pretending* to be regular folk. But they're the Stopwatch Unit. They're *good* at that. And they did it for their kids."

"Then it's OK." Apathy began to shudder. "When I release my pheromones, the soldiers will all go crazy and you'll win. All the blood will be on my hands."

"But we're not *like* our parents! Me, Gene and Millar, we *love* each other."

"Colin told me sociopathy is hereditary." Apathy shook her head, trying to clear it. "How do you know what you really feel? You've nothing to go on except the others on this island."

Poppy swallowed hard.

"I'm not willing to take that chance." She pulled the knife from her belt.

Apathy slid backwards on the bed and threw her arms over her face. Poppy advanced, weapon poised.

Nothing happened.

Apathy risked a peek. The girl had backed away, knife still in her hand.

"I can't," she said sorrowfully. "If there's one thing I've learned here, it's not what we *are* that counts. It's what we *do*."

She tucked the blade back in her belt.

"Please hold on. Just till the children get in the chopper. Please!"

"I'll try."

Above their heads, they heard the sound of gunfire.

"You tell everyone I couldn't kill you." Poppy headed for the door. "Let them know I'm a good person."

"I will." Apathy slumped sideways. "I promise."

"But I have to do whatever it takes to protect my family." Poppy looked hatefully at the knife. "You'd do the same, wouldn't you?"

"Yes, I would." Apathy thought of Emily and D.B. Salty. "Just like my father and mother."

"I *knew* you and I would be friends. If we survive, I'll send for you. I'll probably need a personal assistant."

"I'd be honoured."

"I told you I was a great actress. If you keep my secret, nobody will know what I'm really like."

Poppy looked sadly back at her new friend.

"Nobody ever has."

She locked the door and vanished into the corridor.

Back in the information hut, Brigadier Potter drifted to the library, taking down random books and leafing through them.

"There wasn't much to the village, was there?" he complained. "Anything else interesting on the island while we're doing this damned inspection?"

"Depends on how interesting you find grass." Naish glanced out the window. Two islanders were zig-zagging between the buildings, heads down. She turned quickly back to the room. The other window was obscured by the less than svelte figure of Alison Ainsworth, still standing to attention.

"What about the MacLellan facility?" Potter seemed determined to do more sightseeing now he was here.

"Not much to see there either." Naish glanced out of the window again, but the figures were gone. "The Walton girl is in one of the quarantine chambers on the lower levels. Though we can let her out now, I guess, since she isn't Colin's daughter."

"I've been meaning to ask about that." The Brigadier put down his book. "How do the islanders know exactly when to quarantine a child? How do they know when a pheromone release is about to happen?"

"Their age, mainly." Naish pointed to the corner of the room. "And those."

On a high table sat a tall Perspex box filled with earth, the glass dotted with crawling insects.

"It's an ant farm. How clever," Potter said enthusiastically, wandering over and tapping the glass. "I had one when I was a kid."

"Ants act like an early warning system, as well as a conduit." Naish joined her superior. "Theory was, they'd go into overdrive when anyone on the island was about to release pheromones."

She frowned.

"Only it didn't seem to work with Gene Stapleton. He caught everyone by surprise."

The Brigadier raised an eyebrow. Insects were swarming all over the earthen mound inside the container. They raced back and forwards, biting each other and throwing themselves against the polished surface.

"Well, they're sure as hell acting up now."

"Holy God," Naish sputtered. "Some kid on the island is hot!"

Potter glared at Alison Ainsworth.

"It's news to *me*." Her look of astonishment was obviously genuine. She pulled the walkie talkie from her belt. "I better get Commander Stapleton."

"You better. I don't like the...."

His voice petered out as the sound of gunfire drifted into the hut, followed by a far off explosion. The shelves around the information hut rattled.

Alison Ainsworth reacted first. She dropped the walkie talkie and pulled out her sidearm.

Years on Kirkfallen had not dulled her instincts. Her first three shots took out the soldiers lined along the wall before they had even raised their rifles. Alison dropped to a crouch, kicking over the desk in front of her as the man by the door returned fire. The wooden top fractured, bullets gouging into its surface and the window burst in a kaleidoscope of glass.

Potter scuttled behind the ant farm and Naish threw herself to the floor. Alison rolled onto her side and fired again. The soldier at the door gave a scream and fell as a bullet thudded into his shin. Alison sighted, squeezed the trigger, and the man was silent. The smell of cordite hung in the air, blue smoke drifting across the information hut.

"Well, *this* is awkward!"

"Put down your weapon, sergeant Ainsworth," Naish called.

"Know what kind of ants are in that tank?" Alison replied. "Fire ants. You wanna watch those suckers."

And she fired again.

The glass of the ant farm exploded and a mass of insects swarmed down the sides. Naish tried to get a proper bead on her adversary, but the upturned oak desk made a perfect shelter.

Seconds later, Potter scrambled away from the tank. Ants were swarming over his body, biting every inch of exposed flesh. Alison stuck her arm around the desk and fired again, the bullet thudding into the dirt of the farm. More insects began to pour down the shattered sides, dropping off the table and onto the floor.

The door burst open and the two guards positioned outside ran into the room.

Alison was trained in close-quarter fighting and knew she should stay where she was. But she had lost the advantage of surprise and she was outnumbered.

She stood up and let loose a hail of bullets. They caught the guards in mid-sprint and slammed them back through the doorway.

Naish squeezed off a round. Alison Ainsworth clutched at her chest, looking down in astonishment at her blood-soaked fingers.

She exhaled slowly and sank to the ground.

The Brigadier scrambled to his feet, slapping ants from his body. Naish crawled over to Alison and felt for a pulse. There was none.

"I'm sorry," she whispered. "It was you or me."

"Get on the radio, right now. Muster our men." Potter was purple with rage. "This is treason! I want every adult on this damned island hunted down and killed!"

"You're up against the Stopwatch Unit," Naish spat. "This won't be a *hunt*!"

She ran a hand down Alison's face, closing her eyes.

"It's going to be a damned battle."

55

"The children are ready to go." Deep Singh crouched behind a hay bale at the tunnel exit, walkie talkie in hand. "I suggest we head into the Eastern Hills and go north in a semi-circle. That will give us the most cover."

"That's a negative." Edward's voice crackled back. "It's a tough enough journey as the crow flies. The younger kids will be hard pushed to run four miles on even ground. Take the shortest route possible."

"Very well," Singh replied reluctantly. "But we'll be completely exposed."

"Help is on the way."

As if on cue, Perry and Samantha Gold came dashing up. A few hundred yards behind, some of Potter's troops had peeled away from the village and were advancing towards them.

Singh began pulling children out of the hole and pointing them north.

"Follow the Golds!" he shouted. "Don't stop for anything!"

The group began running, strung out in a line.

"Get us some cover *now!*" Deep yelled into the walkie talkie. "Potter's men are right behind!"

"Cavalry's here!" Fred Wolper burst onto the line. "Keep your heads down."

A giant chopper came sweeping in from the north. Twin gouts of flame erupted from the blunt green nose and the pursuing troops scattered for cover. Singh gave a victory yell and the children put their heads down and doubled their efforts.

In his cottage, Edward issued a final order.

"All members of the Stopwatch Unit who are still in the village, break out. Head through the village and exit at the west side, then make for Jackson Head. Terminate the enemy with extreme prejudice and arm yourselves with their weapons. Fred? You there?"

"Listening." The occupants of the cottage could hear the sound of the chopper's guns in the background.

"Give it five minutes, then destroy Fallen."

"That's our home, Eddie." Annie Stapleton laid a hand on her husband's arm.

"I know that." Edward clicked on his radio. "Bogeyman. What's the status at Reardon Flats?"

On the hill above the village, a lone scarecrow hung on crossed poles. It swung one arm cautiously towards its mouth – walkie talkie clutched in a white-gloved hand.

"The guards there have regrouped." Walter De Guglielmo whispered into the handset through lips caked with grime. "They've obviously been given new orders and they're heading north into the Eastern Hills. If they get above Singh and the kids, they'll cut them to ribbons."

"Understood." Edward traced the movements on the map. "Tell the moles to stop them."

"The soldiers have been joined by forces deployed from the eastern side of the village." Walter cautioned. "Gotta be about sixty men."

"Urge the moles to hold at all costs. The children's lives depend on it."

"Will do." Walter levered himself off the pole and unfastened the gun taped to it. It was a hunting rifle and Walter had spent weeks modifying it himself. In the old days, he had been the Stopwatch Unit's top sniper.

He lay down on the crest of the hill, squinted along the barrel and began firing.

"Good luck, everybody." Edward picked up his weapon. "See you on the other side."

"What about Dan and Emily?" Colin protested. "They've no idea what's going on."

"They've got Geoff Ainsworth with them." Edward crumpled up the map and threw it on the fire. "If that old dog can't get them out, nobody can."

"You need to trust me." Colin placed himself between Edward and the door. "Dan and Emily have *got* to get to Jackson Head. It's vital!"

"Jesus! I'll get them myself."

Annie Stapleton grasped her husband by the sleeve.

"For God's sakes," Edward huffed. "This is the only uniform I've *got*."

"Shut up." Annie swung him around and kissed him. "Don't you *dare* die out there."

"And risk your wrath? Not a chance."

Then they burst into the open.

Doug McCombie and Millar had their eyes pressed against cracks in the shed door. They could hear the pop and crackle of weapons in the distance.

"It's started." Doug laid a hand on the boy's shoulder. "Look, half these guys are leaving at the double. This is our best chance."

He pushed open the door of the storage shed and Millar squeezed through the widening gap.

"Run!"

The teenager sprinted for the hill to the north. The scarecrow was gone, but the cross that held it up was still standing – his sanctuary, if he could make it. Millar's legs were a blur and he sucked air in sobbing gasps, tearing across the flat land and up the incline.

Behind him, Doug McCombie had made it to an abandoned trailer just beyond the shed and was pouring fire at the enemy. A dozen men broke away from the main body and headed after Millar. One raised his rifle and his companion slapped it down.

"He's a bloody kid! We can't just shoot him!"

It was the last thing he uttered. Doug McCombie fired and the man collapsed.

More soldiers came running around the side of the shed. McCombie couldn't defend himself from a double-sided attack, but he tried anyway. He spun round and unleashed a torrent of bullets at the men racing towards him.

Millar glanced back in time to see the return fire slam into his companion. Doug lifted the rifle one last time, the other arm hanging limply at his side. Then the gun fell from his lifeless fingers and he pitched forward onto the ground.

With a wail, Millar ran harder, arms windmilling. The soldiers were catching up but he could see puffs of smoke from the crest of the hill above him. He risked one last glance back. At least four of his pursuers were down.

He kept running.

Walter De Guglielmo had a breech-loading Sharps hunting rifle. It wasn't an automatic but was accurate to two hundred yards. Lying in the grass, he loaded, sighted and fired. Loaded, sighted and fired. The barrel was so hot, it couldn't be touched but he knew the gun wouldn't warp.

Millar was racing towards him. At first, there had been twelve men after him. He'd killed six but the others were closing fast.

Walter De Guglielmo was a killing machine. He and the rifle were one. He loaded, sighted and fired again.

Then Millar swerved to avoid a rock. Walter jerked his head up.

"No!"

The terrified teenager was between him and the enemy. Right in his line of fire. Walter took careful aim and loosed off a shot.

Millar felt the bullet whistle past his head and heard a cry behind him. He didn't think his legs had the strength to go any faster, but *that* spurred him on.

He was almost there.

"Get down, you little fool!" Walter shouted. "I can pick them all off if you just move outta the way!"

But the boy was still heading towards him, head down, oblivious to everything but his dash for safety.

The men following weren't stupid. They changed trajectory, keeping themselves between the fleeing boy and the sniper on the crest of the hill.

Walter struggled to his feet.

"Get down!" he screamed again, motioning with his free arm. "Get on the…"

He spun backwards as a bullet caught him in the chest, the rifle flying from his hand.

Too late, Millar flung himself to the ground. He saw Walter De Guglielmo silhouetted against the sky-line, arms outstretched, mouth open in a silent cry.

Millar pulled the pistol from his belt. As the remaining soldiers moved towards him, he squirmed round and raised the gun, holding it in both hands like his father had taught him.

He emptied the magazine.

When Millar finally dropped the weapon, he was the only one alive on the hill.

Most of Potter's troops were still in a ring around the village. Wolper's chopper floated above their heads, strafing mercilessly, driving the men back towards the collection of stone crofts.

Kirkfallen was in turmoil. The residents were streaming west, out of the village, and had the advantage of complete surprise. They rolled over Potter's troops like a pack of wild animals, armed with axes, machetes and swords fastened out of ploughshares – chopping, gouging and scooping up rifles from their dead adversaries.

Wolper fired two rockets into the outskirts of Fallen, annihilating the soldiers trying to stem the tide.

The Stopwatch Unit poured out of the village and headed after their children.

"Keep going!" Edward shouted. "I'll get the Waltons."

Before the others could say anything, he darted off and headed for Geoff Ainsworth's house.

Geoff was in his doorway, firing at the soldiers besieging his cottage. Edward didn't even slow down. Shooting from the hip, he ran straight into the enemy.

"Eddie!" Geoff advanced down his path, redoubling his fire. "Nicely timed!"

He clutched at his stomach and doubled over. Sinking to his knees, he clenched his teeth and kept squeezing off rounds. Blood began to trickle from his mouth.

D.B. Salty sprinted out of the doorway, heading for a soldier who had ejected a magazine and was desperately trying to fit another into the breech. Dan reached him and swept the gun to the side, head butting the man in the face. He wrenched the weapon from the soldier's grasp and swept it round in a deadly arc of fire. As the last of the troops fell, Emily Walton bolted from the house and crouched beside Geoff Ainsworth. He put an arm around her neck and they staggered back towards the croft.

"Go." The man grunted through his pain as he slumped in his doorway. "There are more soldiers coming. I'll hold them off as long as I can."

Emily kissed him on the cheek and picked up a fallen weapon. Edward started towards his friend.

"No, Eddie!" Ainsworth waved his Commander away. "Go protect the kids!"

Edward beckoned to the Waltons and headed west, glancing back once at his friend, pulling himself up the door frame, rifle still clutched in one blood-soaked hand.

"Edward Stapleton, I presume?" Dan drew along-side him as they ran, pulling Emily behind him.

"And you must be the notorious D.B. Salty."

"I'm going to have that printed on my business cards."

Emily cringed at how quickly the two men had forgotten their fallen comrade. Part of her understood that the islander's fight for survival left no time for mourning. Still, she wondered how much of their callousness came from an inability to feel for others.

Almost all the Stopwatch Unit had passed the western outskirts of the village and turned north, heading after their offspring. Wolper was still laying down a deadly covering fire and Potter's troops were retreating into the village, unaware that they were bunching themselves into a corner that Fred intended to destroy with rocket fire.

"We're gonna win this!" Edward punched the air with his fist as he ran. "It's my son in that chopper!"

A white plume arced out of the village and nar-rowly missed the helicopter.

Edward skidded to a halt.

"Get out of there, Fred!" he shrieked into his radio. "They've got a rocket launcher!"

The chopper stopped firing and began to climb. Another white streak shot out of the village. The helicopter tried to bank and evade the missile but it was a doomed effort. The rocket hit the bird just below the cockpit and it exploded in mid-air.

"IT'S MY SON IN THAT CHOPPER!" Edward Stapleton bellowed, veins standing out on his neck. Baring his teeth like a rabid dog, he took a few steps forward, then back, face twitching uncontrollably. With an agonised sob, he pulled himself together and strode towards the village.

D.B. backtracked and got in front of him.

"What the hell are you *doing*?"

"I'm going after Potter." Edward's voice was flat.

"Don't be stupid, man. You wouldn't get near him!"

"Stand aside before I shoot you."

"No. You're going to *beat* Potter." D.B. refused to move. "You can only do that if you stay in command. If you stay alive."

"Get out of my Goddamned *way*!"

Emily hesitantly raised her gun. She was watching an unstoppable force coming up against an immovable object and wasn't about to let it come to a bloody conclusion.

"For God's sake!" she implored. "There are other kids on this island and they need you both to save them."

"I don't care about the other kids!" Edward wailed. "I only cared about mine!"

"Then it's time you CHANGED!"

Edward's whole body was shaking. His jaw worked silently, eyes pinpoints of hate. He lashed out with his fist and caught D.B. Salty in the mouth.

Dan staggered back but didn't fall.

"You want to commit suicide, go ahead. But my daughter is on this island too." He wiped blood from his lip. "Where is she?"

Edward looked down at his fist. It was clenched so tightly that blood had begun to drip from the palm.

"Please help save *my* child, Mr Stapleton," Emily pleaded.

"I'll take you to her," Edward said finally. "But it won't do any good."

"Why not?"

"Because that chopper was the only advantage we had and our one way off the island."

He wiped his hand down his tunic, smearing blood across the khaki uniform.

"Without it, none of us stand a chance."

56

Deep Singh ran behind the children, egging them on. The smallest were the luckiest - too young to understand what was happening and light enough to carry. Spurred by the desire to keep their little ones safe, the mothers had outdistanced the others, jogging along at an unrelenting pace.

The group had been overtaken by the first villagers out of Kirkfallen and the men hoisted the six-year-olds onto their shoulders to speed up the column. The rest of the kids were still strung out in a line, the twelve-year-olds manhandling their younger companions along, using a mixture of pleas and threats to keep them moving. They knew now this was no movie.

Deep kept scanning the hills to their right. The troops guarding the helicopters had started off further north than his juvenile band and could move far more quickly. If they got to the high ground, the line of sobbing youngsters would be picked off like ducks at a carnival. The fight had gotten too intense for him to believe they would be spared.

The Stopwatch Unit now toted guns they had lifted from fallen soldiers but they were still at a huge disadvantage in terms of firepower and numbers. And there were more of Potter's men stationed at the fence.

Deep knew that, right now, they would be preparing to repel the rag-tag army - and the only way onto Jackson Head was through their defences. He cursed his Commander for trapping them in this dead end, but now there was nowhere else to go.

Edward Stapleton reached the western end of the village, with D.B. and Emily close behind. Sonja Watt and Annie Stapleton were sprawled, face down, between two haystacks. Edward skidded to a halt.

"That's my wife and second and second in command."

Emily bit her lip.

"Oh God. I'm so sorry."

"No need." Edward lowered himself to the ground. "They're faking. Get down and pretend you've been shot."

"What?"

"Just do it, or you'll be dead for real. Potter will be concentrating on cutting off the kids. He's not going to comb the area inspecting bodies."

D.B. pulled his wife down. They lay motionless, hand in hand, only yards from Annie Stapleton, whose head was towards the smoking chopper debris.

Close enough to see her eyes were filled with tears.

Potter's army had split into two sections. Red Force was following the children in a direct line, due north. Without the helicopter to hold them back, they were gaining fast, loping over the rough terrain like hungry wolves. The more northerly Black Force had reached the foot of the Eastern Hills and begun to climb. Another mile and they would be level with the children and on much higher ground.

The moles went into action.

On the flank of the Eastern Hills, nine sections of thatched grass slid aside, revealing holes cut into the incline. Each depression was large enough to hold one man or woman and they contained the best marksmen in the unit, armed with the most trustworthy and longest ranging rifles on the poorly stocked island.

The moles opened fire. The first wave of Potter's troops were mowed down and the others scuttled for cover, returning fire from prone positions on the grass.

Potter and Naish roared up in Wolper's land buggy.

"Get up there and silence these guns right now!" the Brigadier shouted into his radio.

The soldiers rose and headed up the slope again. Above them, a hail of withering fire sliced through their ranks and they dropped back.

"The enemy is pretty well entrenched," Naish entreated. "Can't we just go round?"

"Circling the hills will put us too far behind. If the Stopwatches get to that glorified pillbox called MacLellan base, our casualties will be an awful lot higher. And I do *not* want these men picking us off from the rear when we're trying to mount an attack."

"The kids will never get past the soldiers guarding the fence."

"You think not?" Potter pulled the glasses from his face and furiously wiped mud from them. His face was spotted with angry, red insect bites. "I underestimated my enemy once. I won't be doing it again."

His troops were making short, zig-zagging runs up the hill, searching for any scrap of cover. There wasn't much. The villagers had removed any rocks they could have hidden behind months ago, under the pretence that they were clearing land for cultivation.

Yet sheer numbers began to tell. Though their casualties were high, Potter's men slowly gained ground until they were almost on top of the Stopwatch's defences. The leading men pulled grenades from their belts and flung them at the enemy.

Great wads of earth flew into the air and thick grey smoke drifted down the slope. When it settled, the hill above was silent.

The troops advanced.

But the fight wasn't over. Each Stopwatch position had a narrow hole bored several feet into the hill. As the grenades arced towards them, the defenders had slid down into the crevasse. Now, they emerged and began shooting again.

"Sweet Lord!" Naish moaned. "They're unkillable."

"We should never have got rid of them." Potter couldn't keep the admiration out of his voice. "Edward Stapleton should be a Goddamned General."

He lifted the radio.

"One last push, boys! They're on their last legs."

But it took another twenty minutes to finally overrun the positions. When the fight was over, the hillside was a mass of churned up mud and gore and at least forty of Potter's men were dead.

"We're not gonna catch the main Stopwatch body now."

"I know." The Brigadier got back on his radio again. "Red Force, what's your status?"

"We're right behind the children and encountering fierce resistance," the radio squawked back. "They're moving north along a gulley and every time we catch up, another two or three adults fall back from the group and mount a rear-guard action. By the time we kill them, the main column has moved another few hundred yards."

"Can you stop them before they reach Jackson Head?"

"When they get there, they won't have any adults left." The disembodied voice sounded miserable and apologetic. "But with the fight they're putting up, there's a good chance they *will* make it."

"Keep pushing. We'll be there as soon as we can." He switched channels and contacted his forces stationed at the fence.

"Yellow Troop. The Stopwatch Unit are heading your way. Report."

"We're dug in and waiting, Sir." A different voice this time. "They won't get past us."

"What about MacLellan base?"

"The enemy has possession but there's only one door and I have men covering it. We can't get in but they can't get out."

The voice sounded confident enough.

"That threat is definitely contained."

"I'll believe it when I see it." The Colonel snapped off his radio and slid back into the driver's seat of the buggy.

"Let's get to Jackson Head ASAP."

Edward Stapleton held his wife while she wept.

"I told you not to let Gene go," she sobbed. "I'll never forgive you."

Emily, Sonja Watt and D.B. stood to one side, trying not to watch.

"Annie." Edward Stapleton pushed his wife back and tried to wipe away her tears. "There are twenty-two children running for their lives out there. And they're not going to make it without our help."

Annie Stapleton wiped her nose with the back of her sleeve. Her eyes were red-rimmed and her greying hair fell in curling locks over her forehead. Then, suddenly, the tears were gone.

"I'm going to kill Potter," she said. "I'm going to kill all his men."

"Get the buggies," Edward said to Sonja Watt. "We're the cavalry now."

A murderous look crossed his face.

"Where's Colin Walton?"

"We got separated." Sonja walked over to the nearest haystack. "Or maybe he thought we were really dead. I saw him heading north, parallel to the kids."

Instead of stopping, she pushed her way through the straw barrier. An engine burst to life and one of the three land buggies emerged from the interior of the haystack.

"You and Emily, get in." Edward turned to D.B. "I take it you know how to drive, if my second in command gets hit?"

Sonja Watt coughed in indignation.

"Got no points on my licence." D.B. was staring at the buggy. "In fact, I don't have a licence at all."

"I'll drive the other one." Annie headed for the next haystack. "I've got a lot of pent-up anger I need to get rid of."

Seconds later, she emerged, straw sticking from the wheel rims and roll bars like some giant porcupine. Edward climbed into the passenger seat.

"Head up the west coast. The land is flat and there are no enemy positions. We should reach the fence just before the kids do."

"And then what?"

"Potter's men are in for the shock of their lives."

57

The buggies raced up the coastline and onto Pittenhall Ridge. The sky was cobalt blue and the Atlantic Ocean breathed sighs of ageless power as it swelled and pushed against the rocks below. Edward raised field glasses to his eyes.

To the east, the line of children was approaching the fence. There were almost no adults left and the older children had armed themselves in anticipation of one last fight. Behind the column, flashes peppered the grass where a dwindling batch of the Stopwatch Unit held back the troops following the convoy.

Potter's Yellow Troop had dug in beside the fence on the Jackson Head side. There had to be at least thirty of them. Deep Sing held up a hand. The children gratefully halted, collapsing onto the mossy turf, holding their sides and gasping for breath.

To reach the MacLellan base, they would have to get past the barrier and the men behind it. And the only way through was a narrow gate. Sing pulled out his walkie talkie.

"We're trapped, Commander Stapleton. Can't go back and can't go forward. I request permission to surrender."

"Hold the pursuers off for five minutes more. That's all I ask." Edward handed his wife the glasses.

"You were right." Annie stood up in her seat, training the binoculars on Yellow Troop. "They dug in *behind* the fence."

"Never do the obvious, Brigadier Potter." Edward sneered. "No matter how sound a tactical move it seems. Ploughman one and two?"

"Here, Sir." The voice was high and frightened and instantly recognisable.

"Poppy?" Edward gave a start. "What the hell are you doing on the air?"

"Ploughman one is dead." The teenager struggled to keep the fear from her voice. "He was killed defending the MacLellan base. I'm his replacement."

Annie put her hand on her husband's arm and shook her head.

"For Christ sakes, Poppy?" She leaned over and spoke into the radio. "Isn't there anyone else?"

"I'm already in place, Mrs Stapleton. I know what to do."

"Dammit, Eddie!" Annie slammed a fist against the wheel of the land buggy. "She's only a child!"

Edward Stapleton hesitated. But only for a second.

"Poppy? Take down that barrier."

"We're on it."

Poppy and Kyoko Hayashida – the last of the moles - squirmed along the tunnel that led from MacLellan base to a narrow cave just below the top of the northern cliffs. They pulled themselves over the lip and crawled onto the promontory. Their faces and hands were blackened and seagrass was threaded through their hair.

At either end of Jackson Head were the two rusty tractors, seemingly abandoned. In fact, they had been positioned with military precision. Poppy and Kyoko slid through the scrub brush on their bellies until they were under each vehicle.

Deep Sing and the older children had spread out and were lying in the grass, shooting at Yellow Troop. The soldiers returned fire.

While the enemy was occupied, the 'ploughmen' slid to the rear of the tractors and fastened cables to the tow hooks. The thick wires ran back to either end of the fence, where they were attached to supports at the bottom. Both cables had been coated with pitch and then rolled in grass until they were perfectly camouflaged. Snaking through the tufted terrain, they were undetectable.

Edward spoke into his radio again.

"Wentworth. The ploughmen are in place."

"About damned time." In the depths of MacLellan base, Wentworth Watt sounded more afraid than angry. "Is my wife....?"

"She's alive and with me. Get ready."

Edward reached out and squeezed Annie's hand. "Ploughmen, go!"

Poppy and Kyoko swung into the tractors, pulled keys from their pockets and stuck them in the ignition slot. The vehicles burst into life, dirty black smoke erupting from the funnels. The ploughmen hauled heavy feed bags from under the seats and dumped them on the accelerator pedals.

At the fence, Yellow Troop had forgotten the children and now concentrated their firepower on the tractors. Poppy and Kyoko ducked down and returned fire with handguns.

The tractors surged forwards and the steel cables went taut. The fence shivered as if buffeted by a high wind. Soldiers raced to either end of the barrier and tried to detach the cables - but the steel ropes were stretched taut and couldn't be moved.

Gouts of mud fountained from the tractor's wheels as they strained against the cables. The fence lurched up a few feet.

All of Yellow Troop were firing at the farm vehicles now. The men guarding the MacLellan entrance abandoned their positions and headed for the tractors. As soon as they moved, two of the Stopwatch Unit appeared in the doorway and cut them down, before vanishing back inside. The fence gave another lurch and one end shot out of the earth.

"Ploughmen take cover!" Edward barked. "Wentworth. Hit the switch."

Poppy and Kyoko leapt from the tractors. Poppy landed hands first, rolling into a ball with her arms over her head. Kyoko Hayashida was caught, mid-air, in a storm of bullets. She hung like a bloody, battered kite before plunging to the ground. The tractors roared forwards, only feet from the cliff edge and the entire fence was pulled from the earth.

Inside MacLellan base, Wentworth Watt slammed a lever into the wall.

Ten thousand volts of electricity brought the barrier to life for the first time in many years, showers of sparks cartwheeling from the mesh. The tractors burst into flames as they toppled over the clifftop.

Yellow Troop sprang to their feet, but there was nowhere to run. The fence rattled along the ground, scooping the soldiers up in a crackling net and frying them instantly.

"Shut down!" Edward commanded.

Wentworth Watt pulled the lever back and the current ceased. The fence hit MacLellan base and wrapped itself around the structure as the tractors plunged towards the ocean. The cables snapped, the tractors hit the water and the fence sank to the earth, a harmless jumble of steel and charred remains.

Deep Sing leapt to his feet and urged the children forwards. They raced across the last few hundred yards, firing as they went. The few survivors of Yellow Troop, disoriented and outnumbered, didn't stand a chance. The children reached the door of the MacLellan Facility and pushed their way inside – the defenders herding the stragglers into the interior.

"Move out."

Edward took no pleasure in the victory. The other children might be safe but his own son was dead. For the first time in his life, he was glad that he didn't feel as much as other people. But it still hurt so much he could hardly breathe.

The land buggies rolled across Pittenhall Ridge and headed for MacLellan base, Black Troop still too far away to stop them.

Then another buggy appeared, cresting the hill to the east, heading straight towards them. Edward trained his field glasses on the vehicle.

Brigadier Potter was driving. As much as Edward hated the man, the officer's tenacity was undeniable.

In the back were four soldiers armed with machine guns, harnessed by ropes to the roll bars, bouncing like marionettes as the vehicle raced over dips and hillocks.

"Dammit, that bastard never gives up!" Annie slammed her foot on the accelerator and the buggy shot forwards.

Behind them, Sonja Watt spotted the danger.

"Get in the back and take cover!" She powered down the hillside, her teeth rattling.

D.B. crawled between the seats and into the rear. He pulled Emily from her seat and threw himself on top of her.

And suddenly Dan realised he was back, lying on the floor of a bouncing vehicle. Back in the middle of another disaster, with a woman he didn't know trying to drive him to safety.

Behind them, Potter was gaining. The soldiers rattled off staccato shots, trying to steady themselves in the pitching vehicle. Sonja zig-zagged along the gulley, tracer bullets flashing past her head. The windscreen shattered and Emily gave a horrified whimper.

The ground sped past. They were five hundred metres from the base. Then four hundred. Three hundred.

"We're gonna make it!" Sonja shouted. Seconds later, she gave a strangled gasp. The buggy spun in an arc and ground to a halt.

Dan lifted his head. Sonja Watt was slumped over the wheel, a bloody patch spreading across her back. Potter's vehicle skidded to a stop and the soldiers began pulling at the ropes keeping them in place.

D.B. lifted Sonja's pistol from her holster.

"Stay down," he said to Emily. "I don't want you to see this."

He stepped out of the buggy. Emily grabbed at his arm and missed.

"Don't do it, Dan!" she cried. But D.B. was already heading towards the enemy.

The soldiers in the back of Potter's buggy had put down their guns in order to unstrap themselves. Emily watched her husband marching towards them like some old-time gunslinger. Spotting his advance, the soldiers gave up on the restraints and scooped up their rifles.

Once again, Dan Walton was willing to sacrifice his life to save her. This time, he had no chance of succeeding.

D.B. positioned himself sideways to present the smallest target possible. Emily covered her eyes.

Hearing the rattle of rifle fire, she peered tearfully through her fingers.

D.B. was still standing.

The gunfire was coming from a thicket of gorse on the other side of Potter's buggy. A boy wearing a felt trilby and large camouflaged pants burst from the undergrowth, eyes wild, wielding a rifle that seemed far too large for him. Panicked, the soldiers swung their weapons towards the intruder.

D.B. fired four times in quick succession, so rapidly Emily could hardly follow his arm. The men jerked upright and then swung back, hanging from their makeshift harnesses like puppets with their strings cut. D.B. glanced back at her.

"I've had plenty of time to practise."

In the buggy, Potter sighted his pistol over Naish's shoulder and took aim.

"Dan!" Emily yelled. "Look out!"

He spun around, too late, as Potter squeezed the trigger.

Naish slammed an elbow into the Brigadier's face. He jerked back into the driver's seat, the shot whistling harmlessly into the air.

"I've wanted to do this since I met you." The woman landed a sickening punch on Potter's jaw. "You fucking war-mongering bastard."

The Brigadier's head slumped forward onto his chest. Naish got out of the buggy, patting herself down. Emily jumped from her vehicle and approached the boy.

"And just who are *you*?"

"Millar Watt. All-round fancy pants and genius in residence."

The teenager politely raised his trilby and burst into tears.

D.B. was staring at Naish.

"I recognise you," he said finally. "You helped them do tests on me."

"That I did,"

"You still work for *them*?"

Naish glanced back at Colonel Potter, unconscious in the buggy behind her.

"I reckon I just quit."

The Showdown

Corporations and companies dominate every aspect of western society. Yet, their legally defined mandate is to pursue their own interests, regardless of who suffers. According to Joel Bakan, University of BC law professor, this means that all Corporations can be defined as sociopathic

As far back as 1935, Major General Smedley Butler complained that he had never been more than a 'high-class muscle man' for US corporations – adding, 'like all members of the military, I never had an original thought until I left the service'

At the time of his death, he was the most decorated Marine in U.S. history

58

Edward Stapleton pulled up outside MacLellan base, driving over the smoking remains of Yellow Troop.

"Grab as many weapons as you can carry," he shouted to the Stopwatches, who were emerging from the entrance. "We have to hold this place."

"What for?" Deep Singh materialised from the shadows, soaked with perspiration and covered in grime. "Nobody's coming to help us."

"He's right." Annie wiped sweat from her brow. "Edward, we gotta surrender. Potter must still have over two hundred soldiers surrounding us. We've got what? A dozen adults left?"

"We could hold out for a day or two." Deep Singh agreed. "But what good would it do? With the chopper gone, there's no way off the island."

"Just keep them at bay," Edward barked. "Is Colin Walton here?"

"He's downstairs. What difference does it make?"

"I'm mad as hell, and I *sorely* want some time alone with him."

Edward's eyes were blazing. He unclipped the holster at his belt and pulled out his sidearm.

"Got a problem with that?"

Deep Singh shook his head miserably. The sound of pounding boots rattled along the corridor of MacLellan base and Wentworth Watt emerged into the light.

"Where's my wife?"

"I'm sorry, Wentworth. She didn't make it."

Watt's mouth twitched. He nodded once. Then twice. Then he leaned forward and whispered into Edward's ear.

"There's something you need to see."

Colin was waiting in front of the Communications Room. Without breaking his stride, Edward slammed the man into the wall and shoved the pistol under his chin.

"You played me for a fool, Col." Edward pushed the gun further into the man's fleshy neck. "You came here to *kill* our kids because you figured they were just like Kelty's daughter."

He cocked the pistol.

"You were *counting* on us meeting overwhelming numbers and getting wiped out."

"That was a last resort, yes." Colin didn't blink. "To be used if my main plan didn't work."

"Your *main* plan?"

"Yes. The real reason I brought Apathy here."

"Edward." Wentworth ushered his Commander to the door of quarantine room One. "Look in there."

Edward peered through the observation slit.

Apathy Walton was sitting on the bed, her knees drawn up to her chin. Her hair was plastered to her head and sweat dripped from the end of her nose. She rocked back and forwards, moaning softly to herself.

"She's gonna release her pheromones any second," Wentworth stated the obvious. "Now that MacLellan is filled with kids, the quarantine is useless."

"Get in there and shoot her." His Commander shut the hatch.

"What?" Colin pushed away Edward's gun and threw himself in front of the door. "Don't be stupid! In a few minutes, Apathy will release her phero-mones. Potter's men will go crazy and kill each other but it won't affect you or the kids!"

"The *children* aren't immune!" Edward shouted into his face.

"Of course they are," Colin stammered. "They've all got sociopathic parents. They must be!"

"You utter moron!" Edward roared. "The children aren't *ours*!"

There was silence in the corridor. Wentworth Watt looked away.

"What are you talking about?" Colin whispered.

"Even Army Intelligence wouldn't expect us to give up our own offspring, you idiot! All we did was bring them up!"

He pulled Colin out of the way and flung him down the corridor. The man stumbled and fell onto his knees. Edward turned to Wentworth.

"Get in there and kill the girl."

"Wouldn't that mean we'd have to kill Gene as well?"

"Damn you, Wentworth!" Edward recoiled. "My son is dead."

"Eh? Gene's in here."

Wentworth pulled open an identical hatch on the next door.

"Fred Wolper set him down in the valley when the boy started to freak out in the copter. Before he flew back to the village."

Edward pressed his eye to the slit, his heart hammering.

His son was on the floor, curled in a ball, crying to himself. Like Apathy, he was soaked in perspiration.

"And you didn't *tell* me?" His fury and relief compounded themselves into an outburst of emotion the man didn't know he possessed.

"We were fighting a pitched battle, in case you hadn't noticed!"

"How did he *get* here?"

"Colin found him on the hillside. Joined the convoy and carried him all the way."

Edward yanked on the handle of the door.

"Don't go in there!" Colin scrambled to his feet. "That'll ruin everything and you still haven't heard what I got to say. Please! I've got a way *out* of this!"

Wentworth and Edward looked at each other.

"I told you! I didn't come here intending to kill the kids!" Colin raised his hands. "I had a plan to *save* them!"

"Which now won't work." Edward snapped. "The chopper is gone."

"Forget the bloody chopper! That wasn't my original idea!"

"If this is some feeble attempt to save your niece…"

"Exactly!" Colin grasped at the lifeline thrown to him. "Do you think I'd lure Apathy here just to have her shot?"

"What was your original plan?" Edward levelled his gun at the shorter man. "And you have run out of time to bullshit me."

"You have to get your wife down here. And Dan and Emily Walton." Colin lowered his hands. "You have to do it now!"

"Explain."

"There's no time for that! What have you got to lose?"

Edward holstered his gun and grabbed Colin by the collar.

"Come with me."

He yanked the man up the corridor.

"Put Apathy and Gene in the same room!" Colin yelled as he was bundled away.

"Do it," Edward ordered, dragging Colin towards the entrance of MacLellan base.

Children lined the corridors, wide-eyed and terrified. They watched silently as Edward marched Colin past. One or two reached out tentatively, then withdrew their hands.

"Where's my dad?" Bob McCombie asked in a small voice.

Colin began to shake.

"Whose kids *are* they?"

"Take a good look." Edward swept his hand in an arc. "Don't they seem kinda familiar?"

Colin scanned the passageway. It was the first time he had seen all the children together. Most had straight, dark hair, bright blue eyes and a gap between their front teeth.

"Think of all the times the Stopwatch experiments failed," Edward said. "There was only one person the army had hold of who they *knew* had DNA capable of absorbing a massive injection of pheromones."

He whirled Colin round to face the line of exhausted, fearful faces.

"You!"

"Don't you dare!" Colin backed away.

"You poor fool," Edward whispered. "They're *your* children!"

Colin fell against the wall, digging fingers into his cheeks.

"Oh no. Oh, Jesus, no."

Edward pushed him up the corridor. The children watched Colin leave with haunted, uncomprehending eyes.

The pair reached the entrance of MacLellan base to find the surface in turmoil. The few remaining members of the Stopwatch Unit were laying down covering fire as D.B., Emily, Millar and Naish ran towards them. Fifty yards out, the remains of Black and Red Troop were advancing.

Naish clutched at her arm and fell. D.B. grabbed the woman and pulled her to her feet, staggering on, Naish leaning on his shoulder. They reached a large boulder and scrambled behind, bullets flicking chips of rock from the top.

"They're not going to make it." Deep Singh growled in frustration. "We're totally outgunned."

"We got any heavy firepower at all?"

"Molotov cocktails, but we can't get close enough to use them."

"Yes we can." Colin began grabbing the petrol filled bottles and piling them into the passenger seat of the buggy.

"What are you playing at?"

"Light these," he said. "Light every one."

"You can't throw them all and drive this thing," Deep protested. "You'd never make it."

"You and your wife." Colin turned to Edward. "Take the Waltons, go below and get in the room with your kids. Act calm. Act relieved. Act happy."

He pulled a Zippo lighter from his pocket and began igniting the rags in the tops of the bottles.

"Con them."

Deep Singh moved to stop him.

"Let him go." Edward removed his pistol and handed it to Colin.

"You know what I'm getting at." Colin accepted the firearm. "Don't you?"

"I reckon I've figured it out."

"I'm so sorry, Eddie." The man tucked the gun into his belt. "I was only doing what I thought was right."

"I realise that." Edward put a hand on Colin's shoulder. "Thank you for carrying Gene to safety."

Colin climbed into the driver's seat and turned the key in the ignition.

"Give them hell, kid," Edward said softly.

Colin slammed his foot on the gas. The buggy's rear wheels spun and the vehicle shot towards the advancing soldiers.

"That's my brother!" Emily shouted, instantly recognising the driver roaring towards them, despite the passing of years.

Colin glanced at them as he sped past their shelter, his expression unreadable.

"Colin! NO!" Emily tried to break away, but D.B. yanked her back. He broke cover himself and began firing at the enemy in a doomed effort to save his best friend.

Colin drove with one hand. With the other, he pulled bottles from the passenger seat and flung them in front of him.

Explosions erupted on either side of the vehicle. Black Troop leapt out of his path, pouring a hail of fire at the speeding vehicle. Colin headed for the heaviest concentration of soldiers, holes erupting across the hood and sides of the buggy as the bullets found their mark.

One caught his shoulder and an arc of crimson splashed across his cheek. There were still a dozen Molotov cocktails on the seat beside him.

Colin raised a bottle in his hand and smashed it on the floor.

The buggy exploded.

A sheet of flame spread out across the grass in an arc of destruction. Before the oily smoke could drift away, the group behind the rock raced for the safety of MacLellan base and collapsed in the doorway.

Edward Stapleton folded his arms. Then he unfolded them again.

Finally, he gave a salute.

Behind him, the survivors of the Stopwatch Unit got slowly to their feet and followed his example.

Ash drifted across Jackson Head, covering the silent men and women standing to attention in the fading light.

59

Edward strode down the corridor with Dan and Emily in tow.

"Hold the rest of Potter's men as long as you can," he said. "Close every door and cut out the noise of the fighting. Have someone get me soap, towels and a comb."

"I don't think a wash and brush up will stand you in much stead when we go to meet our maker." Deep Singh commented dryly.

"That's not who I want to impress." Edward pulled off his jacket. "I know what Colin had in mind. But we've got to get this blood off ourselves."

Apathy and Gene were sitting side by side on the floor of quarantine room 1, their foreheads touching.

"Sorry I'm... not more talkative," Gene gasped. "I have to say, I've felt better."

"That's... all right." Apathy bit her lip until she tasted blood. "I like the... strong... silent type."

411

The door to the quarantine room swung open. The teenagers lifted their heads, though even this was an effort.

Edward Stapleton stepped through the doorway, his wife by his side.

"Dad! Mom!" Gene tried to struggle upright. "You're alive!"

"You better believe it."

Gene's parents rushed over and knelt by their son, sweeping him into their arms. Apathy squinted past them, trying to clear the blurriness of her vision. Another couple stood in the doorway.

Her sight crystallised.

"Oh, my God."

Her father's hair was short and brown and he looked years younger, like the man in her photograph. Emily, holding on to her husband's arm, was absolutely radiant.

They, too, hurried over. Seconds later, Apathy was in her parents' embrace.

"We're here, baby." Tears of joy flowed down Emily's face. "We're here."

"We won, Gene." Edward kissed his son on the forehead. He couldn't get near the rest of the boy's face because Annie had his head in a bear hug. "Everything is going to be fine!"

"We're here and we're never leaving you." Emily stroked her daughter's cheek and smoothed back her hair.

"I'll never desert you or your mother again," Dan said. "Never."

"You promise?"

"I promise with all my heart." Her father's eyes sparkled. "If you'll both have me."

Emily let go of her daughter and grabbed him by the back of the head. She pulled him roughly towards her and kissed him full on the lips.

"That answer your question?"

"If that's the reply, I'll never stop asking."

Apathy began to cry, but they were tears of delight. She looked across at Gene, still enveloped in his parent's embrace.

He forced an arm out between their bodies. The girl reached out and grabbed his hand.

Both teenagers began to shudder. Their eyes locked. Gene's grimace slowly turned into a smile.

"It's a roller coaster ride!" he groaned. "But we'll make it. I promise!"

Apathy began to laugh hysterically. The sensation *was* like a roller coaster. Frightening but exhilarating at the same time. Her parents were here! They were all together at last!

"Hold on and try not to barf!" She twined her fingers through Gene's and grasped them as tightly as she could.

"Ready?"

"Ready."

Then they were over the edge. Gene let out a whoop of glee and Apathy joined in.

Emily clutched at her chest, almost falling over. A look of rapture spread across her face.

"Dan.... What the...? What's *happening*?"

She threw her arms around her husband and held on for dear life.

D.B. glanced over at Edward and Annie, catching their astonished stares. For a second, a moment of closeness passed between them. They couldn't experience what was going on. They never would. But it was enough that their children could.

D.B. let out a fake yell of elation, motioning behind Emily's back for Edward and Annie to do the same. They hesitated, then joined in.

Deep Singh stood in the doorway watching the adults and children on a heap on the floor, crying and laughing and hugging each other.

He silently closed the door and went to find his own son.

Around MacLellan base, the firing suddenly stopped. Soldiers got to their feet, staring in horror at their weapons. Potter rose in front of them, chewing his knuckle like a guilty child. Dried blood crusted his top lip.

"What the hell are we doing?" he said to nobody in particular. "Why are we fighting over a bunch of *children*?"

He walked towards the entrance of MacLellan base, hands above his head. The Stopwatch defenders cautiously moved away from their positions, weapons trained on him.

"My name is Brigadier Potter of the United States Army." The officer held out his weapon, handle first.

"I wish to formally surrender."

Millar finally found Poppy, propped against a rock, staring west at the setting sun.

"We beat them, kiddo." He knelt beside his friend. "We did it."

The surf pounded the rocks below Jackson Head like a great beating heart. All around the pair, bodies peppered the ground and the blackened grass was stained dark red.

Millar should have felt sorrow but something was stopping that from happening. He didn't understand. He knew he ought to be crying, but no tears came.

He supposed this was how his parents had always felt.

"This will never happen again." He straightened the teenager's blood-soaked jersey and stroked her hair. "I'll make *sure* this never, *never* happens again."

Poppy's head lolled to one side and rested on his shoulder. He kissed the dead girl's cheek, closing her sightless eyes.

"I promise."

60

The room was long and low, with a horseshoe-shaped table taking up most of the floor space. A line of high-ranking officers, businessmen in suits and scientists sat around it, each face partially illuminated by individual desk lamps.

Brigadier Potter and Colonel Naish stood in the middle of the room with Millar Watt between them. Naish's arm was in a sling.

We're finally in the presence of the originators of the Stopwatch Project, she thought.

At one time, she'd have feared them - but now she wasn't scared of anything. She had absorbed Apathy and Gene's pheromone outburst on Kirkfallen and so had Millar, Potter and his surviving men.

They all had the same purpose now. Almost shared the same thoughts. And, together with the islanders,

417

they had concocted a magnificent falsehood to exact revenge on the men in this room.

"We've read the report." A thin officer with a mass of medals on his chest ruffled a wad of paper in front of him. "Just wanted to hear it from the horse's mouth, so to speak."

"An unhappy coincidence." Potter's delivery was clipped and unemotional. "We arrived on Fallen just at the point when this young man, Millar Watt, was about to release his pheromones."

The lie tripped easily off his tongue.

"Our presence distracted the population and resulted in the boy not being quarantined in time. My men went crazy and most of the Stopwatch Unit died in the ensuing fight."

He laid a hand on Naish's shattered arm.

"Though their immunity to pheromone release meant they were able to mount a spirited defence."

"And the kids?"

"A pilot called Fred Wolper, one of the Stopwatch Unit, managed to get a chopper into the air with the children on board. So they were unaffected."

Potter gingerly touched his swollen lip.

"When the danger was over, he set them down and flew off to get help, but the copter had been damaged by our fire and exploded in mid-air."

"So the project worked," a man in a suit interrupted.

"I went in with over 400 men and less than half survived," Potter replied. "If you call that working, then... yes."

"And these men are alive because?"

"They were too far away to be affected, fortunately."

"They confirm your story, as do the remaining Stopwatches." The General rubbed his fingertips together. "Bit of a mess, all in all."

"I take full responsibility."

"Oh, you will. In the meantime, we'll have a clean-up crew remove the bodies and give the place time to calm down a little."

The General rested both hands on the table.

"We'll say the... incident was a military training exercise that went wrong."

"And this is the boy who caused it all?" A balding Admiral lifted an accusing finger. "The one who released his pheromones unexpectedly?"

Naish put her arm around Millar.

"This very same."

"You're sure he's safe now?"

"He's got ears, baldy." Millar tipped the trilby back on his head. "What he doesn't have is a mother, thanks to you."

"I suggest you keep a civil tone," the Admiral said curtly. "For safety reasons, we're isolated in the middle of nowhere and nobody knows you're here but us.

"You staying alive rests on whether we can depend on your silence."

"I'm not scared."

The children on Kirkfallen would always respect their parents' sacrifice. But, after Apathy and Gene's outburst, none of them would ever feel sorrow or fear again.

"I admire your bravado, son," a scientist commented. "But you're sweating a lot for someone who isn't nervous. We're hard people to fool."

"Oh, I'm not nervous at all." Millar smiled, revealing a gap between his teeth. He wiped perspiration from his brow with a trembling hand and tried to ignore the pheromone build-up churning inside his chest.

"Guess I must be coming down with something."

He grinned.

"And it's pretty infectious."

61

The Stapletons met Dan Salty at Pittenhall. Makeshift crosses lined the Ridge, their whitewashed wood
not yet sullied by gull droppings or the corrosive effects of salt-laden air. Apathy and Gene were fifty
yards away on the clifftop, watching Millar Watt approaching. He was deep in conversation with Emily
Walton.

"Millar is back, as you can see." Edward Stapleton
nodded towards the approaching couple. "The boy
released his pheromones right in front of the people in
charge of the Stopwatch Project."

His expression was stony.

"The base was in the middle of nowhere, so the infection didn't spread. But everyone there has been...
converted."

"Why are you so miserable, then?" Dan asked.
"Doesn't this mean we won?"

"No. Naish and Brigadier Potter still want the children seeded across the world."

"*What*? Who died and left *them* in charge?"

"Well... most of *us*." Edward swept his hand around the field of headstones. "There are only eleven adult Stopwatches left."

"What about Apathy and Gene?" Dan nodded towards their children. "They were the ones who caused the original pheromone outbreak. Isn't what happens next their decision?"

"They may have caused it." Edward sighed. "But Millar absorbed it. He's like the others now. Apathy and Gene are as alien to him as we are. They have no authority here."

"The pheromone outburst has changed everyone normal beyond recognition." Annie broke in. "Naish, Potter and their men. Millar and the other kids. Even your wife. They've all changed."

"Yeah, I had noticed," Dan retorted sourly. "Emily has hardly said two words to Apathy or me since the outburst. Spends all her time with Potter's men and the children."

He pursed his lips.

"They call themselves *The Colony*. Y'know? Like ants?"

As if on cue, Emily veered away from Millar and headed towards them.

"The fact that they all think and feel the same thing is disturbing enough."

Edward pulled loose a splinter of unpainted birch from the cross marking Colin's grave.

"But they want everyone else to be like them, too. They intend to make the whole world part of their Colony."

"What if the kids get scared?" Dan protested. "What if they release alarm pheromones across the world instead of Mandibular ones?"

"They don't feel fear anymore, remember?.."

Edward pulled a cigarette from his pocket and lit it, cupping his hands to stop the tiny flame from being extinguished. "They're zealots, out to mould humanity in their own image."

"You telling me we're back to square one?"

"Square zero more like," Annie broke in. "They don't seem to feel anything at all. Not sorrow. Not joy. Certainly not love."

She gave a shudder.

"They're worse than us."

"Whatever happens, we're in deep trouble." Edward took a drag on his cigarette. "In the new world order these children intend to create, I doubt our kind will be tolerated."

He gave a bitter smile.

"I guess Kelty will get his master race after all."

"Let me talk to my wife one more time." Dan waved to Emily as she approached. "She used to care for me once."

Emily didn't wave back. Uncombed hair hung messily around her shoulders, framing a face devoid of makeup.

"Why is everyone hanging around here?" She ignored the crosses that sprouted on either side. "The chopper will be here in a few minutes to evacuate the children."

"We don't think they should go," Dan replied. "Their *mothers* and *fathers* don't think they should go."

"They're not the real parents, though, are they?" Emily patted Colin's headstone absentmindedly.

Dan winced and Annie clenched her fists.

"Besides, the children *want* to do this."

"Your daughter would rather stay here."

"I can't do anything about that." A flicker of regret crossed Emily's face, but it was gone in a second. "We're all grateful to her and Gene - but no individual, not even Apathy, is greater than our cause."

"I think this discussion is ended." Edward took a deep breath, then enveloped Dan in a hug. "Be seeing you, neighbour."

He stepped back and patted his heart.

"Remember. We have more here than they realise."

Dan's jaw twitched. A small lump betrayed the concealed pistol in Edward's jacket.

"Got that right, Eddie."

Emily threaded her arm through her husband's and watched the Stapletons walk back towards the village.

"I promised Colin I'd keep him safe. That I'd rescue Apathy. And you."

Dan looked at the ground.

"Promises I couldn't keep. Do you know what that's done to me?"

"You also promised to stay with us." Emily seemed oblivious to her husband's pain. "I know it was just to stop Apathy releasing the wrong kind of pheromones but I'm holding you to it, anyway."

"You don't know that at all."

"It doesn't matter. You always keep your promises, remember?"

Emily stood on her toes and kissed his cheek, lips cold and dry.

"After what she's done, Apathy deserves to have a mother and father. You play along and no harm will come to you."

She tugged at his sleeve.

"Let's go."

"Wait a damned minute." Dan shook her off and got down on one knee next to Colin's grave. He clasped both hands in front of his chest and closed his eyes.

"I'm sorry I couldn't save you, Colin," he whispered. "But it was a good con, even if it didn't work out."

His voice broke as he tried to utter the last words.

"I appreciate a good con."

Emily put both hands on her hips.

"The helicopter is going to be here any minute," she cautioned. "And the sooner these kids are on it, the better."

She glanced warily at the remains of Kirkfallen village.

"I don't like trusting the future of the human race to eleven sociopaths."

She turned on her heel and walked away without a backward glance.

Dan stood up and shielded his eyes. In the distance, an army chopper surfed the hilltops, heading towards the village like a fat fly.

"Twelve sociopaths, if you include the notorious D.B. Salty." He said softly. "And you just handed us an escape route."

He felt inside his own jacket where Edward had slipped him a homemade knife.

"As you said, Emily. My promises no longer mean anything to you. But I'll save my daughter. You have my word on *that*."

Apathy and Gene watched the ocean batter against the cliffs of Pittenhall Ridge as it had done for thousands of years and would do for thousands more.

"How does it feel to be the new Adam and Eve?" The biting wind whipped hair around Apathy's face, hiding her expression.

"At least we don't have to start out naked." Gene sounded exhausted. "It's freezing here."

"We can't let the children leave Fallen." Apathy shivered and rubbed her arms. "They're walking time bombs."

"They may just save the human race. Have you thought about that?"

"How? By flushing self-will down the drain? By taking away people's ability to think for themselves?"

"If humans used that gift properly, democracy would work and we wouldn't be in this mess."

Gene's voice was soft and low. He seemed much older than the boy Apathy had met a few days ago. "Maybe we *need* to all think the same."

"Maybe," she agreed. "Only... *I* don't want to be part of it."

"You wouldn't say that if you were abused or dirt poor or living in a war zone. Most people are."

"I know. But we're not."

"That's the curse of having choices," Gene admitted. "You appreciate how terrible it is to have them taken away."

Millar Watt finally reached them, perspiration beading his forehead.

"Are you two ready to go?" he said. "We have a new world to build."

"Don't you mean a new world to conquer?" Apathy grunted.

"That's an old way of thinking," Millar shot back. "We'll *all* be part of the new order. The smart ones will lead. The strong ones will build. The fertile ones will breed. The weak ones will be weeded out."

"And so will outsiders." Apathy's scorn was withering. "Outsiders like us."

"Don't you get it?" Millar looked shocked. "You only have to wait until Marcie Gold releases her pheromones. Then you'll be part of the Colony as well."

"And if we don't *want* to be part of it?"

"What's got into you guys?" Millar slapped Gene on the back. "Get your stuff together. I'm packed already."

"You'll have a job getting all your precious books on the helicopter."

"Books?" Millar looked puzzled. "What will I need books for? I know how to hunt, fish and farm. And I know how to fight."

He glanced in the direction of Kirkfallen village.

"I'll be in charge of mopping up any threats to the Colony. But you'll be safe, don't worry."

Millar looked at them in awe.

"You *made* us."

"Give us five minutes, Millar. Could you do that?"

"Sure thing." He tipped his hat back and headed back the way he had come.

Gene watched him open-mouthed.

"You were right," he said softly. "He didn't even look at it."

Apathy read the inscription she had carved with Dan's Swiss army knife on the headstone next to her.

Poppy Ainsworth
Fallen Star

"You win," Gene said sadly, "If we humans are too stupid or short-sighted to prevent our own destruction, so be it. The planet will get along without us just fine."

He laughed bitterly.

"But it already has enough ants."

Apathy glanced across the graveyard at her father. Even from that distance, she could see sorrow etched into his posture. A man whose makeshift moral compass had finally let him down.

She reached out and took Gene's hand.

"Can we really go through with this?" She felt a lump forming in her throat.

"The Stopwatch Project has to end forever." Gene knelt by Poppy's grave and thrust his hands into the freshly turned soil. He removed a gun, brushed the earth from it and got to his feet.

"We're the last of the Kirkfallen Stopwatch," he said grimly. "We do the jobs nobody else will."

Apathy took the Swiss army knife from her pocket and held it up, allowing the weak sunlight to glint off the blade. Dan nodded, drew his own weapon, and quietly set off after Millar and Emily.

On the crest of the hill, Edward Stapleton re-appeared. The survivors of the Kirkfallen Stopwatch were bunched behind him, all armed to the teeth.

Apathy and Gene stood, hand in hand, watching the ocean crash endlessly against the rocks with a power beyond their comprehension.

Savouring one last moment of innocence.

Ants operate a social system where the population operates together as a complete unit, sacrificing individual instincts to ensure the survival of the colony – a process enforced by hormone excretions known as pheromones

Ants existed on earth a hundred million years before humanity. They are still far more numerous than us, possess more cities and occupy more ecological niches than the human race. They can survive massive climate change, global pollution and even nuclear explosions

In terms of numbers, longevity and adaptability, humans are not the dominant species on earth

ABOUT THE AUTHOR

Jan-Andrew Henderson (J.A. Henderson) is the author of 40 teenage, YA, adult and non-fiction books. Published in the UK, USA, Canada, Australia and Europe, he has been shortlisted for fifteen literary awards and is the winner of the Doncaster Book Prize, the Aurealis Prize and the Royal Mail Award.

www.janandrewhenderson.com